I0671677

SANDPRINTS OF DEATH

Nash Black

IF Publishing
Jamestown, KY

This is a work of fiction. The events and characters described herein are imaginary and are not intended to refer to specific places or living persons. The opinions expressed in this manuscript are solely the opinions of the author and do not represent the opinions or thoughts of the publisher. The author has represented and warranted full ownership and/ or legal right to publish all the materials in this book.

Sandprints of Death
All Rights Reserved.
Copyright © 2011 Nash Black
v3.0

Cover Photo © 2011 JupiterImages Corporation. All rights reserved - used with permission.

This book may not be reproduced, transmitted, or stored in whole or in part by any means, including graphic, electronic, or mechanical without the express written consent of the publisher except in the case of brief quotations embodied in critical articles and reviews.

IF Publishing
Jamestown, KY

ISBN: 978-0-578-08370-4

PRINTED IN THE UNITED STATES OF AMERICA

For Gretta Kircher with thanks

for a wonderful idea.

Characters

Ono County
Jim Young – recovering from an accident
Maud Tosh – recovering from the death of her husband
Matt Young – recovering from a football injury
Isaiah Young – recovering from a lost love
Phillip Andrews – recovering alcoholic

Seamew Island
Thayer "Thay" Townsend – Sheriff of Seamew Island
Marshall "Marsh" Leviticus — manager of Seamew Inn
Louise "Mamma Lou" Leviticus – mother of Marsh and Orta
Orta Wallace – laundress, maid, Shell's mother and a sister to Marsh
Shell Wallace – nephew of Marsh Leviticus & busboy
Nialis Lapier – maid and Shell Wallace's friend
Moses Southly – meteorologist
Virgil Landers – Chief of Police on the mainland

Seamew Inn Guests
Phedra Lavin – on vacation prescribed by her doctor
Dr. Lemuel Lavin – Phedra's husband
Lettic Forbenshire – Phedra's sister
Wally and Fanny Longer – vacationers from Minneapolis
Kevin Stevens – FBI agent and Roger Barker's supervisor
Roger Barker – FBI agent
Stanley Collins – Special Investigator for the Department of Interior
Rhodes Thornton – lawyer for Dr. Lemuel Lavin
Rick Riley – searching for his sister
Jane Riley – cousin of Phedra and Lettic

Prologue

Flying is wonderful! I got to see the tops of the clouds. My tummy went whoosh as the plane took off. They served a little breakfast. The Bloody Marys were decked out with teeny bamboo umbrellas stuck in stalks of celery.

The trip was short, but we had to wait an hour to land at the Atlanta airport. Five times the plane flew a big loop over a barn that had "Chew Mail Pouch Tobacco" painted on the roof. I loved sitting by a window. It's like the porthole in a ship. I could see everything. From the air, the houses resemble a child's play-yard.

Thank you. I don't think I could have endured those last months without your help. When Rupert started using the bed (too nasty to use the slop-jar)— I'd have to clean him up. I came near to killing him, myself.

This hotel is almost empty. I can't see how they can afford to keep it open. I did meet a young woman who has been staying here for some time. We were the only people in the dining room so I invited myself to join her. I would never do something like that at home.

She was saying goodbye to her man when I arrived. Her husband is a doctor and couldn't stay for a vacation. She lost two children in accidents and a head-doctor sent her here to recover from her depression. Scientific word for grief, which anyone knows is perfectly natural. Best medicine in the world is talking to a stranger.

I found a perfect sand dollar on the beach. It's the start of a collection of seashells for me to bring home so I can remember my trip.

I don't know why I was foolish enough to make you a promise to write. I'm sending this letter to your office in Buckston in an envelope I stole from a real estate firm on the mainland. I don't want those post office guys gossiping in Clydesville. They go on like Boots Randolph's, "Yackety Sax."

It isn't seemingly to be sending letters to a man when Rupert is barely dead.

Maud

Chapter 1

Damn. The sand swallowed my boot. When I squat to yank it on, a flat white pebble glows in the pale light. I pick it up and flip it over with my thumb. Two-bluebirds with their beaks together like they're kissing are painted on a chip from a plate. The old chip is like me, polished off and washed up.

Me. Jim Young, dirt-track driver, scratched from the big time before even one lap was completed. My future is as barren as the dunes that surround me with their dead winter grass. Black-headed gulls screech like banshees, laughing and jeering at my attempt to walk without a cane.

Yesterday, after lurching down this beach, I drove back across the causeway for a pair of shop-goggles. Grit is hell to clean out of an empty eye socket. My rubbing grinds against the scar tissue like polishing it with double-0 steel wool. The cobalt eyeglass Abel found in an antique shop doesn't help. I end up with water running down my t-shirt looking messier than a kid who can't find his mouth with a spoon.

Kane insisted I come to this desolate seashore. The hard thump of the waves against the shore keeps his sarcastic voice pounding in my head. Harsh words that stung worse than the sharp wind hitting my face. I'd ignored my business. Let the bills pile up without paying them. I'd let Lon Chambers and Elroy Harris run my shop and yard. My greatest sin was to worry Mom with my drinking.

Not one new engine has passed through the garage doors in the seven months since the accident. He doesn't know how my feet ached when I tried to stand on the cement floors. I screamed inside as I watched Elroy polish a cylinder, knowing it should be for the C-9. Word gets out fast in the racing world. I'm finished in racing. Young's Enterprises is washed up like the gunk on this beach beneath my crippled feet.

The deep sand sucks my boots into a quagmire of stumbling misery. It's a match for the wretchedness of not having a future. I shove my foot back in the boot and turn to go back to my cottage. I can escape the nightmares if I sleep during the day.

"I'm sorry, Ma'am. I didn't see you." I bumped her on my left side. She totters before I can reach to steady her. I've almost knocked a woman down with my blind clumsiness.

"Mrs. Tosh!"

"You know me?"

I tug off the goggles and my knitted cap. "I'm Jim…Jim Young."

"Oh! What are you doing here? You looked like an alien from outer space with those goggles."

"What are you doing here?"

"Jim, I asked you."

We'd spoken at the same time. "Kane sent me."

"Kane? Your brother?"

"Yes, Ma'am. John Henry Burton told him how they cure muscle injuries in race horses. The trainers strengthen their legs by running them on beaches and in the surf."

"Horses? When did you get a horse?"

"Oh no, Ma'am. My feet and legs. Kane's notion was that if it was good for horses, it ought to help me. You're a long way from home." I change the subject fast. It's hard enough to face a stranger, much less someone from Clydesville.

A yellow slicker covers her down to her red Indian-rubber boots. A green hat like a Turkish turban hides her ears, but wisps of gold-red hair blow in the wind. She studies my face for a moment with her head slanted to the side as if deep in thought. What is she doing on this beach?

"Healing? Yes. Seems like we've both come for the same purpose."

"Mr. Tosh."

"Good a reason as any—same intention."

She is flustered, searching for something to say and drops the grocery bag she's holding.

"Let me get that for you."

"Careful Jim, what's left of Mr. Tosh is in that poke."

"Huh?"

I almost drop it again as the stench of decay invades on the off-shore wind. He was a big man, but the sack has little weight. I hand it to her and she smiles.

"These are his ashes. I didn't mean to shock you."

My cheeks burn. How could I be so dumb? Mom went to his memorial before the holidays. The grit in the air is making my eye blink like a nearsighted owl. I pray it isn't parts of Mr. Tosh.

"Let me help."

"Oh no, Jim. This is my job."

Her voice lowers until I can barely hear her above the bump of the waves. "He came to Clydesville when they built the dam, so he didn't have a family burying plot. I heard on a *Nova* show that life came from the sea. Now, I'm giving him back."

"Yes, Ma'am."

"You go sit on those steps while I finish the job. Then we'll chat."

Jim has a heap of troubles for a young'un. He lets his shoulders slump as he heads for the steps. His hands are brushing hard at his clothes before he rams them deep in his pockets. His steps, are hesitant as if he's enduring pain beyond the physical, but too proud to admit it.

He smiled when he greeted me. That deep clef in his cheek below his eye patch is devastating. It's different from a dimple, just breaks into a crag on the left side of his mouth. A hard shove is what he needs. Sympathy will destroy him.

"Rupert, this is the last time I'll speak to you. How did you like my scientific story? Jim is too young to know about men as rotten as you.

"'From dust thou cometh and to dust thou shalt return,' even if you do get wet. You deserve a good dousing. We could have had a fine life together if you'd given our marriage half a chance. All you saw in me was a charwoman my daddy palmed off on you.

"I've always wanted to see the ocean and face its roar in a storm. What's left of you is in this sack. You can't smell the salty air, but I can. It's as sharp and tasty as pickling brine. Your dust doesn't even have a stench.

"I squandered some of your insurance money. Today I have the Atlantic Ocean for a front yard.

"Rupert, you didn't know it, but I hated you though I love your name. It's different. The only decent thing you ever gave me. There isn't another Tosh in Brewster, no Ono County. Its hard to remember that silly new name.

"Pa thought you were a fine catch for me. An engineer with a good living. You didn't show your colors until after the ring was on my finger, although through my nose was more like it.

"I was your little woman. *Me!* Up against the door frame, in my stocking feet, I top five-foot nine on the tape measure. I heard you tell Doc Flanders to take out my insides because you didn't want any squalling brats. I wanted to die that night. Doc Flanders knew what happened, though I told him you were drunk and didn't know your own strength. He didn't want to get involved between a man and his wife.

"Let me tell you, I'm proud I didn't have to bring any of your get into this world to make another women miserable. I'm doing what Mitzi Gaynor did in *South Pacific*. I'm washing you out of my hair.

"Speaking of money, Rupert. Those bonds and your insurance savings left me well fixed. You didn't name a beneficiary, but Elton Fightmaster made sure I got it all as next-of-kin. Our marriage license was good for something.

"Have to thank you. It was a complete surprise when Phillip Andrews brought over the insurance check. Too tight to even go to the doctor or have someone in to help me with the lifting of you. Me, working and skimping like a dog, believing we were broke when you couldn't work anymore. I also got your government insurance and will have your pension after I'm sixty-two, but that's some years off. I earned every penny waiting on you hand and foot.

"I love my job, putting those old records in order so a body can find something. I get to decide how to do it because no one else knows anything about historical record keeping. It doesn't seem like I've been working for four years waiting for you to die.

"You milked every day. I couldn't go out in the backyard, but what you were yelling. But I got even. I started feeding you sleeping pills in your morning coffee. You never noticed with all the sugar you demanded. Then I had breakfast at the Kricket and let Callie Rogers comb out my hair before I went to work.

"You were too gone in your head to know, but Phillip Andrews helped me those last months. He loaned me the strength to hold things together until you passed.

"Phillip is pushing me. He doesn't understand that I don't want to be married ever again. Hear that, Rupert. A real man—a good man wants me. He's lived next door to us for nearly twenty years and knows all our ugly secrets, yet he's never said a word.

"Love is one thing and it's just fine. I do love that handsome man. He looks like a movie star, too pretty to be real. But loving someone as fearfully as I do him doesn't mean marriage. I'm not a coward, but being hitched to you was enough for this lifetime. I'm free to make my own decisions. I can live my own life. Me, Maud Tosh.

"Jim must think I'm an old fool muttering to myself. He never expected to meet someone from Clydesville, least of all me. He looks sad sitting over there shaking out his boots.

"His sister-in-law is telling it all over town that he's a drunk. I've never liked Vera. She can't pass a mirror without admiring herself. Wanting to be a singer when she can't carry a tune in a thunder mug. Bet she was surprised when Jim got the Throckton money. Catherine's will is filed in my office at the courthouse. The child wrote it the morning before she was run down.

"That's the last of you, Rupert. Have a turbulent rest tossing in the sea."

<> <> <>

Mrs. Tosh is taking a long time as she pulls handful after handful of dust from the bag and throws it into the wind. She gives the bag a final shake and rips it in little pieces, scattering them on the waves. The sun is full up now. There is a glow around her head like a halo. What she's doing must be right, but it's a strange way to bury a husband.

Her coat crackles as she walks toward me with both arms swinging at her sides like she wants to follow the gulls. "Come on, Jim. I can use a cup of coffee. They have a nice restaurant in the hotel."

"Mrs. Tosh, I can't go into the hotel...haven't shaved." Green eyes almost level with mine look me over. She knows I'm lying. I've never had much of a beard.

"We'll both go get cleaned up."

"I've got the makings for breakfast in my cottage."

"Dry cereal doesn't keep a body together. I don't want to eat alone. Not today, after scattering Mr. Tosh." She looks toward the ocean as if she is watching her husband drift away leaving her stranded on this barren shore.

"I'll buy your breakfast."

"Ma'am, I can't let you do that."

"Nonsense, of course you can. You forgot to renew your license plate. Mary was worried you'd get stopped for driving on an expired tag. I brought it with me. I promised your mother I'd treat you on your birthday. It's today, January 10th. You're twenty-six years old. You were born the year I married Mr. Tosh."

She laughs at me as my face gets red. I'd rather live in a city where everyone ignores you than in Clydesville where everyone knows you.

"Jim, take a hand full of sand and make a ball...like a snowball... then throw it in the ocean. Let the water have your troubles. They'll never come back in the same form. The ocean has a way of dealing with hurts. It's healing, like the spring at Lourdes. I did."

"Yes, Ma'am." I scoop up a blob of wet sand. Shape it into a rough ball and fling it with all my strength towards Europe.

January 10, 1976

In the afternoon it warms up, but early mornings when I walk on the beach I'm glad I brought mother's sealskin coat. The wind cuts through you. You'll have to help me shake it when I get home, the sand gets in every fold. Today I wore a slicker because of the fog. It was so thick it oozed.

When I walk across the floor of my room, I can hear a crunch under my feet even though the maid runs the vacuum every day while I'm eating breakfast. Pure luxury, freshly ironed sheets and fluffy towels every day. Their laundry bill must be fierce.

I found Jim Young. I got here two days before he arrived by flying. Tell Mary he is keeping his word and not to worry. I did what she suggested and got him out of hiding. Imagine, that boy has been eating dry cereal and drinking instant coffee made with tapwater in his cottage rather than let people see him.

I bumped into him early this morning on the beach. He caught me as I was throwing Rupert's ashes in the ocean. I was so lost in ugly memories I didn't expect another soul to be around at that hour. The sun was just coming up as the last of the fog was rolling out. I don't know what he thought of my bizarre behavior.

I felt bare to have someone from home catch me, but he seemed to understand. Mary Young did a fine job with her boys. His manners remind me of Elton Fightmaster. Who always does the right thing no matter what is happening.

He apologized for running into me, when the truth of the matter is I backed into his path. I didn't recognize him until he took off his stocking cap and goggles. He waited on the steps for me to finish with Rupert and walked me back to my cottage.

It must be very painful to walk when all the bones in your feet have been broken. He was wearing barn boots and heavy clothes that made him look as if he'd gained thirty pounds.

You'd think when you inherit money all your troubles would be over, but look at Jim. Seeing Catherine Throckton hit by that car, then being one of her heirs. Bartlett Throckton did everything he could to convince Dan Sommers Jim killed her.

There was a lot of ugly talk at the time, Then when it all died down, he had that terrible accident. I think Vera made up the story about his drinking. He wasn't breathing hard when we collided.

Jim is very attractive with that patch over his left eye, rather rakish looking. I always admire a well set-up man, reminds me of you. Listen to me, I'm sounding like Callie Rogers, repeating gossip.

Maud

Chapter 2

Double doors open out to a wide porch, which faces the ocean. Tall palms in huge pots, like the ones in the yard of the hotel, stand beside the doors. It's hard to imagine this place was once a home. It's too big, overpowering as if people don't count for much. I heard the porter say the wings had been added, but I can't see where they're joined on the outside. The builders must have used new clapboard.

I feel as if someone is watching me, but I can't see them. It's uncanny, like a belligerent spook got left behind seeping in from the swamps when the old folks moved on. I'm glad I have one of the little cottages near the beach. They're comfortable. There I don't have to strain my neck to find the ceiling.

It's dark now. In the daylight we can see the water from our table by the windows. The walls of the dining room are the color of buttercups that bloom in the woods in early spring. Their glow doesn't relieve the feeling of oppression. The fanlike leaves of the palms make spectral shadows against the soft yellow.

Mrs. Tosh chose a table near the window to watch the birds diving into the ocean. The chairs are made of bamboo with tropical patterned coverings of large yellow and red flowers. Our waiter is pulling the drapes closed, shutting out a nippy wind seeping in around the doors that makes my feet cold. The splashes of color turn the room into a garden, but still, I feel something lurking in the dark behind the curtains.

While Mrs. Tosh went to church yesterday, I found a haberdashery like Lair & Oldham's in Buckston. I was surprised they were open on a Sunday, but resort towns are different from country places. I purchased a gunmetal gray suit, some white shirts and two ties. I tried a pair of shoes, but I couldn't walk in them. Had to settled for black tassel-loafers, which don't look too bad. I didn't want her thinking I don't know how to dress when squiring a lady to dinner.

I'm early because I like watching her enter from the vestibule with a smile so bright every diner has to respond. A secret joy floats about her as if she expects to find treasures under every leaf she turns over. Her eyes share the secrets, each with a different person.

January and the first of the week, not many people eating tonight. Yesterday I was glad we ate in town after she went to church. This room was still packed with people waiting in the lobby when we got back. I wouldn't want to face the long drive out from town over that shifting causeway in the gathering night shadows.

The people who're staying at the hotel are polite and don't stare at me. They watch Miss Maud with her burnished, curly hair bouncing in time to her long steps. Tall for a woman, but all the parts are well distributed and in good repair. She's some kind of cousin to Marcy Lane, the movie star who died awhile back.

Tonight she is wearing a crimson Pendleton pantsuit with a green turtleneck sweater like Adam wears. I saw the label when I helped her put it on last night. The strong colors show the world she is a fine figure of a woman. It's hard to tell a woman's age. She may be around Mom's age. I stand to help her into her chair. She smooths the crisp tablecloth with a rough hand and points to the doors.

After a quick peek between the closed curtains, the glum busboy drops our menus on our table and hurries to the kitchen while looking at his watch. His abruptness is the first sign of the haughtiness I'd expected to find in this fancy place.

Miss Maud's eyes follow him over the top of her menu. "I'd say he has a hot date. He's sure in an all-fire hurry." She winks and looks down to study the evening's offerings. Our waiter puts tall glasses of water and ice tea on the table then takes our orders for the special of the day.

"I found something strange in the sand the morning I met you on the beach." I dig in my pocket for the fragment I've been carrying since my birthday and hand it to her.

"The dishes from the Wren."

"Yes, Mom bought some coffee mugs and a big platter when they had the fire-sale."

"They used willow dishes at the Wren as far back as I can remember. My father always took us there for Mother's birthday, even during the depression. Rupert took me for our anniversary. It was the same night Marcy Lane came home.

"I've always regretted not asking her for an autograph, but he wouldn't permit me to speak to her. I did wave, when he wasn't looking."

"I'm taking it back to Mom. Her coffee mugs have fat blue birds, these are skinny."

"You got a good one, sir."

I look up, our brown waiter stands beside the table holding our soup plates. We hadn't heard him.

"People have found these before?"

"Yes, sir. Not often, but once-in-a-while. Them pieces are good luck."

"Where did they come from?" Three couples and several lone men are busy with their meals, but we're the only people sitting at a round table tonight. One woman spoke to Maud as she came in— they seemed to know each other, but I've never seen her around the hotel.

I don't feel guilty keeping him talking as he lays our places when so few dinners are in the room. The menu said Frogmore stew with sausage, shrimp and crabs. Whole shrimps and crabs, still in the shell!

Our waiter smiles and hands us large white towels and nut-crackers, and then places little bowls of water with a slice of lemon floating on the surface on the table.

He removes a big china tub resting on a large platter from the serving cart, and places it slightly above our places, but within easy reach. It's filled to the brim with more stew. The atmosphere and smell of the old hotel may be cloying, but the kitchen doesn't stint on food. If you can figure out how to eat it.

"Hurricane in 1893, took out an old hotel. Them pieces came from it, been in the water close to a hundred-years. They wash up every now and then. Congratulations, Sir.

"Excuse me, please." His eyes shift to one couple. The woman who knew Maud.

She is on her feet with an angry toss of her head, which make her brown hair bounce around her shoulders. The man jumps up and reaches for her arm. She slaps him and storms from the room. It's as fast as the blink of an eye, but the look he gives her is pure hatred. If it wasn't a public place, he'd wring her neck.

He turns as the waiter hurries to their table, the look is gone, replaced by a tight smile on his pitted face. The print of her hand is red against his pale skin. He says something to the waiter, then stuffs bills under his plate, and hurries after the woman.

"Jim, you're staring. Couples have tiffs. They blow over."

"You know them?"

"I went shopping with her before you arrived."

"Excuse me. I've never seen a couple fight in public."

"That is a mild way of describing it. She was angry."

"Yes, Ma'am. But for a second he looked as if he hated her."

"Men hit on women in private."

"But, she hit him!"

"Thick makeup doesn't cover the bruise on her cheek."

Her voice drops low like it did on the beach, as if talking to herself. "Not to my eyes. I've tried it."

I hear her. No one ever mentioned her husband knocking her around. My brother, Adam says only cowards, drunks, and misfits beat on women or children who can't defend themselves.

Mrs. Tosh reaches around the china pot and pats my hand to erase her words, then smiles as she changes the subject.

"Those are finger bowls to wash your hands after you peel the shrimp. The stew is named for a small town on an island down the coast. It's messy, but good. I had it the night I arrived. Dig in, there's no other way to eat it."

I can't help looking over to the empty table. The waiter is watching the sullen busboy clear the remains of the wasted meal. I dip my spoon into the stew with my eye on deserted table. The fiery taste singes my tongue. I take a huge swallow of ice tea, which doesn't help one bit.

She grins at my discomfort and goes on calmly eating the liquid inferno. "Eat slow, and wait until you've finished to drink. The cold only heats up your taste buds."

"Yes, Ma'am."

"Takes a bit to get used to, but it's worth it. I'd take up stealing for that tureen with it's matching ladle and tray."

"It's a pretty bowl."

"Jim! It's Coalport, it came from England. It matches my great-grandmother's china."

"I'm pleased you recognized it, Ma'am. We have a few pieces left from before the soldiers camped here. I saw you looking at it in the drawing room. A notion told me you'd appreciate it, since we're not too busy to do the fancy tonight."

Our waiter is deftly removing a bowl of shells and replacing the finger bowls with fresh ones. The plates have a wide, pale-green border. The edges are gold with a single full-blown rose in the center. The man's a marvel. He appears out of nowhere.

"I have four place-settings of my great-grandmother's wedding china of the same pattern. It was brought up the Mississippi and Cumberland Rivers on a paddle boat. Her pieces were packed in barrels of flour and corncobs. When I get home, I'm going to unpack it and use it. You're right, one should use lovely things, not keep them stuck away in the attic. Thank you for reminding me of how people should live." Her work-worn hand caresses the handle of the ladle as if it were solid gold.

"What are you going to have for dessert?"

"Mrs. Tosh, have you tried the chocolate pie?"

She laughs, a tinkling sound like the Christmas bells still on the blue front door of the hotel. "Good choice, I'll have some too. Don't worry about...."

She doesn't finish her sentence, but I think she knows the real reason Kane insisted I spend three weeks on Seamew Island. Exercise to strengthen my feet and legs is secondary to drying out. She didn't order any wine with our meal, but maybe it isn't consumed with stew. I'm so ignorant about how things are done. I've let her choose our food and watched her use a little fork to pull the meat out of the crab's claw.

Did Mom send her to keep tabs on me? Mom is a keeper of secrets and Mrs. Tosh isn't family.

"Jim, you can call me Maud."

"Yes, Ma'am."

"Fate has strange goals. We're both far from home on a mission."

"A mission?"

"To rid ourselves of past demons. We both needed a sojourn in a strange place. New experiences, nothing humdrum." She grins over the remains of the stew, which is good, though I've never eaten miniature corn, cob and all.

I just learned. Never put your spoon down if you haven't finished eating. As soon as I did, the soup plates and tureen were whisked away to be replaced by our dessert. It comes in tall stemmed glasses with a short flat bowl on top. The carving in the glass sparkles in the candlelight throwing prisms of rainbows across the white cloth.

She doesn't want to talk about personal things any more than I do, so we busy ourselves with our pudding. But she's right, it's much more comfortable eating with someone.

She joins me admiring in our French chef who owns the one real eating place in Clydesville. "His food is first-rate. If Lon Chambers or Elroy Harris called him, no matter what time we finished working on the C-9, he'd have a great meal waiting for us."

"He's equal to any gourmet cook you see on TV. I won't tell him how fast you've gone through that chocolate pudding."

"Miss Maud, the waiter called it a mouse." Her left eyebrow pops up like Kane's, but she doesn't correct me.

"Same thing, just uses more egg whites than cream."

"Oh."

The waiter removes the glasses when she takes her last bite. He places a silver teapot and thin china cups of the same pattern before us. It's amazing how Miss Maud can get any man, no matter what color, to start showing off to please her.

Humdrum—I should say not, first my mouth is scalded then it was cooled with a fluffy chocolate mouse. Now I'm drinking tea from cups over one hundred fifty years old while wearing a suit. Jim Young, you're a long way from home.

"I think we've had our excitement for tonight." She glances at the other tables, now set for breakfast and picks up her jacket. "Walk me to my cottage. Tomorrow, if you don't mind you can drive me over to the mainland. They have some nice shops. I'd like to get a few presents."

"Maud," her first name feels strange on my tongue, "I'm willing if you'd help me find something special for Mom?"

"Be glad too. I hope they made up. She was looking forward to his coming back for a few days. I don't like to be sad. I've had enough of that to last me a lifetime."

I sign the check and lay a tip on the table. Maud Tosh slips her hand under my arm and we leave the dining room as if on a real date. A lone man is sitting at a table behind me. He's drinking coffee from a heavy white mug and watching us with fog-gray eyes. Eyes that see beyond us into the dark. Flat seeing eyes—I shrug my shoulders. I hadn't imagined being watched, but he wasn't sitting there when I seated Miss Maud. Damn these people who come and go without making a sound. They give me the creeps.

Light flakes of snow glitter in the lights as I walk down the path to her cottage. I glance back at the hotel. It's impressive, with long porches facing the sea, but I feel better out here with the falling snow. Even the cold wind hitting my face is somehow clean, not laden with the sullen smell of smoldering wet logs.

January 12, 1976

> *The beach is stark like some of those surrealistic paintings Prentice Throckton collected. I love sitting on the steps and hearing the rush of the waves in a hurry to get back to the sea. It's like I can hear my own blood rushing through my veins.*
>
> *Nialis Lapier, a maid, is airing out my cottage. Remember the sand dollar I found? It was alive and died. The stench is awful. She told me not to worry it was a mistake hotel guests made all the time, but to buy one in town that had been dried for my collection.*
>
> *Jim is a sweet boy, but he is naive about life. He believes his life is over when it has barely begun. I watch him drive himself like he drove his cars, fast and hard.*

Yesterday, he carried me to town and fooled around while I went attended the late service in a church that was built before Clydesville became a place. Then we visited one of those little crab shacks that line the road out to the island for dinner.

I miss you and not sharing my happiness. It's in the little things, not the big problems. Those are a burden no one wants to wish on someone they love.

It's January, but at the edge of the boardwalk going over the dunes, a little yellow flower was braving the elements to bloom. I watched a man stomp the flower, he didn't even see its bright face. After he left, I brushed the sand from my flower, the soft sand had cushioned it from his big feet.

Everyone has troubles, but you don't bury them inside of you or parade them around in public to condemn the world for blighting you. Phedra Lavin flaunts hers while Jim tries to dig a hole to bury his. He doesn't realize what he is doing, but Phedra does it like a litany she has rehearsed over and over. Tonight she was in the dinning room with a strange man. She had a bruise on her cheek. She used makeup to advertise it, not hide it.

Writing to you made me realize what I'd actually seen. A woman knows. She was punishing someone for hitting her, not hiding it from public view. First impressions are not always correct, but Phedra has a streak of vengeance she keeps hidden under the makeup.

Don't fuss. I've made reservations for next year. I've made up my mind. If I'm careful with my money I can come every year at this same time when the hotel isn't crowded. I'd hate to see the lovely beach all spotted with umbrellas and sunburned people. When you look out to the ocean, you see what our ancestors saw.

It will be my special time that doesn't belong to anyone but me. I know it sounds selfish, but being near the ocean is as important to me as breathing. I want you to understand, it's for me. It doesn't have anything to do with you.

20

I love our hills; they were once under an ocean. The shells in the rocks tell you it's so. They tumble like the ocean waves if you can get up high enough to see it, but here the sea is mine. At high-tide, which comes twice every 24 hours, it reaches the steps leading to the hotel, breathing in and out like a living person.

The little cottages are so cozy, they have milkhouse heaters set in the wall to take off the chill. My bed is big, what they call a queen size. I feel snug and lost at the same time, if that's possible.

Maud

Chapter 3

Below a barrier of high dunes the sand is wet, it's like hardpan. High tide doesn't reach the tall mounds of sand with sparse growth, as if little can live in this cracked and barren world. A few plumes of a tall sea-grass bend in the wind like goldenrod gone to seed. Tufts of last night's snow cling around the base of the stalks.

The deep cracks are like the ceiling of my hospital room. It was the only view I had for weeks. One fissure was a cat chasing a dog around a race track—endlessly pursuing, never catching.

My family has scattered like the grains of sand on this beach. Adam and Kane remain at home. Catherine understood how being the runt of a litter of nine left me out of their lives.

Twins are strange. Kane and Abel are so close no one else exists. They know where the other is even though they haven't spoken in months. Isaiah and Isaac are just the opposite. They almost hate each other. No, they bicker constantly when they are together, but no one else can voice a criticism of the other in their presence. Four brothers, two so alike they are duplicate sides of the same coin, while the other two are so different folks wonder if they had the same mother.

I'm catching my breath from my run. It's easy to park on the steps leading down from the boardwalk that crosses the dunes to the cottages. A little platform with a broom for brushing the sand off your shoes is below the step...a fine place for resting your feet. Maud sits down beside me bundled up to her ears in a long black fur coat and hands me a cup of coffee.

22

"Thank you." I take a drink, put the cup down and pull on my parka. The wind is stiff and cold.

"I made a reservation for next year."

"You're coming back?"

"Yes, my treat to myself. Can't afford it any other time."

"But, why? There's nothing out there." I indicate the desolate beach from where I'd just come. It wasn't bad in the dark last night. The snow was soft, but the sun takes a long time to come up in the winter.

"Jim, I don't know that I can explain. It's like a kinship with that rough ocean. The sun coming up over the edge of the world turning everything a golden pink."

"It's been day over on the other side for a good while. It is pretty."

"It's more than pretty, it has gotten in my bones. A…what is the word? It's on the tip of my tongue. I know, primeval. The beginning of the world and I'm part of it. My heart feels like it once emptied into this vast ocean to mingle with the fishes. Like Mr. Tosh, bits and pieces of me floating on the waves." Her hair spirals out from her hat in match-like flames as the sun catches the fine wisps.

She sighs, quiet-like as if in church. "I can sit here forever watching the sun climb. That rosy-yellow light glinting off the sand, the ocean turning a deep turquoise-green. At home I've seen that exact same shade in the sky at sunset like a reflection."

I wonder if Rupert Tosh knew what a fine woman he'd had. I'd seen them around town. He always had a hard grip on her arm as if he was afraid she'd run away. Strange to remember that. His hand clamped like a vise on her arm. Seems to me the harder you hold on to a person the further they'd move away. Mom never held onto us once we were grown. She pushed us out of the nest like a mama bird, forcing us to fly on our own.

"Enough. Let's go find some breakfast." She reaches for her bag, but the sleeve of her coat catches it, toppling it backwards. Her stuff spills between the steps.

"Damn, let me scoop up my things." She bounces up and goes around to the back before I can get to my feet.

"Jim." Maud's voice is weak. She sounds scared. "There's...a foot."

I follow her. A woman's foot wearing a stocking is sticking up from the sand. Maud bends down, but I catch her arm.

"Don't touch, we've got to get help. They'll know who to call at the hotel."

"Jim, we can't leave her."

"We'd better or we'll be in a heap of trouble. She's not going anywhere."

<> <> <>

Maud and I watch from a seaside window as the Sheriff and the ambulance driver bring the body up from the beach. He is same man who watched us last night. He beckons to me and I go out to the side courtyard. He unzips the black bag on the stretcher.

"Ever see her before?"

"Yes, Sir. She's the girl who was in the dining room last night. You saw her."

"Go in and finish your breakfast."

"Breakfast?"

"I'll be along as soon as she's stowed."

Those dirty frost eyes raked me as if I'm both stupid and squeamish, lingering on my patch.

While I was outside Maud had our plates moved away from the window and we sit with our backs to it. Neither of us can look at those barren dunes without seeing the furious woman who'd stormed from the dining room.

"Where's the man she was with last night?" We laugh because we'd asked the same question, but our sound is somber. She glances around, but there's no one in ear-shot to hear. Maud tilts her head a bit to the side as if her fur turban has slipped. Her eyes are still as a forest pond as she studies, not me, but a world I don't know beyond my shoulder.

"Can't help but wonder? If you ask around, you could find out?"

"Me?"

"Yes, you. Ask the waiter we had last night. They always know what's going on. He won't talk to me. It wouldn't be proper."

"What are you talking about?"

"Jim, you find out things. You discovered that Laurence Bradley staged that wreck to rook the insurance company. That's why Mr. Andrews offered you a job."

"How did you know?"

"He asked Elton Fightmaster about you, one morning while we were eating at the Kricket. Besides, I work in the courthouse and have my hair done at Callie's. You can't send a postcard home without all the guys at the post office reading it." Her smile is all-knowing as if she sees me in my BVD's.

"Do as I ask and pretend to eat. Here comes the sheriff. Sheriff Townsend is a strange man, those lifeless eyes are cold like the North Sea."

"Yes, Ma'am." I answer quickly, shocked by her harsh words.

Maud lifts her coffee cup and peers over the rim, only her eyes glimmer above the edge. "Good morning, Sheriff. Did you wish to see us?"

"You're the only ones here. I'd say it's obvious." The man smiles and it transforms him. He enjoys a pretty woman flirting with him, and that's what she is doing, using her cup like a fan, as you see in the movies. "May I join you?"

25

"Of course." Her hand indicates the chair to my right, so I can see him without making a production of turning to face him. Damn, she's the sharpest woman I've ever met.

"Don't mean to spoil your meal, but will you indulge me for a few minutes?"

"We're finished, just enjoying the coffee." Neither of us has eaten more than a bite or two.

"The young woman you discovered under the steps. Did you know her?"

He looks directly at me, so I answer.

"No."

"But you have seen her?"

"She was having dinner in this dining room last night."

"And."

"What did you see?"

"We don't pry in other people's business."

He takes a small notebook from his pocket, flips the pages and looks at his notes. "Mrs. Tosh, the woman took some hard licks and was strangled. Her body was buried in the sand under the steps soon after her death. Killer didn't count on the wind combined with rigor mortis. She wasn't stiff when she was dumped under the steps, body contractions may have jerked her knee up like you found after she was buried. Tide was low last night, the wind may have displaced the loose sand. I won't know until an autopsy is performed.

"Please remember, I was in this room last night. It isn't prying to tell me what you saw."

Maud is hesitant to answer, so I plunge in. "Sir, I don't understand. You saw the same thing we did."

"No, people see things from different angles. You didn't know I was behind you until you left."

I study his words. They're true. I hadn't seen him until I got up to help Maud with her jacket.

"I didn't see much until I turned my head at the sound of her slapping him."

"It's recent. How did you loose the eye?"

I brace myself and growl, "A racing accident."

"Where're you folks from?"

"Other side of the mountains. Clydesville, Kentucky."

"Here on vacation?"

"Yes."

"January is a strange month for a vacation?"

Maud's laugh tinkles. "No, not if you have to mind your pennies."

"Wouldn't you save more with one cottage?" His sarcasm drips with ugly innuendo. Maud breaks a brilliant smile, showing even white teeth except for a little lap of the two front ones.

"His mother would tan my hide for a floor rug, but thank you for the flattery. We'd planned to go into town to purchase a re-membrance for her before I discovered Phedra's body." Her head rises as she looks him directly in the eye. The Sheriff knows he's just been chastised. But from the expression on his face, I'd say he's having trouble figuring out how she did it while smiling at him. He drops his eyes first. She won that round.

"Mrs. Tosh, it sounds like a good plan to me. Don't let this morn-ing ruin your vacation. I won't keep Mr. Young, but a minute."

"You gentlemen please excuse me. I need to freshen up before we leave." Maud rises from her chair. We follow her lead and stand until she leaves the dining room.

"May as well drink our coffee." The sheriff points to the table. It's a command and I sit down. He takes a sip and grimaces. "Marsh, bring us some hot coffee. We may be awhile."

The waiter appears by the table on his silent feet with fresh cups and a steaming pot. The sheriff ladles two heaping scoops of sugar into his cup, but I like mine without fixings.

"Lose that eye recently?"

I grit my teeth as I answer, "Yes."

"Up and coming driver, until the accident?"

"Yes."

"Mrs. Tosh a family friend?"

"Yes."

"I followed you back to your cottage last night."

"You what! Why?"

"Figured to put a stop to the one-word answers." His smile is anything, but friendly. "No particular reason. Just like to keep an eye on hotel patrons this time of year. What were you reading until so late?"

My ears start burning, the heat of my face melds with the coffee to sting my eye as I take deep swallow of the scalding brew. What I was reading isn't any of his damn business.

"One of those nixey-dixie books. I passed four times and you were still at it." He's hesitant, as if he is not accustomed to giving out teasing.

"No, Sir. I have a new job waiting at home for an insurance company. Doing their investigations. I was reading, *The Young Detective's Handbook*. All I could find on how to be a detective."

"Learn anything?"

"Some."

"Well, keep your detecting to books. Mrs. Tosh had bad luck when she dropped her purse. Never saw a guy blush. Different." He grins, then saunters away from our table.

His warning won't jibe with Maud's instructions.

<> <> <>

Shopping is dilatory when you're under orders to get off the island. Maud picked out a cashmere shawl for Mom, all pale blue and pinkish like the morning sky. I never felt wool so soft....

"Jim, look out! He's going to hit you."

Maud's voice is sharp, then drops in pitch and fades into a gulp. I check the rearview mirror and see the grill of an old Jeep Wagoneer bearing down with no place to go. My hand changes gears as I double clutch, but I've got no get-up-and-go. The Rover isn't built for a fast get-away. I can't outrun him.

"Damn fool."

I yank the steering wheel hard over to allow the old station wagon room when his back-end gets loose as he tries to brake. He skids on the sand as he passes me. He barreled around that blind curve, nearly rear-ending us. I pull off to the edge. Maud is pitched down between the seats.

"Are you okay?"

She leans back and shakes her head. "I'm fine, Jim. If I hadn't been reaching for my purse and seen the hotel wagon, he would have hit us. You were quick to dodge out of the way."

Her voice is shaking and her hat is down over one eye, but she seems fine. Then she laughs and points.

A great blue heron, just like we have a home, staggers out of the mud and takes lumbering flight across the hood of the Rover. We have disturbed his fishing. Maud sits up straight in the seat, tucking curls of hair under the edge of her hat.

"Give me a minute. That was quite a ride. Is that how it feels when you're racing?"

"Racing? Miss Maud, I wasn't going thirty-five. My poking along caused the problem. The driver was the busboy from the hotel. Damn fool should know how treacherous it is to drive on this causeway."

"Jim, he wasn't paying attention. It looked like he was having an argument with the other man. Shell was shaking his fist when he came around the curve. I saw him, plain as day."

"Shell?"

"Shell Wallace, he's Marshal Leviticus's nephew. He's working at the hotel as a busboy to earn money for college."

"Please excuse my language. If he'd have hit us, it would have destroyed the hotel's wagon. The Rover is built like a tank. It will go anywhere. It would be like hitting a stone wall as slow as we were moving."

The tires spin for a moment in the soft sand as I pull back on the roadway. I'd almost put us in the drink. There is black mud, covered with tall brown grass like wheat on both sides of us. I wouldn't want to try to drive in that muck.

"Jim, I was married for many a year. My ears can take a few male phrases. I use a few myself, in my mind. I'm okay, really I am, just shook up. Where was he going in such an all-fired hurry? Haven't seen the man with Shell before. You couldn't miss that carrot hair."

Chapter 4

*S*he's dead. Phedra Lavin. The woman I went shopping with. I found her under the wharf this morning—she was murdered.

My words sound blunt and crude, but I don't know how else to tell you. I was stunned, I'm still not thinking clearly.

It isn't fair. She was grieving for her children. She watched a car swerve off the road, jump the sidewalk and hit her son before she could get to him. The driver fled the scene of the accident. It was an ordinary black sedan. The police acted like she was lying until her husband explained to them that she never paid any attention to cars. They believed him, but wouldn't believe her.

Then her daughter died in her crib. Again the police kept questioning her. She was at the hospital visiting her mother when the baby died. Her husband had to get the nurses to tell the police where she was, but she felt like she was going crazy when they wouldn't believe her.

I feel terrible that I was so critical of her in my last letter. Now she's alone in the morgue and I feel there is something I should be doing to help her. I did ask Jim Young to question the waiter about her. You know how he finds out things.

She had been at the hotel for five weeks before I arrived. Her husband brought her to the island, but he returned home. Another man visited her one afternoon, but the waiter didn't know who he was. While he was here, they went for a drive around the island, then he brought her back and left right away. He didn't stay at the hotel.

She didn't mention him when she was talking to me. Must have been the psychiatrist, she was seeing. The one who recommended she come to the island.

Something so awful throws a damper over my trip. Why kill her? She was a nice girl who loved her children.

Please keep an eye on the water pipes in my house. The television said the temperatures are below normal on the other side of the mountains.

Maud.

Tall stalks of sea-grass sway on the wind like spectators watching a death dance. Out here, even though I'm wearing the patch and goggles the wind stings my face. The sharp particles of sand have gouged tiny scars in the plastic lenses. I can't see 'em, but I can feel the rough surface. When I use aftershave the cuts on my face sting and burn.

The fog swimming over the beach hides the rising sun and blurs the colors of the sea. Everything is a pale gray, mists of time rising from Maud's primeval pond in a distant land. My body feels disconnected from my soul as if it could float away on the streamers of vapor.

The forlorn boom of a distant foghorn pounds in a strange rhythm almost like the sound of Isaiah's bongo drums.

I force the picture of the woman buried on the beach from my mind. I'm glad I really didn't see the body. Watching a woman die is something I never want to see again. Maud said her name was Phedra Lavin.

She made an impression on Maud, like her strange, yet lovely, name. She liked the woman and hates what happened to her, but

I can't see that we can do anything. Though I get the notion Miss Maud expects me to find answers to her questions. The sheriff as much as told me to mind my own business.

I turn. The wind is not so sharp against my back. I find the strength to run on spiny feet as the sharp odor of saltwater and decay floats on the fog. The spurt of sprinting in the sludge cramps my calves as the tide slides out. My legs feel stronger, but my feet complain.

"Sheriff, you might as well join us. We're the only ones here. Mr. Leviticus won't have but one table to watch." Maud waves a hand toward a chair, which he pulls out from the table.

"Mr. Leviticus? Oh, you mean Marsh, Ma'am."

Maud reminds me of Mom when people say things that don't strike their fancy. Their hackles spark. They take on a pugnacious don't-mess-with-me quality.

"I'm an officer of the court. When Lon Chambers brought in Elton Fightmaster's papers for his guardianship of Talmus and Sunshine Burrows, I would not have dreamed of calling him Lon."

He laughs, which takes the sting out of Maud's sharp words. "Not even when you had the same great-grandfather?"

That explains it. I hadn't realized. The sheriff and the waiter both have eyes the color of the battleships I'd seen parked at Norfolk.

Maud beams; "Kin is kin, no matter which side of the blanket. What does he call you?"

The Sheriff looks discomforted. He doesn't wear a uniform like Dan Sommers. This morning he is wearing a light gray shirt that is tight across the shoulders, and old cords with knee-poked bulges. He draped a plaid wool jacket over the back of his chair. Maybe it's his age that makes him un-sheriff like. But before he can answer we turn to watch a new couple seat themselves at a table in the middle of the room.

The woman is so thin she's like a stalk of the winter-burned grass blanketing the marsh where the causeway crosses to the island. Shell sets water and menus before them without looking our way and darts back to the kitchen. I itch to have a word with him about his reckless driving. This makes me feel like a old busybody even to myself.

"Harry, how can you tolerate the slothfulness of a hotel staff that puts us in a room that hadn't been made up? All you did last night was apologize for being a bother. They were expecting us. We had reservations. I told you thirteen was an unlucky number. A very bad day to travel. We should have left right then and there. Canceled our reservations."

Harry's face is mottled and round. His nose turns up like a snout. "Lovie, we arrived at two a.m. Where would we have gone?"

It's a reasonable question, but the skinny woman ignores him and keeps talking. "We wouldn't have gotten lost if you'd let me read the map. The travel agent assured us this is a first class hotel. Looks to me like a moldy pile of rotten boards...."

"Sheriff Townsend, what would you like for breakfast?" Mr. Leviticus is arranging our plates and managing to stand between us and the new hotel guests.

The sheriff looks up at him and grins as if he's teasing him. "What happened last night?"

"Strangest thing. Nialis says she made up that rooms fresh about three on Monday afternoon. When I took the Longers up, the bed had been stripped. I got fresh sheets out of the linen closet. Two sets of sheets were in the hamper for Orta to launder. No one has used that room. I don't...."

"Waiter. We're waiting." Her voice bellows around the room like a frog with laryngitis.

Mr. Leviticus excuses himself after taking the sheriff's order and hurries to their table.

The woman pokes her nose in the front page of a newspaper as she hands her companion what looks like the sports section, ignoring the waiter she beckoned. "Wally! The papers says a murder was committed here Monday night."

The man is giving his order, "That's nice dear! What do you want to eat?"

"Wally. You know I take coffee and toast. This is exciting. Listen, she was found on the beach. When you finish we'll go down and have a look."

Sheriff Townsend rises and walks over to their table. "Ma'am, I'm sorry, but the beach is off limits until the investigation is completed. I must request that you restrict your walks to the hotel grounds. I want to thank you for your coorporation." He turns and starts back as the waiter delivers his breakfast.

Mrs. Longer lifts her crooked beak from the paper and stares at his back. "Young man, we are hotel guests. We were assured the complete use of all the facilities, which includes the beach. Who are you to tell us what we can do?"

His posture stiffens like Mark's, but he doesn't turn around. "I am the sheriff."

As he sits down, the waiter whispers in his ear.

"It's not a problem, Marsh. Just keep them off the beach. Maybe the storm building up the coast will send them on their way."

I look at Sheriff Townsend. He is smiling as if they're sharing a private joke. "You were in the Marines?"

"Yes, how did you know?"

"Your walk. My brother, Mark is a lieutenant. He took his basic training at Paris Island."

"They prefer southern boys. We know how to take the heat and no-see 'ems."

"We call them gnats, at home. Have you made much progress on Mrs. Lavin?" Maud does ask abrupt questions when she has a mind to.

"No, Ma'am." He lowers his voice to prevent his being over-heard. The Longers, both of whom are doing their best to hear our conversation, lean toward our table. "I haven't been able to con-tact her husband. Nothing much in her room except clothes and cosmetics."

"I'm sorry, Sheriff. I didn't know the beach was closed. I ran down there this morning."

"I know, I watched you. Your feet are giving you a bit of trouble, even running, you're careful how you place them."

"Oh."

"Same accident that took your eye?"

"Yes." He gives me a long look from those flat colored eyes.

"Mrs. Tosh, I owe you an apology."

"You do?"

Shell is making a major job of clearing the Longers' table. A look of contempt flashes across his face as he watches Mr. Leviticus make change for the couple. He picks up the tip from under the edge of the man's plate and sticks it in his pocket. His head is sunk in his shoulders as he pushes the cart back to the kitchen.

"I didn't answer your question. Marsh calls me Thay, when he isn't being a royal pain. We grew up together. Don't let him pull your leg. He owns this end of the island. This hotel belongs to his mother. My father was the sheriff, preacher, and justice of the peace. Dad died while I was in the service, and I became sheriff by inheritance. Never have much call for the law duties, since most everyone who lives full time on the island is either family or friends."

"I'm recording and arranging all our county records. I know about families and land."

"Right on target. Our some great-grandfather bought this island from the Indians like the Dutch bought Manhattan. The purchase was near the middle of the 1600s. Same family and their indentured servants have always owned and cropped it. The first Townsend took an Indian mistress, then made it legal. Another one brought a few slaves from St. Croix, when they were trying to grow rice and indigo. After the Revolution they started raising a special long fiber cotton from the southern islands."

His laugh has a bitter sound. "I'm sorry, I didn't mean to get started on my personal hobby-horse."

"Thay, you drink your coffee, then go home and get some sleep. With Shell's help we'll keep things going today."

"Thanks, Marsh. It was a long night."

Full daylight is slow in breaking over the rough dunes. Maybe it is the sheriff's gloomy history of the island. Or maybe the lone woman who lies in the morgue on the mainland with no one to claim her. But the constant grayness of the day has invaded my cottage.

The iron bedstead and wicker furnishing are painted white, but look as if they are overdue for a fresh coat. Insulation has been added between the walls and paneling. The walls are painted light blue with a white wash layered over the blue, but the wood grain shows through. It makes the room look like the sky shrouded with thin clouds. Strange, and yet comfortable.

I tried to take a nap after breakfast, but I slept in rough fits and starts to the thump of a loose shutter flapping on its hinges. A screwdriver would fix it, but I lack the energy to walk to the parking lot for my toolbox.

I didn't bother to go back to the hotel for lunch, not good company today. Maud told me how the murdered girl had come to the beach on the way to town. She said Phedra Lavin looked sad and lost as she strolled along the dunes. Maud didn't disturb the young woman, but retreated to the hotel to get a book from the parlor.

She regrets her action, though I don't see that she could have done anything else. It wasn't like Mrs. Lavin was a friend.

Munching on Nabs and drinking a Pepsi, I watch Maud from my window. She's wearing her red boots and the yellow raincoat, the only bright spot on the beach. She stops near the steps, picks up a shell and drops it in her pocket, then moves on, looking out toward the ocean.

Small fissures in the clouds let streaks of light dash across the breakers as the ocean rushes toward the shore and then retreats. The waves built the island. At home the rain and wind tear down the land, taking it away by the rivers to the Gulf of Mexico.

I don't think Maud wants company this afternoon; she doesn't seem alone out there. She is in a deep study. I half-heartedly wave when she looks my way, but she doesn't see me. I can't let her down. I must ask more or better questions, but of whom?

The sheriff doesn't know much more than we do, or if he does, he isn't saying. From what Mr. Leviticus said to him this morning he must have been walking around the island most of the night. Wonder what he was looking for, like why was he spending time watching me read? How do you inherit a job as a law officer?

A strange man, the sheriff?

Chapter 5

A large hand clamps my shoulder. "I knew I'd find you eating."

"Matt! What are you doing here?"

"Had a few days, so I came down to check on you." He pulls me from the chair in a one-armed hug. "Still as skinny as ever, I see."

"Put me down. You're showing off."

He sets me on my feet so as not to damage the freshknit bones. "You know Mrs. Tosh?"

"How are you, Ma'am?"

"I'm fine Matthew. When did you arrive?"

"Call me Matt. Matthew sounds like I've been misbehaving."

All the while, they're bantering, Matt is eyeing the sheriff. "Sheriff Thayer Townsend, may I introduce Matt Young."

Matt can charm the scent off a skunk. He reaches his big paw across the table and shakes hands as if he'd waited all day to meet the man.

"Matt Young, you play professional football?"

"Yes."

"You're brothers?"

"Yes."

"I recognize a family trait."

Matt brown eyes flicker with puzzlement, but I laugh.

"Mr. Leviticus, we will need another place-setting and a menu."

"Yes, Ma'am. If Mr. Young will autograph the menu, you can call me Marsh."

Matt takes one of his business cards from his pocket and pulls his right arm out of the sling. He writes a note on the back and then hands it to the waiter.

Marsh reads the note. "Right away, Mr. Matt."

"Waiter. We're waiting to be seated."

Wally and Fanny Longer stand just inside the door. Her demand stops him from taking our orders to the kitchen. He starts to seat them at a table near the front, but Mrs. Longer charges like a front lineman to the table beside ours. Like a trailer in tow, Wally waddles behind her. Marsh follows them with a scowl on his face.

He gives them menus and retreats to the kitchen. Her ears waggle like loose antennas as she changes her seat to have us in full view. "Wally, that's Matt Young. You watched him broadcast the last game of the season."

"No, Lovie, he couldn't be. Matt Young is in Minnesota."

"No, he isn't. He's been fired. I read it in the paper. The Vikings dropped his contract. I never forget a face. That's him, over there with that so-called Sheriff."

Matt shrugs. "So much for my secret. I'll tell you about it later... right now I'm hungry. Mrs. Tosh, what brings you to Seamew Island?"

Maud pats his hand in sympathy. "Matt, we're all on a first name basis. I'm on vacation, just like you and Jim."

"Thank you, Ma'am."

I want to ask him about his contract and what happened, but it's clear he doesn't want to discuss the matter in public.

"Sheriff Townsend was telling us about the island at breakfast. I'd love to hear more."

"We'll have what they're having. Don't put sand in our food like you did this morning. Wally couldn't eat his cereal."

Marsh stutters with outrage, "Sa...nd! No one put sand in his cereal."

"Yes, you did. He said he had grit."

"No, Lovie. I said...."

"Wally, don't interrupt me. I know what you said. We want the flounder and make sure it's fresh. Do you understand me?" Her voice gets louder as if Marsh is hard of hearing.

"I will bring your order...right out." Marsh's broad shoulders are shaking while he uses the towel he carries over his arm to wipe his face as he almost runs to the kitchen.

"My, her voice does carry." Maud raises her napkin to dry lips. Matt is about to double over, making it tough for me as I sit facing Fanny Longer.

"Thank you, Shell. I'd love an ice tea with my meal, but I believe your uncle wants you to serve the Longers first. You wouldn't want to slight the paying guests." Thayer Townsend's face is solemn and his voice soft, but he winks at Shell Wallace.

The busboy doesn't seem to understand the Sheriff's instruction. His sweeping look dismisses our table before he turns with a single glass of tea to deliver to the Longers.

"I'm so full, I feel like the Thanksgiving turkey. That stuffed flounder was terrific." Matt looks at us with a grin, while I'm trying not to belch.

Sheriff Townsend smiles at Matt. "I've eaten Mamma Lou's cooking all my life. This is a new offering. What did you write on that card you gave Marsh?"

Matt wipes butter off his square chin and finishes his roll. "If he'd call me Matt, I'd call him Marsh and I was starving for fresh seafood."

"You went to Mamma Lou's heart. She created this recipe on the spot, just for you. This is different from what she sent the Longers." The sheriff seems almost human since Matt has joined us. His slate orbs gleam with laughter.

"Mrs. Longer's eyes almost jumped out of her head. What was on her plate?" I ask because I am sitting facing her and saw her reaction.

"Exactly what she ordered. Fresh flounder. Shell caught it this morning. They live in shallow waters."

"Oh, the cook left the eyes." Matt smiles his lazy smile.

"Yes, but flounder are not ordinary fish. Both of their eyes are on the same side."

"What?" I gape at the sheriff.

"After they're grown, they turn sideways then lie flat on the bottom. Sand covers them as camouflage from predators. The eye on the underside migrates topside. What is it, Shell?"

"Mamma Lou wants you in the kitchen."

"Excuse me. After this meal, I'd best answer her beck and call."

The sheriff isn't gone but a few minutes. While he is in the kitchen, the Longers finish their meal and leave. Their absence makes the room more comfortable to my way of thinking.

"Gentlemen, our cook informs me she is running short on oysters. Would you be up to joining us for an after-midnight harvest?"

"Would I? Will we need a fishing license?" I've been wanting to wet a line since I arrived.

"No, a strong back will do. Low tide is around 2 AM, which should give us plenty of time to get some sleep.

"Jim, you have boots and a heavy coat, bring them. Matt, Marsh will find something for you. Meet him in front of the hotel at one o'clock, and he'll show you how to get to my place. You don't mind using that big Rover of yours, do you?"

"Are you kidding? I've never been fishing for oysters."

Matt laughs at me, "Jim, you don't use a pole for oysters, a maddox is a good tool."

"Sheriff, I didn't realize when the menu says fresh, it's right out of the ocean."

"Miss Maud, the sea is our front stoop. Why not take advantage of its bounty when there isn't a hotel full of guests to feed? It's different during the summer. Then Marsh has the produce delivered from the mainland. It's still fairly fresh, but the commercial guys take over the delivery. The oysters come frozen. It's illegal to harvest them during the summer months.

"Jim, before I forget, give Marsh your keys so he can put the baskets and buckets in the back."

"I must meet Mamma Lou. She is a woman after my own heart. She vexed Fanny Longer who has been so obnoxious. Then put you fellows to work for our dinner. When do you think the Longers will be leaving?"

"Miss Maud, you have a devious mind."

"Well! At least, I have one, not like some people I've seen."

As if on cue, Marsh starts removing our plates. "We have chocolate-pecan pie for dessert, still hot from the oven."

The sheriff looks up at him, "Reserve my place at this table as long as your guests are here."

"Trying to be funny? You eat here every day."

"Oyster dressing wrapped in a fillet of flounder. Bourbon cream on the pie? Now she got us out in the middle of the night for more oysters. Tomorrow night she's going to shuck grilled oysters here in the dining room. I know preferential treatment when I taste it."

"Humph! It's to get everyone's mind off the murder. Shell, push that cart to the kitchen."

"Marsh is a football fanatic. He keeps his own stats by following every team. Played in high school before he went in the Army. He knew who you were as soon...."

"Lemuel, she'll show up. Probably went shopping. Stop worrying, let's eat."

A voice, honeyed yet shrill enough to cut steel.

We all turn. A man and woman stand just inside the door.

The woman is wrapped in mink from head to toe. The man has an impatient air as his dark eyes dart around the room looking for someone.

"Matt." Her rapier voice pierces the air as she drags the man to our table. "Matt Young, what are you doing in this god-forsaken place?" She grabs his hand and holds it. Except for Miss Maud, we all stand, the sheriff is first on his feet.

"Having dinner, Lettic." The charm has lowered by perceptible degrees. Matt doesn't have any use for this woman, but he isn't backward. He looks at us like a trapped coon. "May I introduce, Lettic Forbenshire and her brother-in-law, Dr. Lemuel Lavin. Where is Phedra?"

"We've been looking for her."

"Dr. Lavin and Miss Forbenshire, please come with me. I'm Thayer Townsend, the sheriff on Seamew Island. I must talk to you." He gently takes the doctor's arm and steers him toward the door.

"Tell Marsh to bring some coffee to the small parlor off the lobby." The woman gives Matt a saucy look and follows in their wake.

"Who are they? You asked about Phedra." Maud is gripping Matt's good arm.

"Lettic's father owned a semi-pro team outside Minneapolis. He died recently and the sisters inherited the team. She collects trophies. I don't intend to be one of them.

"Phedra is Lettic's sister and Dr. Lavin's wife. Why did the sheriff hustle them out of here? He hasn't finished his dessert."

"We found his wife's body on the beach." Maud's voice is low and reverent, but she has a strange look on her face. She shakes her head as Matt almost bellows.

"What?" He stares at us. "I thought the sheriff was trying to beat Jim's time with you."

"Matt, he acts like we're suspects. He follows us. He told me he patrolled at night. He spent one night watching me read. At least, he did until you arrived."

" I doubt that my presence can lend you respectability. Can't you stay out of trouble on a deserted beach?"

"Discovering Phedra Lavin's body isn't doing anything. I only asked a few questions."

"Jim, damn it. If someone killed her, they can sure knock off a nitwit hillbilly poking around in their business. Kane will have a fit. We just got you put back together."

"You don't have to tell him. Besides, Maud found her. I was sitting on her."

"You what?Marsh, may we have more coffee and another sliver of pie?Thank you, put the bill on my room.

"This is fascinating. When did it happen?"

Maud leans her head sightly to the left making her red curls just brush her shoulder. "Matt, are you positive that man is Phedra's husband?"

"Sure. Dr. Lavin emergency-set my shoulder before the ambulance arrived. You don't forget that kind of pain. He is always around the locker room after a game helping the team's physician with minor injuries."

She gives a little shrug as if dismissing something. "Matthew, we found her body Tuesday morning. According to the sheriff she was beaten and strangled sometime during the night. That's all we know."

When Matt raises his eyebrow, it isn't like Kane's with a look of disdain. It wobbles, having been cut in half by a cleat. It looks as if he's trying hard not to laugh.

"OK, Gumshoe, spill it. There are some details, I think I missed. Like how did you get so palsy with the sheriff who suspects you of killing a woman you never met?"

Damn him. He's gotten me bumfuzzled, making fun of me in front of Maud. I'd said more than I intended and it came out sideways. How dare he treat me like a rube who has never left home?

Chapter 6

"The walls in the hotel are too thin. I heard every step the porter took while I was trying to take a nap. Tomorrow I'm going to move out to the beach."

"Matt, they don't have a night porter."

"The kid, Shell, I heard him talking to someone on the verandah. He insisted on taking my bag to the room before dinner. He'd of unpacked, if I'd let him.

"Matt, the fawning is called service. We're in the deep South. It's like stepping back in time. Takes getting used to, besides, not many paying customers around this time of year to pass out big tips. Shell Wallace is Marsh's nephew. He works in the kitchen, and helps in the dining room as the bus boy. He's a veteran and trying to get accepted at Howard University for law school."

"He'd better kick his habit first. He's a user."

"Are you sure? That stuff's dangerous."

"Didn't you see how his eyes were dilated?"

"How did you know?"

"I've seen it in locker rooms. But Abel clued me in about 'Nam. A bunch of kids who should never have been there in the first place came home with the habit. Their muster-out pay from hell." Matt is angry.

"Don't mention that while we're out on their boat. Marsh might drown you for bad-mouthing his nephew. Their entire family works here in some capacity or the other. The cook, Mamma Lou is Marsh's mother, and she owns the hotel. For that matter, they're also kin of the sheriff. He told us they had the same great-grandfather."

"My, my, you are being nosey. Why don't you take up genealogy? We don't know a damn thing about our family. Let's fix a flask to take with us to brave the cold."

"I promised Kane I'd dry out. I've already cheated with Mamma Lou's bourbon cream."

"That pie was wicked. It was so rich, my eyes sweated. I knew it would put you to sleep and make us late." He clamps his left hand on my shoulder and shoves me sideways up the path to the hotel.

"The hell with Kane. He's never had a carbuckle, never did anything wrong. Mr. Perfect. Every family has the same burden to bear. My shoulder is giving me fits from driving."

"That's your fault. The Porsche is great looking, but doesn't handle worth a damn. You drive too fast."

"Look who's talking."

Chapter 7

Marsh's directions take me the length of the island through pitch-black tunnels of Spanish moss that floats like phantasm in my headlights. The red eyes of deer stare at us before bounding away from the monster encroaching on their feeding grounds. We turn beside a dirty-white farmhouse whose yellow porch light is a faint beacon surrounded by a shoal of shadow.

The shell road ends at a dock, which extends out into a lagoon called *Port de Refuge.* The name sounds odd, like a guttural swallow.

Lanterns hang from hooks that extend out over two boats. Flat-bottomed and shaped like a john boat, these skiffs are longer and broader. Six-horsepower trolling motors rigged from each stern are tilted out of the water. Long poles are attached to the gunwales like handrails. Flat ladders bolted to both sides of the dock let you climb down to reach the skiffs.

Going down the ladder, I notice that the posts of the dock are whole tree trunks driven into the muck. There is some water under the boats, but not much. When I put my weight in the boat a waft of rotten eggs engulfs me. The air below the dock oozes of decay, rotten fish, and wet salt. The sky is like crawling under a huge cast-iron pot. Crushed under the weight, I'm trapped by the burden of closeness.

A lantern bobs in the dark, then descends with the sheriff. He's laughing. Marsh hands down bushel baskets and a galvanized washtub.

"Hold this while I batten down the cargo." He hands me the lantern. "I sent Matt with Marsh. They can talk football to their heart's content. Here, take off your jacket and string these through the sleeves then put it back on."

He removes a pair of heavy gloves attached by a thick cord from around his neck. I can see another pair dangling from his jacket's sleeves. They look like mittens for giants.

"Won't need them for now, but when we pull up the oysters, they're a blessing. You can shave with their shells. Good gloves cost a fortune and they're easy to drop overboard in the dark."

All the time he's talking, he's fastening the washtub into cleats on the bow seat and distributing the baskets down the sides. He is careful to step around the large bent prongs of a long-handled-rake that is lying in the bow.

"That's a clam rake, but it comes in handy with oysters if the incoming tide catches us. Not much chance tonight as we've got about five hours before it gets too deep to work the beds.

"We'll follow Marsh. He and Shell too, for that matter, can find their way through every slough between here and the river, without getting in the main current. His given name is Marshall, but we shorten it because he spent all his free time out here. Never could find him unless he wanted to be found."

"Oh. Where's the river?"

"We're on the backside of the north end of *Seamew*. *Port de Refuge* was named before it filled in with silt, not much of a port now. Once it was a hiding place for pirates. There is a dense estuary running to the mainland. Four miles of tidal mud flats, with little creeks and arms of a river delta. Smaller, but like the mouth of the Mississippi. It's like a maze and is always changing. Navigating in the dark-of-the-moon takes an expert and a keen sense of direction if you're not using a compass."

I hear slup-glug and watch the dot of light on Marsh's boat bounce like giant firefly. A large owl glides just above the dock, I can feel the brush of his powerful wings on the still air.

"They're poling until they get in deeper water. Here, take one of these, and I'll show you." He hands me one of the long poles. Its over two feet above my head. The pole is worn smooth with frequent handling.

"We have to pole in unison or we'll go sideways. Push it down in the mud about two inches. Don't waste energy trying to shove it deeper. You'll get the feel, enough to move it forward then lift it clear and move it up beside that first basket before you put it down again."

I copy his hold on the pole using the faint light from the bow. I know how to row with two oars or paddle a canoe, but poling is new to me. Below my feet, under the skiff, I can feel a slight shift in the depth of the water. It isn't like the movement of the tide on the beach, but it has the same rhythm like my pulse beating through my feet.

"Let me move us into the current. I'll tell you when to start poling." He's like a shadow against the dark as he maneuvers the awkward craft out from the dock, using the huge sunken pillars to push us backward.

With my first pole, the skiff skims over the surface, faster than I'd imagined, as if I've shoved the bottom out from under my feet. The silence is deafening. Nothing but the slup-glug sucking sound of our poles as we pulled them from the water, which is thick with stirred gunk. I lean over farther and farther to touch bottom with each pole.

After a good struggle, I find the rhythm of his smooth movements. This will put shoulders on a man as easy as power lifting. Sweat is running down my face, getting in my eye, but I don't dare let go of the pole to wipe it away. My arms are aching when I hear the chug-chunk of a flywheel being pulled.

"Almost there. They're around the bend in deep water. There's a rake, sorry. To you it's an oyster bed to your left, but it's too close to home. Marsh doesn't care to take from that one unless it is an emergency."

"Hellfire and damnation."

The curse rings in the silence. "Thay, stop poking along. Start that motor and get over here."

They were farther away than I figured from the sound of Marsh's voice. He is tugging at a grimy cloth, like a tablecloth.

"Jim, hold that lantern up high. Thay, help me get this damn thing off. It's hung."

My feeble light bounces off piles of oysters clinging to the rotting ribs of the hull of a ship.

"Remains of the *Amelia*. She got tossed up here during the same hurricane that put the old hotel in the ocean."

Thay takes us in close and they jerk the cloth free. It's attached to a broken mast by twisted ropes.

"Damn near ruined the motor. It was floating below the water line. Wrapped one of those ropes around the prop."

Matt asks my question. "How did that get here?"

"Came in on the tide. Ropes got tangled on something and held it when the tide went out. Happens all the time. Shell's supposed to check this area for debris. He didn't say anything, I'll wring his neck."

The sheriff sees Matt's scepticism at Marsh's explanation. "Standing where you are now, when the tide's in, only your hands would be above water."

Marsh is looking at the broken end of the mast, "Fresh, twisted then tore off, looks like it got caught in a crosswind. Fool didn't know enough to haul down his sail."

Matt is standing by the transom with his arm extended above his head. "Good measure. Not like the Bay of Fundy, which has 54-foot tides. Our tides send what amounts to a wall of ocean inland. They are much smaller, from five to seven feet high. This shore has two during every twenty-four hours. Tiny sea animals, the can't-see stuff in the water are the oysters' food."

"Stop showing off with talk and help us twine the sail around what's left of the mast. We'll take it back with us."

After tugging, twisting, and shoving we get the soggy cargo stowed under the seats, out of the way of our feet. Then we start harvesting oysters, which is hard, grueling work. Matt works beside Marsh's boat and I stand outside of Thay's breaking off chunks of shells with a claw-hammer and tossing them in the boat. Standing on the polished-glass surface of the bed in rubber boots is murder.

They don't trust us to do the sorting. The bad ones, those punched by a oyster drill, and empty shells are thrown back. Thay shows me the tiny hole in the shell from the oyster drill, which is a snail. I wouldn't have seen it in the near black, even with my improved night vision.

The galvanized tub is filling with starfish. Matt was excited with his first find and being able to identify the familiar sea creature until Marsh demonstrated what they do to an oyster.

"Take your hand and pretend it's a starfish. Close your fingers around it like covering a football, then push the fleshy part of your palm out. Your palm is the starfish's stomach. Suction cups on the underarms pull the shell apart enough for it to push its greedy stomach down to the meat, which it sucks right out. One starfish will consume six to eight oysters a day, bunches of 'em will destroy a bed. Toss it in the tub. Ground up they're good fertilizer."

The hours fly, but I'm losing my taste for oysters. I've learned too much about them, too fast to digest.

Matt carefully climbs over the pile for one last look before we head back. His head disappears over a crumbling hill of discarded shells. The moon sheds shafts of light through the drifts of scudding clouds, making it easier to see in the near black.

"Marsh, there's another sail over here all rolled up. It's almost covered with water. I can't lift it. It keeps sliding."

"Stay there, we'll work our way around."

When we get to the backside, Matt is standing beside the roll, staring. "Sheriff, there's a hand on this side. It's wearing a suit."

Thay Townsend jumps as I steady the boat with the pole against the ribs of another ancient ship. Marsh tosses me his line and follows him, pulling a flashlight from his pocket. The Sheriff is all business as he carefully uncovers the body. I can't see much. I'm glad, as I hold both skiffs off the clumps of oysters. However, Matt is looking rather peaked.

I look down at the body as a shaft of moon light strikes his face. It's mottled grey with staring eyes that bore into my brain. The man is wearing a suit. The once-white collar of his shirt is now a grimy brown. His tie begins to float in the water as the tide rises around us. My stomach starts to roll, but I clamp down hard with my teeth and take in gulps of briny air. For a moment, I think I know him, but the thought evaporates as my insides fight for air.

"He's been garrotted! Sliced above his shirt collar."

"Thay, that's the man who took Mrs. Lavin for a ride around the island."

"Are you sure?"

"Yes, he asked for her at the desk."

Chapter 8

"I'm sorry, but you'll have to stay here until the ranger from the Port Authority gets over here to take our statements. You were a real help, but he'll want to question everyone who was out there. Take a seat while I make the call on the radio."

We're standing in the den of Thay Townsend's home. It's a beautiful room with a broad fireplace across one end, with long windows that reach the floor and face *Port de Refuge*. One wall is lined with books, like Elton Fightmaster's office with the same style of furniture that have open shells carved in the wood. The pieces are upholstered in deep green leather. The chairs and davenport by the fireplace are worn smooth, the color almost gone on the arms. Between the windows is a tall cabinet, which the Sheriff opens. He folds down a long narrow table and pulls out a microphone.

"Marsh, it'll take them a half hour or so to get here. Rustle up some food, I've got some sweet rolls and coffee in the kitchen. Better fix enough for six, they'll expect substance for our getting them up before daybreak.

"Mayday! Mayday!" He speaks into the microphone.

"Sweet rolls! A person could starve to death on what he keeps in his kitchen. He'll have to tell them the whole story before they'll come out. Can you make coffee?"

"Sure." Matt answers, but looks at me.

"I'll take Thay's truck and see what my sister has in her larder. She'll be wondering about all the lights. There's a big urn back there," Marsh is pointing down the hall. "somewhere. Use it. Be right back."

We follow Marsh down the hall and he ducks out the back door. The kitchen is huge.

"What's on his mind? He was in a hurry to get out of here."

"He was telling the truth, look in this refrigerator. It's bare except for a can of coffee. Never saw one this big with glass doors." The Sheriff may not cook, but someone did. There must be a couple of dozen copper pans hanging from a rack above a dark granite sink.

"Jim, stop thinking about food. Marsh was worried about something as soon as he saw that body. He didn't say one word coming back, but kept glancing down at that rolled sail. It was an old one; it had been mended. You're too trusting."

"Matt, there's a connection between this new murder and Phedra Levin's. Marsh identified the body as the man who took Mrs. Lavin for a ride a few weeks before she was murdered. I promised Miss Maud I'd help, but tonight was too much."

"I know. Bodies with slit throats are out of my line. Jim, I can't tell you what to do. Your head knows the score. Problem is I don't think your heart will listen. You let other people rule your actions. Coming here in the first place. Why here? It's gloomy enough without two murders."

"Kane didn't want Mom to worry about me."

"Don't you dare let Kane lay a guilt trip on you. Did Mom say a word to you?"

"No, but I saw the look in her eyes when I was on the floor and couldn't get up. Vera was yelling at Adam to get his drunken brother out of her house. I wanted to die right there.

"Matt, I wasn't drunk. My cane got caught in one of those braided rugs she has all over the place. Mom's eyes were so sad."

"Stop feeling sorry for yourself. Think of someone else. Ever consider maybe she was sad for Adam?"

"Adam?"

"Jim, get your head out of your ass. Look at us, *all* of us."

"I don't know what you mean."

"Take Adam, for instance. He's never had much of a life. Had to be the man of the house when he was ten years old. Vera only married him because she thought he could provide the money for a career in Nashville. She has been riding him raw since Catherine Throckton left her estate to us. Mom can see the truth if Adam can't."

"Their marriage was rather sudden."

"Sudden hell, she trapped him. Told him she was pregnant when she wasn't."

"But she lost a baby."

"That was later. She made sure he wouldn't dump her until she had her hooks in tight. She'd screw anything in pants if she thought it would get her to Nashville."

"You mean the same way Lettic Forbenshire came onto you? Seemed rather silly to me with Maud sitting there looking like Mom."

Matt starts laughing. "Maud looking like Mom! Where in the world did you get an idea like that? Maud Tosh doesn't look like anyone's mother. She looks more like one of those French courtesans from the seventeenth century. Give me a cigarette."

"Huh." I toss him my pack of Pall Mall's. Matt doesn't smoke, and besides, what are courtesans?

Matt cups his hand around the match flame and lights the cigarette. His dark eyes glitter above the flame. "How could Kane let you out of Clydesville? It's too dangerous."

"Will you stop jumping around? I'm not dumb."

"Didn't say you are, just naive and innocent. You don't know a blessed diddly about women. It's a good thing it was Isaac who went into politics. You'd be a nice juicy lamb for the wolves to fight over."

"There you go again. What's Isaac got to do with women?"

"Sit down, Little Brother, you are going to get a crash course in women."

I'd gotten up from the bed where I was half lying as Matt had settled into the comfortable wicker rocker by a low table. I stand watching the waves hit the beach while I massage the muscles in my leg. The sky now is devoid of clouds and the moon has turned from gray to the burnished silver of a polished piston. "I'm fine. Need to stretch my leg."

It isn't true. He is pushing my buttons. He saved my life, but he doesn't have to treat me like an idiot. I've had girlfriends. Not many, but a few.

"Look, let's say it this way. Maud Tosh is class, even though she's never been away from home. She's a woman of the world. Look at her eyes. She knows all about you."

I'd had the same feeling when we had dinner, like she was seeing me in my BVD's.

"She flirts with every man she meets, but it doesn't mean a thing. She's in love with someone. You can see it, all other men are just desserts to her because she's interested in you as a person. If you cross the line, she'd pat you on the ass, send you off to bed alone, and you'd love her for it."

"Matt, her husband just died. I watched her pitch his ashes in the sea. She loved him when she married him even if he was rough on her."

"No Jim, she's in love with a living person. She endured Rupert and by throwing him in the sea she got him out of her life, a grand symbolic gesture. Maud's deep. It's what makes her special."

"Who?"

"How should I know? It's none of our business."

"You're right, but I still don't understand what you're driving at.

Matt stabs the cigarette at me like a teacher's pointer. "Plain and simple. Lettic Forbenshire is expensive trash, she carves notches on her bedpost."

"But where do Isaac and Vera fit in?"

"Vera wants to be a Lettic, use people, but she is too self-centered." He looks down at the burning butt and pitches it in the fireplace. "Can't prove it, but I know she started those tales of you being a drunk. She pitched a fit in the hospital when Kane told them to send him all your bills. Gave Adam hell, saying he didn't care enough for his family when you were hanging between life and death. She raved about his leaving her and their child while you were in trouble. Mark lost his temper. He marched her out of there like she was a raw recruit. Told Adam to take her home and drown her."

"I didn't know."

"Of course not. Remember we were all there for four days not knowing if you would make it. Not being able to do a damn thing, but wait and hope, which is hell."

His story made me feel small that I'd put my family through such times. My right leg is shooting pains to my shoulder as I lean on it, listening to him. I collapse on the bed and light another cigarette to give my hands something to do.

"The gist of the whole matter was Kane used the family fund for you, but won't spend a dime on her.

"Isaiah says she hasn't the drive to make it in the music business. She makes a play for him every time he comes home. She wants him to take her homemade tapes to Nashville. Rather than cause a row, he flees to Capital City to fight with Isaac or pull Levi's strings."

"Now you're back to Isaac."

"Didn't mean to go around the barn. Isaac is a lady's man almost like Maud is a man's woman. He needs to win his next election and with our help he will, but he isn't ready for a wife. He attracts them like flies. What woman can resist his looks? Like Maud, underneath the camouflage he's a one-woman man, but that won't necessarily mean marriage."

Lack of sleep is catching up with me as I yawn. "What about you, Mr. Know-It-All?"

"I'm going back to the hotel. School's out."

"You didn't answer my question."

"See you on the beach at 10 hundred hours."

"What's…that?"

"Military time. Ten o'clock." The door bangs.

It's six am, four hours to beach time. I set the clock. Whatever happen to rest on a vacation?

January 16 , 1976.

> *I have so much to tell you and I haven't got much time to make the morning mail.*
>
> *Matt Young joined us for a few days. He lost his contract with the Vikings because his shoulder isn't healing properly. Like Jim, he hasn't said anything about his troubles.*
>
> *There is a silly couple staying at the hotel, Fanny and Wally Longer. I've learned the meaning of the term "dumb broad." I haven't heard an intelligent word out of that woman's mouth. Jim says she sounds like a drowning bullfrog.*
>
> *Last night, while we were eating, Phedra's husband and sister arrived. They didn't know she had been murdered. No one has seen them since the sheriff informed them of the tragedy. They are staying in their rooms, but ordered rolls and coffee from room service.*

Odd. Her husband isn't the same man I saw Phedra kissing, nor is he the man she slapped the night before she was killed. Wonder what all this means because I've now seen or connected Phedra with three different men. Her sister has her eyes on Matt, but he isn't buying. He knows them from Minneapolis, or at least knows the family.

The cook fixed a marvelous dinner last night with fresh flounder. Fresh here means right out of the ocean. Imagine!

I just learned this. After midnight the sheriff and the manager of the hotel took Matt and Jim with them to harvest oysters. They caught more than they expected. Matt discovered the body of a man hidden in the oyster beds.

The sheriff just stopped by my table to tell me. I'm eating alone as the boys are still sleeping after their late night. He asked if I would mind going to the mainland to view the body for identification. Jim must have told him about my seeing her kissing someone.

The postman is at the desk. Talk to you later.

Maud

Chapter 9

"I thought I was...in shape. How do you run in those dumb boots?"

Like mine, Matt's breath is coming in gasps. We'd run for two miles down the beach. We warmed up going out and raced back to the steps.

"Enough sand in this boot to take the beach home. Early morning is my favorite time. Maud brings me a cup of coffee, then we watch the sun come up. She's been up for hours today."

"Those boots must weigh a ton." He holds up his worn sneakers, his little toes are sticking out the sides.

"Practice. I've been here for a week. Legs hurt like hell, the first few days. You'll freeze your toes, I looked at the thermometer on the way out, 30 degrees. It was warmer last night."

"Jim, I run in Minnesota, zero in January is a warm day. How did you meet up with Mrs. Tosh?"

"On the beach the second morning I was here, she was throwing her husband's ashes into the sea."

"Fitting. Life came from the sea."

"She said the same thing."

"When I was around home, I heard stories. He mistreated her. When did he die?"

"Near Thanksgiving, best I can remember. Mom took food to church for the reception after the memorial service."

Matt is seven years older than me. I turned twenty-six on the day after I arrived. He's my special older brother. Adam, the oldest, has always been like a dad, and the twins, Kane and Abel are a law unto themselves. I know I owe him my life. He pulled me from the wreck that took my eye last May.

"Last night was something, wonder who the guy is?"

"Sheriff didn't do more than put him in Marsh's boat. The killer didn't intend for him to be found, is my guess."

"I didn't mean to find him, either. Almost fell in the water when I was tugging on that sail and his hand popped out. Then when the sheriff moved him and I saw he had that extra mouth. I came near losing it."

"I wouldn't have been surprised if you had, I kept sucking air like I'd run full-out for six miles. Then your riding back with him at your feet. Just thinking about it was enough to make my stomach rumble."

"Didn't hurt your appetite. Marsh really did go to get supplies."

"Seems to me those two shore patrol guys did more than their fair share with the groceries."

"Thay is a cold blooded guy. Took it like it was all in a day's work. Where did you find the woman?" Matt is standing, doing stretches.

"Just to your left. Her foot was sticking out of the sand." He jumps. "Maud found her."

"Marsh mentioned the guy asked for her at the desk and took her for a ride around the island the day we found her. Can't help wondering how she knew the deceased?"

"Jim, what are you talking about?"

"Phedra Lavin and the guy you found last night."

"I've never seen him. He wasn't with them at any of the games, when I was playing host. Forbenshire had a box at Memorial Stadium. Their father was a good guy. He always brought the family. Public relations insisted players visit with the box-holders. That part of the game I don't like. "

"Are semi-pro teams important?"

"Yes, they give the smaller towns a taste of professional football. Sometimes, they help injured players get back in the game. Mr. Forbenshire died a few weeks back. I told you that last night. With Mrs. Lavin dead looks as if Lettic will have her dream—an entire football team at her beck and call. I don't want any part of it."

"You can sit here and puzzle on murders, but I'm hungry. No coffee delivery."

"Hey, I'm not the one doing the pondering."

"I sort of promised Maud I'd find out what happened to Phedra Lavin, but last night changes everything. I don't want any part of it, besides, the dead guy belongs to the Port Authority. Townsend's jurisdiction is the island."

"Don't mean to rain on Miss Maud's parade, but you keep your nose out of it. Thayer Townsend is a nice guy, but poaching on his turf is dangerous. I get the feeling he'd be happier walking the planks of one of those old pirate ships, wearing a patch over his eye."

"You noticed that, how he's always watching me?"

"Can't miss it."

"I thought I was being paranoid." I glanced at my watch. We've been out for two hours. It's noon. Late nights make you lazy.

"Come on, get off your butt. You know we're both "on the beach."

Matt doesn't want to go near the subject of his canceled contract. "You nuts? We are on a beach."

"'On the beach,' is an old sailors' cant. Means you're stoved up and can't get a job on a ship. You can't drive and I can't play ball."

With that somber note, Matt drapes his good arm across my shoulder like I'm a little kid and we climb the stairs to the hotel. He ignored me last night, too. Is this as close as he'll come to answering my questions? Maud is coming toward us carrying two large paper cups of coffee.

"Go get out of those sweaty clothes. I told Marsh to start your breakfast when your heads cleared the steps."

"Yes, Ma'am." Maud doesn't ask any questions. She would have gotten the news from Marsh. I reach for a cup of coffee to take with me and Matt follows suit, taking to Maud as they head for the hotel.

By the time we get to the dining room our breakfast is sitting on the table. We dig in like hungry wolves. I'm ashamed of myself for not trying to carry on a conversation. Maud asks what happened last night and Matt tells her. I'm content to sip coffee and sort things in my mind.

"Jim, will you take me into town when you finish?"

"Of course."

"The sheriff wants me to look at the man you all found last night."

"Why? Do you know him?"

"He thinks I may have seen him. Marsh remembered my coming into the hotel to register. Phedra followed me in, Marsh believes she may have been out a second time with the man you found last night. He doesn't know where she had gone that afternoon, but her car didn't leave the parking lot."

"Where is the good sheriff?"

"He's taken Dr. Lavin and Phedra's sister into town to formally identify Phedra's body. Actually, I think he had in mind to show them both bodies."

Matt's eyebrow wobbles. "There's an answer to one of your questions if Maud did see him in the parking lot."

Chapter 10

After several wrong turns on one-way streets we find the hospital. I'd sworn I'd never enter a hospital again. Hospitals buy interior paint from one supply house in barf green.

We're down in the basement. A long corridor runs like a tomb under the parking lot. We entered the front door first, but were directed around the building to steps leading underground.

"Thank you for coming, Mrs. Tosh. He's over there." He points to a table covered with a white sheet.

The rank odor of formaldehyde is worse than the rotten eggs smell from the marsh bottom. Immediately I remembered the biology lab at school. I'd opened a specimen jar and dropped it. The lab smelt the same way for days—awful. In this closed room with no windows the odor seeps out of the walls.

"Didn't Dr. Lavin and Phedra's sister come with you?" Maud is holding a lace handkerchief to her nose. A faint whiff of lavender stirs the malingering air.

"Yes, they're over at the funeral home making the arrangements to have her flown home as soon as I complete my investigation and release the body."

"Rather fast, isn't it?"

"Has to do with his religion, but the procedure will take a few days. This way, please. You fellas don't have to go through this again. Wait over by the door. Some fresh air seeps in around the hinges." He grins at our discomfort.

The sail the body was wrapped in is lying over a table against the wall, drying. The damp cloth's briny smell is a fresh sea-breeze blowing across the formaldehyde. It's fairly white, unlike the torn sail Marsh caught in his propeller.

"Sheriff, this isn't the man I saw with…."

The door swings wide, pinning us behind it so we're looking through a small window with chicken wire imbedded in the glass. Two men, wearing uniform suits not much different from the one on the body, walk toward the sheriff who turns to face them. I can see the corpse's head between Maud and the sheriff. His hair is dry, it's bright as a carrot. He's the man who was with Shell when he almost rear-ended us.

"Sheriff Townsend? We thank you for your endeavors in bring this matter to our attention." The men are average. Their brown hair is cut short in a standard military style. Medium height—five nine or ten, built the same and wearing gray suits that are neither dark nor light.

Matt plants his number fourteen on my foot. "Feds."

For a moment the only sound is the buzz of the florescent lights. Slate turns to granite, and with a voice saturated with contempt the sheriff responds, "I beg your pardon. Who are you?"

Maud lowers her handkerchief and places her hand on the sheriff's forearm, as if to stop him from decking the man.

"Look, Townsend, this is our jurisdiction." Both men hold out brown folders to the sheriff. "We're here to remove the body."

"Gentlemen, I don't care who you represent. The deceased was found near my island. He is connected to a previous murder. The rangers from the Port Authority have a prior interest in a body found in their waters."

" We took care of the locals. Your murder is not our problem. We have instructions to remove the body to federal facilities." One man reaches inside his coat. I jump a little, but the sheriff gives him a cold stare and takes the papers he removes from his inside jacket pocket. They are both wearing guns. I can see the slight budge under their coats.

"How can one guy own an island?"

Sheriff Townsend looks up from reading the papers. "Ancestor selection."

I look at Matt and whisper, "Did he insult him?"

"Slicker than a greased pig."

"These are in order, your game." Townsend hands back the papers and closes his hand over Maud's then smiles at her. It's a soft look as if he is saying thank you.

"Barker, get the gurney and driver down here." A barked command by a superior officer.

Barker is startled to discover us standing by the door. His face is nondescript, with pale blue eyes set deep under his heavy brows. He doesn't seem too pleased to find witnesses.

The other guy is talking to Sheriff Townsend. "You may leave, we'll finish up in here."

"I have the key to the door. Your papers said nothing about locking up."

The boss guy knows when he's reached a stalemate. They aren't going to get a chance to be alone in the morgue. Though why they would want to be in here is beyond me.

"Barker, stop wasting time. Get over here." The man turns and spies us.

He has the same bleached blue eyes as Barker. Isaiah comes to mind as I return his blank stare.

"Who are you?" Matt stomps my foot, and I bite my tongue to keep from yelping.

"Transportation for the lady." As he answers, he hoists himself up on the table onto the damp sail. How he did it without showing he is using only one arm I don't know, but I follow suit.

Matt's presence is intimidating. Coal black hair, dark brown eyes, scar in his eyebrow, a nose that has been broken three times, and shoulders that match Lou Ferrigno's. At six-four and 240, wearing a Vikings sweatshirt that has been split down the front to make it easier to put on with his gimp arm, he makes these guys look like pygmies.

Barker keeps staring at him like he's trying to place him, but turns to help get the body on the stretcher.

"Leave the sheet. It's hospital property." Thay Townsend's voice is brook-no-argument sharp.

They don't say another word, but march out the door like soldiers in a dress review taking the corpse with them.

"Thank you, Mrs. Tosh, for your help." He smiles again and releases her hand. "Quick thinking. In their officialese, they neglected to inquire how he was found. What made you cover the sail?"

Matt holds up the edge of the sail and pulls his sweatshirt around. There is a small darn, it matches the edge of the sail.

"Orta's work. Orta Wallace is Shell's mother. She does the hotel laundry for Marsh. I saw it last night. The sail is off Shell's skiff, the one we used. I checked both boats after the traffic cleared, and the sail was missing. Marsh read him the riot act last night before I got a chance to talk to him. I drug him over here first thing this morning. He swears he's never seen FBI Agent Kevin Stevens."

No wonder Marsh was so nervous last night. He recognized the darn on the sail. Not only did he need to get some eggs and bacon, he wanted to find his nephew. Matt said Shell was a drug addict and he's also a liar. Is he involved with this second murder?

Sheriff Townsend continues to talk as he locks the morgue. "The body was in the water, which throws off the time of death. But Doctor Harrison says Mr. Stevens hadn't been dead more than ten hours when you found him, Matt.

"Few marsh creatures had been working on his flesh. The sail is puzzling me, because Shell's skiff has been tied to my dock since he brought in the flounder yesterday morning. He used that sail while he was fishing. I helped him stow it, myself. Last night, he was working in the dining room and he'd been at the hotel the entire day."

Outside, I'm deep-breathing fresh air, fanning my jeans to dry them, and listening to him. The sheriff watches the brown ambulance round the corner at the end of the street with a deep frown on his face.

"Sheriff, someone must have taken the boat while everyone was busy at the hotel."

"Miss Maud, I don't know. Shell came in before the tide turned."

"How does that make a difference?"

"Matt, there are two tides each day. The body was dropped during the high tide, which was before noon when the oyster beds are covered with water. We went out on the peak of the low tide and it was coming back for over four hours when you discovered the body."

"Oh! Then...."

"Whoever disposed of Mr. Stevens didn't want him found. There were good size stones in the sail."

I'm listening to every word. Turning them over in my mind against what I've learned. "Whoever dumped Stevens wasn't familiar with the tides."

"That's my conclusion. I'd best round up Dr. Lavin and Miss Forbenshire and get them back on the island before those desk jockeys decide to take an interest in Mrs. Lavin."

I'm curious, "Who was the guy giving all the orders?'

"His shield said, 'Stanley Collins, Special Investigator for the Department of Interior.' Roger Barker is with the FBI. Strange companions. Generally those guys don't speak to each other, much less work together. Collins was giving the orders and Barker wasn't liking it."

"How did they find out so fast?" I look at him. Somehow events have made us friends, maybe because he understands family. He's laying his cards on the table and I can't tell him we saw Shell driving Mr. Stevens to the island since Maud hasn't mentioned it.

"Jim, the Port Authority reported the discovery to all concerned federal agencies before they left for the mainland. His identification was in his pocket."

"I see. From their attitude, you're low on the totem pole."

He grins, but there is strain around his eyes as if he has a headache, "Bout right."

"I'd go back and get that sail, those guys may decide to come back after we've cleared the deck. I didn't see any blood stains on it, so that means the guy was dead before he was wrapped in Shell's sail. Getting your throat cut would leave an awful mess somewhere."

"Thanks, Jim for reminding me. I missed that point completely. These murders have me stymied. Mrs. Lavin was killed in her room and taken to the beach. The clothes she was wearing in the dining room were hanging in the closet. One shoe was by the bed, she was wearing the other one." He hands Maud into the front seat of the Rover like she's a queen. Elton Fightmaster couldn't have done it better.

"Take this lady out for a good lunch. *The Barn Door* serves excellent steaks, even Marsh likes them. But save some room for supper. It will be late tonight.

We wait in anticipation for the hard won oysters. A driftwood fire started in the late afternoon sends clouds of fragrant smoke down the beach. Maud retreated to her cottage to write letters. She never mentioned the red-haired man during lunch. Matt and I'd used the time after we returned from the morgue to catch a nap. I could smell salty wood smoke seeping under the door as I slept, a fresh clean odor after the morgue.

The dining room is almost full. Lettic Forbenshire and Dr. Lavin sit at a small table by the long front windows in isolation from the crowd gathered to face the door to the kitchen. Marsh warned us not to bother with dressing for dinner. I'll admit to being more comfortable in a flannel shirt and jeans.

In the center of our table is a huge bowl of salad greens with anchovies and baskets of cornsticks. We serve ourselves. Shell, his mother Orta, and Nialis Lapier are weaving among the tables re-filling glasses with iced tea, passing out white bibs and crisp salad crackers made with corn meal. Matt is making two bites do for each cornstick as he empties the basket for an appetizer.

"Pass the basket. Maud and I are hungry, too."

"Sorry, but I love these things. Mom always makes cornbread in a skillet."

"Feeding your tribe, I'm not surprised. It saves time. My moth-er had a collection of irons. When she died, my sisters and I divided them, each of us got five. Each one had a story," She butters the end of a stick, "So much gets lost with time, it's so short. They're some-thing else I'm going to start using when I get home."

For a moment Maud's face becomes pensive like she's lost in memories. Then she smiles and looks at the cornstick in her hand as if she can't remember why it's there.

Fanny Longer insists on having a rare steak, she isn't about to eat half-cooked seafood, then complains the meat wasn't cooked to her specifications. Her harangue brings a small smile to Dr. Lavin's careworn face. I can't help but glance their way. Lettic will reach out and pat his hand. She hasn't stopped talking since they entered the room, but no one can hear what she is saying.

"Is this chair saved for me?"

"Sit down, Sheriff." Maud indicates the chair to her left. Matt

71

scoots over a bit to give him room. Wood smoke clings to his clothes bringing the outside indoors.

He surveys the room and laughs, "I see word got out. People drive for miles when Marsh has an oyster roast. The show is about to begin. Watch closely. I can shuck oysters as well as any islander can, but Mamma Lou has no equal."

Marsh and Shell come through the kitchen doors, both carrying washtubs filled with oysters. They place them on small tables set behind a big table stacked with heavy paper plates. Marsh opens the kitchen door, a large wicker wheelchair rolls between the small tables and stops.

The guests in the room, with the exception of the Longers, rise and start clapping. They are acknowledging a queen. We join them as the sheriff goes over and kisses the most beautiful woman I've ever seen. She looks like that Egyptian queen.

I hear Matt utter a low, "Oh, my God!"

Maud responds, "No wonder she rules the island."

A regal nod of her head, which is crowned by thick hair so black it glints blue, is her response to the ovation. Her hair is pulled back from her coffee-cream face in a twisted figure-eight roll. Gold hoops dangle from her ears, dancing in the light. She waves Sheriff Thay away with an elegant hand crisscrossed with fine scars from the sharp oyster shells she's handled most of her life.

Marsh's wish to take everyone's mind off the murders for one evening has been granted. All attention is focused on Mamma Lou as she settles a mottled-blue granitic paring-pan filled with roasted oysters on her apron, pulls on heavy rubber gloves, and picks up one of the four knives on the table.

The knife is a bulging triangle, which looks like a hoe blade ground down to work around corn stalks with a shield next to the handle. She inserts the sharp blade between the bivalves and flicks her wrist. The shell pops open. Her hands fly and service is fast.

Her family members remove the top shell and place the half-shelled oyster on a heavy platter as fast as she pops the lid. Then they rush the filled platters around the room, while I study her face.

Sheriff Thay catches me staring and mistakes my interest, "Her hips were crushed during a storm when I was small. Don't worry, she can operate that chair like you drive. We never knew where she'd turn up, but frequently it was when we were doing something we shouldn't have been. She's a witch or sorceress may be a better word." I can hear the love and admiration for Louise Leviticus in his voice, which is low and very gentle.

Shell and Marsh are winding among the tables dumping empty shells in a tub and collecting used paper plates. No elegant hotel service tonight, I believe most of the people in the room are friends or family. Talk is loud and laughter frequent. I'm ashamed of myself, but both Maud and Matt have piles of shells on their plates as high as mine.

"Oh, look." Maud is pointing to an oyster on her plate.

"You got a hitchhiker. It's a pea crab. Good eating."

"A what?"

"Jim, they live inside an oyster. We call them pea crabs because they are so tiny. Biologists call them oyster crabs. You find them frequently during an oyster roast. Ignore them, a little extra protein."

Maud puts the oyster on his plate, "Thayer, I'll take your word for it."

"Mrs. Tosh, don't let him spoil your supper. He's right, the little crab cleans the oyster's gills so it can breathe." The voice at my elbow is low with musical overtones. Mamma Lou can move her wheelchair as silently as her son walks. Her hand resting on the arm of the chair draws my eye. It is just like Maud's. Long, tapered fingers ending in smooth, polished nails, and the rough scars aren't ugly. They show the strength of those hands. Mom and Isaiah have the same shaped hands.

"Is everyone on the island a marine biologist?"

A laugh deep and free rings like thick church bells, "No, we're islanders. Sea knowledge is spawned in the bones. Thay went to college, studied marine biology, and never studied a lick. He takes advantage of anyone who'll listen to him go on about our ocean and its life."

She has removed the rubber apron and given it to Orta Wallace, who has assumed the shucking duties. Marsh's mother's skin is as smooth and glossy as the bolts of silk satin I buy for Elroy and Lon to check pistons for invisible spurs. She must be near Mom's age, but it doesn't show in her face, just little lines spraying out from her chocolate eyes that deepen as she laughs. Black eyebrows like bird wings rise above her eyes as if to take flight. The bones under her skin are like mine, yet softer and broader, showing a faint Indian ancestry.

A frown clouds her expressive face. I turn my head to follow her gaze. The Longers are leaving and have stopped by Dr. Lavin's table. Fanny extends her hand, but he ignores it as he introduces her to Miss Forbenshire. Fanny drops her hand, says something to Wally and charges from the room with her beak in the air. Wally waddles behind her, stopping by the desk to sign the check.

"I didn't want those folks bothered, Marsh. They have enough troubles."

"Mamma, I tried to stop her, but she refused to listen. Doctor Lavin handled Madam Nosey."

He is standing behind me. "Marsh, It's been so quiet, I'd forgotten they were here."

"Mamma, she was giving Mr. Wally a rough way to go for having your special, but I put her behind some Broomtown folks. She said oysters were kitchen leavings for the poor."

"After all my hard work, she called this ambrosia 'kitchen leavings?'" Matt's eyebrow wobbles as he tries to wink. "You're going to have leftovers for breakfast. Oysters in scrambled eggs would look like the brains and eggs Mom always fixed after a hog killing. I'll exclaim loud enough for her to hear so I won't have to share. I owe her a favor."

Our table erupts in laughter. Fanny Longer has gotten stale, the woman leaves a bad taste in my mouth. "Marsh, what do you have for dessert after this wonderful meal?"

"Ambrosia with pecan cookies. Help yourself, it's on the buffet."

"Don't look now, do it when you go to the buffet. Agents Collins and Barker just sat down at the Longers' table."

"Are these men people I should know, Thay?"

"No, Mamma Lou, they're spooks who gum up wheels. Miss Maud, may I bring you your dessert?"

"Thank you. I want to visit with Marsh's mother. I have a friend who'd love to have her chocolate pecan pie recipe."

Chapter 11

I'm not sure what I should do. The man Matt found is the same
man who was with Shell Wallace when he ran us off the road.
Oops! I didn't tell you about that. Shell was driving too fast, but
Jim got his Rover out of the way.

We were in the morgue when two government men came in and
took possession of Mr. Stevens' body. The man whose throat was slit.
He was an FBI agent and had carrot-red hair like Vernon Osborne.
I was starting to tell the sheriff when they arrived, then things got
mixed up. The sheriff wasn't happy about their taking the body, but
there wasn't anything he could do. I stopped him from losing his
temper. I just knew he was ready to ready to do something he would
be sorry for later.

Jim and Matt sat on the sail that had been wrapped around
the body. Then Jim told the sheriff to go back into the morgue and
get the sail. That's suppressing evidence from federal officials. The
sail belongs to Shell Wallace. Sheriff Townsend said it did, but Shell
is his cousin. It all happened so fast and Jim didn't say anything
about seeing the busboy with Mr. Stevens so I kept my mouth shut.
But it's bothering me. Everybody is hiding something from the authorities and I can't discover why.

Writing to you helps clear my mind. I'm sure Jim had a reason for
not mentioning it. His legs get stronger every day now that he can run
with Matt. They race on the beach and it's good for both of them.

Did my water pipes make it through the cold snap? It is getting warm here, a good sweater is all you need. Mamma Lou says a storm is brewing down the coast. They call it a "Nor'easter." It will be here in a few days.

Don't forget to water my plants, they are the only things Rupert didn't destroy in one of his rages.

When I get home, I will unpack my family treasures I hid from him and use them. I learned that from the hotel manager. Good things are meant to be enjoyed, not hidden away in a secret place.

Maud

"Brrrr, the temperature is dropping."

Maud is faithfully holding our coffee as Matt and I come up from the beach. The gray drizzle isn't helping the temperature.

"Maud, you're an angel." Matt takes both cups.

He hands me mine, "Go change. We'll meet you in the dining room." He puts his bad arm around Maud's shoulders as I hurry to my cottage. My wet t-shirt holds the cold like a sponge soaked in ice water.

I shed my hooded-slicker and knitted cap in a little room off the lobby.

Matt is at our table by the window with Thay Townsend when I get to the dining room. He's using a pair of binoculars to watch the sandpipers and plovers feed on the edge of the beach. There must be dozens out there as they scurry and stop, then scurry and stop again. They look like little dots moving up and down the beach. Along the floor next to the French doors is a roll of heavy carpeting to block the wind.

I rub my hands against my plaid flannel shirt to warm them. Matt is wearing cords and a brown fisherman's sweater over a turtleneck.

"We're going to get a Nor'easter within the next forty-eight hours. I hate them. They play havoc with the estuaries and marshes." Thay's face is lined with a concern I didn't see when he worked with the victims, It's as if the fate of the island is more important to him than murder.

"What's a Nor'easter?"

"A major winter storm that blows in off the ocean. Normally they track further north up around Virginia. We will have very heavy rains and high winds driving the waves onshore. For us, it may begin in the middle of the night with the sharp drop in temperature—like a hot knife slicing butter. The winds are blowing in a circle around a low-pressure zone."

"Like a hurricane?"

"A hurricane comes from Africa. A nor'easter starts forming in the Gulf and blows up from the south where it hits cold air from the Arctic coming down from the north. The force of the strong current of the cold air hitting the warm air drives heavy waves onshore. The tides can't get out fast enough before a new tide starts in.

"Everything gets churned around, it's hard on both sides of the island. The beaches and dunes take damage from the waves, but there can be a real disaster in the sound. All the water from the ocean backs up against the water coming from the main land and has no place to go. It washes out the land and scatters the oyster beds."

Marsh sets a platter of pancakes in the middle of the table. "Hard on me too, trying to keep guests entertained indoors with not much to do but play cards. Help yourself while this syrup is hot.

"The feds took rooms last night and were up late. Barker came down for coffee in the middle of the night. I've been running up and down those stairs all morning. Dr. Lavin and Miss Forbenshire ordered coffee in their rooms. The Longers heard them and followed suit. Shell didn't show up this morning, Orta said he didn't come home last night."

Maud comes into the dining room wearing the red pantsuit and green turtleneck sweater. We stand while Marsh seats her.

Thay looks at Marsh. "Are you caught up in the kitchen?"

"As soon as I get your eggs and sausages out? If you folks don't mind eating family style?"

Matt laughs, "Marsh, family style or any style, just make sure you use big bowls. I'm so hungry I could eat a sand...witch."

"I want to see that. Bring him some of Fanny's sand with plenty of butter." He almost puts his fork in my hand.

Maud flashes her warm smile, "Marsh, bring another platter of pancakes, a large coffee pot and join us. Take a break. I heard Fanny complaining her coffee wasn't hot enough from the bottom of the stairs before I came in the dining room."

Marsh's face is a picture of shock. I don't think he has ever been ordered to join guests for breakfast. He has no idea of the before opening breakfast that Wilson fixes at the Kricket.

As he starts to the kitchen, Barker stops him. "Are you the manager of this hotel?"

"Yes, Sir. My mother owns it."

"She has a busboy by the name of Shell Wallace?"

"Yes, Sir."

"We need to see him."

"I'm sorry, Sir. He isn't on duty."

"Locate him and bring him to our table."

Sheriff Townsend walks over to the two men. "Mr. Barker, is there a problem?"

"Sheriff Townsend, you're interfering with a government investigation. We need to see that busboy." Barker snaps at him.

Collins unfolds the newspaper in his hand and walks to a table.

Thay looks at Barker, who remains by the door. "Mr. Leviticus has told you. Shell isn't on the premises. He doesn't know where he is."

"These people always know where to find their own."

I'm surprised at the blatant sneer of prejudice in Barker's voice, but the sheriff remains stoic.

"Mr. Barker, Mr. Leviticus is short-staffed this morning and we have a storm brewing. He doesn't have the time to go looking all over Seamew Island for a busboy. May I help you?"

"Townsend, Collins told you to tend to your own business."

Maud coughs and clears her throat. Thay glances at her, she gives him her dazzling smile and winks.

He studies Barker for a moment. "Shell Wallace is unavailable. Please join Mr. Collins and order the pancakes. They are delicious, perfect for this cold day." He nods to Marsh, sending him to the kitchen, and returns to our table.

"Miss Maud, your breakfast is on me this morning. Thanks for the signal to watch my temper."

The sheriff stands up almost immediately, "Please excuse me. I've enjoyed breakfast."

"You haven't started eating."

"Momma Lou'll make me a sandwich of the leftovers. Right now, I need to talk to the widower and sister."

I turn around. Dr. Lavin and Miss Forbenshire are taking a table near the door even though they had ordered coffee in their rooms. We won't be able to hear a word of their conversation. The doctor looks like he's been run over by a tractor, but the lady gives Matt a wave by wiggling her fingers. Collins and Barker sit at attention when Thay joins them. But like us, they aren't seated near enough to eavesdrop.

Our meal isn't fun anymore. There are too many currents in the room, and they aren't coming from the wind creeping around the door pad. Lettic Forbenshire gets up from the table and heads our way, her booted feet almost stomping. "Here comes your trophy collector and she isn't happy."

"Jim, another stupid remark and I'll dump you in the ocean, boots and all."

"Don't you start," I snap. There is too much tension. "You sound like Kane. I was just kidding." Maud pats my knee and shakes her head.

"Mattie, the sheriff told me to have coffee with you while he talks to Lemuel." Matt cringes as she runs her fingers around the back of his neck.

"Introduce me to your friends."

He reaches up and removes her hand which has come to rest on his shoulder. "You met my brother and Mrs. Tosh the night you arrived."

"How sweet, being on vacation with a companion." She sounds like she'd run on the beach, but her words are insulting.

"Mr. Leviticus, please set a place for Miss Forbenshire. Sheriff's orders."

Marsh is tricky, he puts her as far away from Matt as the space will allow. She can't reach him to play footsie under the table. Her bottom lip juts out in a pout.

Maud's eyes dance as she examines Lettic's mink-vest and pink, scooped-neck, knitted-dress which leaves nothing to the imagination. I can see bits of the fuzzy yarn on Matt's sweater sleeve. Her dress sheds like a Persian cat.

"I don't know why Phedra wanted to come to this desolate island. So inconvenient for Lemuel. Look, what it got her."

"I'm sure your sister didn't expect to be murdered. Why're you here?"

"She's been strange since Poppa died. I wanted to talk to her. Let's talk about something more pleasant. It's so gloomy. Doesn't the sun ever shine?"

Maud tries to get a civil conversation out of Miss Forbenshire, but her valiant efforts fail. Matt clams up tighter than the oyster shells. She makes me uncomfortable as she stares past my shoulder at the table with Dr. Lavin and the sheriff. They talk for a long time.

Collins and Barker order more coffee and proceeded to read every ad in the *Washington Post*. I can see the masthead above Collins's left hand when he moves to turn a page. Again, I have a flash of Isaiah, but it is gone in an instant.

Marsh never takes a break. He keeps buzzing around the room adjusting window curtains, moving plants, arranging chairs, and setting tables for lunch. His obvious nervousness infects even Maud.

We're trapped in a vortex that centers on the table where Dr. Lavin and Thay sit in earnest conversation. When they leave the room it's like a breath held too long is suddenly expelled, leaving a vacuum. Collins and Barker fold their papers, too studied to be accidental, then saunter after them. Lettic swiftly follows, not even bothering to take leave of Matt.

"Mr. Matt, would you folks like some fresh coffee with a bit of left-over pecan pie? It's too nasty out to do much else."

"Marsh, bless your heart. Everyone's gone. Join us."

I look out the window. It's as dark as late afternoon and pouring rain. The sheriff and Phedra's family are gone. Chocolate pecan pie and coffee will fill the hollow spot in my stomach, which isn't from hunger.

Before Marsh can get to the kitchen, Fanny and Wally Longer stagger in from the lobby. He is soaked to the skin. She marches up behind Marsh and pecks him on the shoulder.

"Waiter, get us some hot tea, Earl Grey would be best and something sweet. Wally insisted we go somewhere to get a decent breakfast."

Marsh starts to say something, but she waves her hand to silence him. "He got soaked coming from the car. He must keep his strength up so he won't take a cold." She points to the table next to ours and marches our way like a battalion sergeant. Wally pulls a handkerchief from his pocket and blows like a foghorn.

Why didn't they go up to their room and change clothes before coming in here to soak the upholstery? Maud pats my leg again and smiles. She knows what I'm thinking, but common sense is beyond Fanny Longer. The woman is no longer funny. I wish they would leave, as she keeps threatening to do.

"Marsh, not the pie." The look on Matt's face is pathetic.

"Wouldn't waste it on the likes of them, Mr. Matt. I have some of Thay's stale sweet rolls in the freezer."

Maud grimaces, her distaste for Fanny Longer evident in her sharp words. "The last thing that stuffed walrus needs is something sweet."

Chapter 12

This Sunday the dining room was nearly empty—different from a week ago. The after-church crowd is avoiding the island as the rain and wind have created a quagmire of the road and parking lot.

Before going to bed, I latched the storm shutters, stacked wood on the hearth, laid a fresh fire ready to light, and got the oil lanterns out of the closet in case of a power failure. I've always enjoyed spending a winter night at Mark's place. This cottage is smaller, but it has the same sense of peace. If I wasn't so comfortable in my nook I'd move to the hotel and save myself the cold wet walk. But sleep eludes me, as I turn the day's events over in my mind.

Thay and Marsh left for the mainland as soon as dinner was served to bring additional supplies for the hotel in case the increasing surge of backwater damages the causeway. They took my Rover and the old station wagon. Nialis Lapier and Orta Wallace finished cleaning the dining room while we guests entertain ourselves around the huge fireplace in the parlor.

We played three-handed Canasta and then change to Gin Rummy. Maud is a deadly player. I owed her three dollars by the time we quit. The women kept an urn of hot chocolate and small sandwiches under damp towels on the registration desk for nibbles.

Matt changed his mind about moving out of the hotel. The four cottages above the beach are restored slave cabins. He's squeamish about staying in one because of their past. His reaction surprised me. I don't have any truck with spooks and haints. People get born and die in houses all the time. I know the dead can't hurt me. Only memories of them invade my nights and I've lived with nightmares of Catherine's death for five years.

Marsh assured Maud no slave ever lived in these cottages. The originals were destroyed during a hurricane in the 1920's. He and his father with Thay's help rebuilt them on the old foundations in the late 1950's when their hotel began to overflow its summer capacity. Marsh showed Maud an album of pictures taken during and after the Civil War. One was of several former slaves in uniform and some Union soldiers loafing on the front porch of a cabin exactly like my cottage. It is a little duplicate of the big house without the wings and double porches.

The rain is back to drizzle so I leave the hotel for a walk to clear my head. I enjoy a cigarette, but there are limits to the scorched fumes of raw tobacco. Late in the afternoon a grizzled old man settled in the parlor. He took the *Washington Post* Collins had left on a table and retired to a wingback chair by one of the long windows to smoke a foul-smelling pipe. I swear he was smoking corn shucks mixed with catalpa bean-pods like Levi and I once tried. We called them Indian cigars.

Huge live oaks line the shell road running through the center of the island. I try, but I can't stretch my arms around one monster with crooked limbs that reach across the road. Long strands of Spanish moss, soaked with water trail down to the crushed shell road. The wind makes them dance on the crude pavement. This is the same lane we took to Thay's home the night of the oyster harvest. If one believed in haints, this is the place to find them.

The wind is heavy with damp that has washed the salt water and marsh odors away. I can feel the cold inside my nose as I breathe, which quickens my steps. I'm almost stomping like Lettic as I turn back toward the hotel. Resentment of the brush-off Barker handed Thay Townsend fuels my steps. Does their federal badge give them the right to come onto a man's land and order him around?

Four different law agencies have an interest in Mr. Stevens' death. The sheriff of Seamew Island, the Port Authority, the Department of Interior and the FBI all have a hand in the investigation. Why has the murder of Kevin Stevens drawn so many people to the island?

Mrs. Lavin's death hangs in the air, while her husband and sister are stranded on the island until an official on the mainland releases Phedra's body. Her death has been ignored by the experts, but Thay Townsend spends each day going over the tiny threads of evidence, which lead to dead ends.

Who gave her the savage beating? Who choked her? Who buried her body in the sand? Is her death connected to the death of Mr. Stevens? If so, how?

Shell Wallace was driving Mr. Stevens to the island, but Stevens never came to the hotel. Maud believes they were having an argument, which was why Shell almost hit us. Matt identified Shell as an addict. His sail was wrapped around the body of Stevens. He was in the hotel the entire day of the murder. It isn't mentioned, but his family is worried. Shell hasn't been seen on the island for two days. Barker is using the strength of his job to demand access to Shell. Where is the busboy?

The questions tumble in my brain as I return to the hotel. Questions that have no answers. They're like a puzzle without a border.

Maud is sitting on one of the sofas by the fire listening intently to the old man who appreciates his lovely audience. She changed her suit jacket for a brilliant jade cashmere shawl, which gives her a softness totally at odds with her inquisitive face. It's draped around her shoulders like a cape with a star-shaped pin holding it in place.

The old man is wearing a high collared white shirt, yellowed with age, but spotlessly clean, and a broad striped tie. His rough tweed jacket with leather elbow patches looks as if was made for a larger man. The pockets bulge from the weight of his tobacco pouch and pipe.

"My Martha told me to come up to the hotel for supper. It gets bad when the wind's a-blowing out of the north. The wind creeps into Martha's bones on nights like this, making her ache something terrible. She is not able to do much in the way of fixings these days. When the north wind blows in the night she weeps in her sleep and I hold her. Martha doesn't say, but I know my holding her hurts her bones.

"You are a nice lady. You must come by to visit my Martha. She would love to talk to a pretty lady like you." He pats Maud's hand, his crooked index finger is stained and the nail rimed with black where he packs that pipe.

Maud smiles, "When the storm lets up I would love to visit your Martha. I won't be disturbing her will I?"

"Oh, no, Missy, nothing disturbs Martha now, but the sound of the wind when she cries. She gets angry if I find her crying. She ceases to weep once the storm passes.

"I put my pail on the porch. Louise will let me take some extra chili home to Martha. Louise always fixes chili and soup with biscuits filled with leavin's from the dinner roast on cold windy nights. It warms Martha's bones. Martha does not like for me to drive the car when there is a storm brewing.

"Louise comes a-visiting when the weather is good. That chair of hers will go anywhere. She understands why Martha cries. We have been together since we were young'uns. We worked our farm and prayed for children. But none ever came, it is just as well, they would worry Martha with their noise. She loves the quiet when the sea is peaceful."

His gnarled hand strokes the folds of the shawl on Maud's shoulder. "Martha would love a soft scarf like yours to wrap around her bones to keep them warm." The clouded blue eyes gaze into the fire as its flames shoot sharp blades of blue, yellow and green against the crusted heat reflector.

Mamma Lou rolls her chair to the doorway. The old man looks at her as if from a distance. He has Maud mesmerized, her stillness pervades the room, yet her knowing eyes recognized the rambling nature of the old man's references to his wife. I slip into a high-backed chair and prop my feet on the fireguard to dry the soles of my Bass Weigens.

Mamma Lou places a small covered pail in the man's hand. There is a sack taped to the lid. "Mr. Morgan, Marsh is waiting with the station wagon to take you home. He'll check the fires at your place before he comes back."

The old man struggles to his feet, but refuses assistance and lifts the pail. He walks straight to the door. His back is ramrod stiff with pride.

"I must be getting home to Martha. You have been good company." But he's talking to the wind as Marsh holds the door.

"Poor soul."

"How so? He seems right spry to me."

"Physically he is, but Martha has been dead ten years."

"But he told me all about her and her illness."

"I heard. He tells every stranger the same story. Martha wasn't his wife, she was his daughter-in-law. Folks around here believe he killed her and threw the baby in the ocean."

"She was murdered?"

"Neck was broken and the baby was gone. Thay's father was sheriff. Mr. Morgan's son was convicted of manslaughter. She was my youngest sister. His son, Innis had the courage to marry Martha just before the baby was born. His father flew into a towering rage and disowned him." Her head goes up in the same stiff manner of the old man, a deep pride in her person. "He's not island-born, but is growing old on this shifting land living with his ghosts."

"Oh!" Maud raises her hand to the place on her arm he had stroked as if it hurts.

"Don't worry, Miss Maud. You were kind to listen to him, he's been like that since the night she died. If Mrs. Lavin had been killed on the beach, I'd swear he did it even though Innis is in prison for it. They died the same way."

Matt is standing behind Mamma Lou in the doorway, listening to the conversation, his right arm back in the sling.

"This damp cold is making my shoulder hurt." He answers my silent question, yet his presence lightens the gloom left by Mr. Morgan's sad story.

Mamma Lou laughs, "We have a left-handed spoon just for you." She twirls the chair. "Supper will be served as soon as Marsh gets back. I thought I heard a truck on the drive. It should be Thay."

"How could a man whose hands are like claws strangle a young woman? He could barely hold the bail of the pail." I open my mouth to stares from both Maud and Mamma Lou. I look to Matt for assurance that I haven't asked the wrong question.

Matt doesn't answer, but he raises the sliced eyebrow.

Marsh leans over to place a tureen of tomato bisque above Maud's plate. Matt and I are having chili, but we both steal some of the beaten biscuits filled with country ham that accompanied Maud's choice. The old man was right. Fluffy biscuits with thin slices of pot roast come with the meatless chili. A perfect meal for a frigid night. The temperature has dropped to 20 degrees, which is extremely cold for this southern island.

As Marsh rises, "Thay requests Miss Forbenshire share your table tonight. He has business with Dr. Lavin. Two deputies from the mainland are here to see the doctor."

"You know we don't mind. She's adrift and doesn't know where to turn."

"Why do you say that, Maud? I've never known Lettic to be a helpless female."

"Matt, I know you don't like her, but she's unhappy and trying hard to hide it. If I don't miss my guess, all of her attempts to get your attention are a cover. She's in love with her sister's husband."

I stare at Maud and start to ask her how she came to that conclusion as Lettic Forbenshire arrives at our table. Instead I take a spoonful of chili and try not to splutter from the fiery soup. I should have known, after my experience with Frogmore Stew.

"Mattie, the sheriff sent me down while he talks to Lemuel about Phedra. I hate to eat alone, the sheriff said to join you."

Lettic Forbenshire is wearing a black dress that is far from mourning. Every muscle in her body spells sin in capital letters. Her smile shouts bedroom though her light brown eyes are fogged with despair. No man in his right mind would hesitate to comfort her, but the image is spoiled as she clenches a fist. This woman is fighting anger behind a public face.

Maud smiles, "Lettic, sit by me. The tomato soup is delicious." Maud fills one of the large low mugs with soup and places it on the plate before Lettic. "Be careful, it's hot."

"Thank you." The response is automatic. Her eyes are glued to the door into the lobby as she takes a small sip of the soup, before pushing it away and pulling a cup of coffee forward. She wraps her hands around the cup, more to keep her hands still than for warmth.

"Matt, what are you going to do next season? There's a place for you with us."

"Have to see what the team physician has to say about the shoulder when I get back. Right now, I'm on vacation with my brother, a little R and R."

"Why here, of all places? The food's good, but today was awful. That Longer woman took every magazine out of the parlor. Nothing on TV but college basketball games or shouting preachers. Why would Phedra come here? She hates the sea. She didn't enjoy Dad's beach house on Lake Michigan."

Maud puts her hand on Lettic's arm, "I had dinner with your sister, and she told me her doctor suggested Seamew Island."

"Phedra told you that? Lemuel is her doctor. He didn't send her to this weird island in the middle of nowhere. Lemuel has a home in the Bahamas she uses for vacations."

Lemuel Lavin and the two deputies walk up to our table. Sheriff Townsend is standing behind them wearing a gray suit. A badge is pinned to his lapel.

Dr. Lavin's face is an ugly, pasty white, but he lightly pats Matt on the shoulder, "Mr. Young, put the sling back on, you're putting to much pressure on those fractured bones." His voice is professional, but a slight tremor hides behind the kind words.

"Lettic, call Rhodes Thornton. The deputies are taking me to the mainland."

"What for?"

Dr. Lavin runs his right hand through his hair, making the tight curls stand up in spikes. He looks as if he is seeing his wife's ghost.

"They believe there is evidence that I killed Phedra. I'm under arrest!" The man is in shock, and even I can see he is stunned by his arrest.

"You couldn't have, you were...."

"Please not now, just call him."

Her napkin falls on the floor as she leaves the table on the run.

Chapter 13

"Hey, aren't you going to leave any for me?"

"Isaiah!" Matt jumps up and gives him a hug with his left arm. I reach out to grip Isaiah's hand, ashamed of my rough hand against his cool palm. Isaiah's Blazer is in the parking lot. I've been staring at it for some time, lost in the fog of my own thoughts.

That mustard yellow box couldn't belong to anyone else. He bought it from Elgin Carstairs. It was practically new, but Carstairs ended up teaching at the university where the officials didn't approve of hippies on their faculty. Adam had built special racks for the back to hold Isaiah's instruments and canvases.

Isaiah is our tallest brother at six-five, but he won't make a shadow standing sideways. He's four years older than I, one of the twins, but people don't recognize Isaac as his twin. It's more than their difference in height and looks. Isaiah is the only one of us who doesn't have brown eyes. His are a changeable hazel, deep set under thick black brows in a face carved like a mountain crag.

"Marsh, we'll need another breakfast. You'd better make that two. I see Thay's truck pulling in the parking lot. Isaiah, when did you arrive?"

"Just a bit ago, Ma'am."

"Passing through?"

"Well, yes. I have an opening in New York, the first day of February. This will be an exciting year to be in New York. The bicentennial celebration is generating all kinds of special events. The curator of the gallery where my paintings are being shown wants me to open with a concert. That piano off the lobby is a nice Steinway. I was tinkling on it—needs tuning, but I can get in some practice while I'm here."

"With all that activity, I think you deserve a vacation. Your mother told me you finished your doctorate in December."

Isaiah flushes a light pink around his collar. He is embarrassed to learn Mom's been talking about his achievements.

"Yes, Ma'am, I completed my work, but the committee must review everything before I'm granted the degree. I may have to sing for my supper. The work took every spare cent I had, which is another reason to go to New York. I must sell a few paintings for walking-around money. This hotel is cheap compared to what they charge for lofts in the Big Apple. A friend is going to be studying in Paris this spring. I'm sub-leasing his place."

"You don't have to worry about selling paintings. A friend gave me the little oil you did of the courthouse for Christmas and I love the portrait you did of Marcy. Elton is so proud of it."

"Phillip Andrews told Mom about you begin here, meeting up with Jim and finding the body on the beach."

I don't have to worry about talking. Isaiah is here. His chatter can go on forever. Matt isn't saying much either. He's sitting there smiling as if he is showing off a game-winning ball. We all do it, even Isaac doesn't hit on Isaiah about his talent, though they fight about everything else.

"Your mother sent you to keep her baby safe from the grieving widow?" Maud's green eyes dance with glee, she's flirting with Isaiah like they both hold secrets.

"No, Ma'am. Well, she did suggest I stop by to keep Jim from doing anything foolish. She didn't know Matt was here to keep tabs on him."

"Don't worry, Sheriff Townsend is monitoring our behavior." Maud is like a queen bee, beaming around our table filled with

Youngs. Mom always grumbles about having to step over so many long legs when we're at home, but Mom is short. Maud is delighted to add the sheriff to her collection and is teasing him as he crosses the room for his mistake about our relationship.

"Another brother?"

"Good morning, Sheriff. Marsh will have your food out in a jiffy. I ordered what you didn't eat yesterday. Sit down."

"Yes, Ma'am. Which Young are you?"

"Isaiah, Sir."

"I talked to Dan Sommers last night. Nine of you. Will we be seeing the entire team?"

"No, Sir. I play left field when no one is on base."

Thay laughs at the sally, which is Isaiah's polite way of saying none of your business. I can never think fast enough to make remarks like that. Thay is being plain nosey and it sucks like a gummed up piston.

"Why did you call our sheriff?" Maud asks.

"In case you've forgotten I have two murders on my hands. Wanted to find out if there was any connection between you and the victims."

"Connection?" Unexpectedly, Matt is rumbling like a thunder cloud about to settle on a mountain. "The Lavins are from Minneapolis. I've met them a few times, but my family has never seen them." He is being big-bother protective, but I'm not sure why. They've been friendly since he arrived.

Maud smiles at the sheriff. "If you talked to Dan, sheriff to sheriff, then you know all about us."

"Yes, Ma'am. You're a widow whose husband died in November and you work at the courthouse. Jim Young is recovering from a racing accident, lost his eye, feet and legs were banged up pretty bad. Matt Young is recovering from a football injury. That business about watching your pennies was phony. You're comfortable from a financial aspect. Do I have it right?" His slate eyes wander around the table, but there is a faint gleam in their depths.

"Except I didn't know about the money until Rupert died. Dan Sommers is an old gossip. I'll wring his ear when I get home."

"Not necessary, ma'am. It was like pulling a hen's tooth to get information out of him. I have a suspicion he told me what was in the local paper."

"Are we in the clear?" She is looking at him over the edge of her cup. Maud enjoys putting the sheriff out of countenance. So far she hasn't batted her eyelashes, but there is a teasing grin hidden behind the cup.

"Yes, Ma'am, in some respects, but you told me you were from Brewster County and there is no Brewster County. Clydesville, Kentucky is in Ono County." Thay is playing back to her being very serious. He can't be serious.

"What? When?" Matt booms.

"But...but, that's only true since the first of the January. I keep forgetting that silly name."

Isaiah can't resist telling the story. "That's true, Sheriff. Tom Clement explained it in the *Gazette*. He called it gerrymandering. When the Corps of Engineers built the dam the county was cut in half by the lake. You have to go through two other counties to get from one part to the other.

"After almost thirty years the state decided to clean up the mess for extra votes in their camp. They took bits of land from other counties and created a new county. The Board of Supervisors were to select a new name and no one could agree. Everyone just kept saying 'Oh no!' to any suggestion. The judge lost his temper after hours of listening to their wrangling and ruled the most popular name was Ono."

"He did what?" Matt is laughing and trying to talk at the same time. "How do I explain that piece of folly when they announce I'm from...Ono County on TV? I'll never live it down."

Isaiah knew about the name change when he arrived, but saved the story until now to change the subject. He's good at deflecting embarrassing questions and giving a person time to think. I'm keeping my mouth shut. I didn't even look at the new license plate Mom sent by Maud, just unscrewed the old one and slapped the new one in place. Don't see how it changes anything, it's still home.

"Sheriff Sommers explained the situation. I was teasing Mrs. Tosh, but I am concerned about an important neglect." Sheriff Thay looks hard at Maud and she stares back.

"You didn't tell me you went shopping with Phedra Lavin or that you saw her kissing a man in the parking lot the day you arrived. Come to think of it, you also didn't say anything about the man not being her husband."

"Just a minute, Sheriff. We've barely talked to you since Dr. Lavin and Miss Forbenshire arrived. You sit down to a meal and then dart away faster than a cat after a mouse. Who squealed? Who knew I'd seen Phedra kissing another man?"

Sheriff Thay is laughing at Maud's indignation. His steel eyes are dancing like the balls in a pinball machine. "Miss Maud, Nialis Lapier isn't as much use as a headache, but she is worried about Shell. She saw you arrive, when you both witnessed the affection. She finally told me about the incident this morning. She was above you on the upper porch sharing a joint with Shell."

Maud is huffy at losing a battle in their game of mental chess and rounds on me, "Jim, did you tell him about our shopping?"

"No, ma'am. I thought you did."

"Marsh told me, the morning you found her. I'd been waiting for you to tell me yourself."

She looks contrite, "Sir, I think everyone has been less than forthcoming. We went shopping, but she didn't purchase anything. She had her hair done while I explored. She carried me over to the mainland. We met here in the dining room the night I arrived, both of us were alone so we shared a table."

"Did she say anything to you?"

"No, we talked about her children's deaths and the island. I told her I'd lost my husband, general things you say to a stranger."

"Miss Maud, that will get you off the hook for now, but I'll need a formal statement from you about all you know in regards to Mrs. Lavin."

"I will be more than glad to write it out for you, but will it help Dr. Lavin?"

"I'm not sure, I think they've jumped the gun arresting him. He wasn't going anywhere until they released his wife's body. Now we have to wait for his lawyer to arrive to clear their mess.

"Yes, Marsh, we'd like some more coffee, but please clear these dirty dishes. I hate to see them left on the table. Still no sign of Shell?"

Marsh walks like an Indian. He's standing behind me, again.

"No. Mother is worried. It's not like him to stay gone so long. You know he sticks close to the hotel, and his boat is still tied to your dock.

"Welcome to Seamew, Mr. Isaiah Young. The sheriff normally has better manners than he's showing this morning. Don't let him make you think we don't know how to behave. Talking about murder at breakfast stirs up the *sparits*."

"Marsh, they can't get in the hotel. You've got every door on the island painted blue, including mine."

Marsh loads the dirty dishes on his cart, gives Thay a hard look and gets the last word. "Don't go asking for trouble, got enough as it is." He stalks to the kitchen with his head in the air.

It's a bleak thought. Thay watches him with troubled eyes as he rubs his earlobe as if it itches. A silent message passed between the cousins, which I don't understand.

The rain has let up for a moment, but it's still dark and dreary with a high wind. It whips Lettic Forbenshire's fur coat open as she darts across the parking lot to a Mercedes. She peals out making the back-end skid on the loose shells. I can hear the squeal of her tires as she flies between the stone pillars that mark the entrance to the hotel.

"Where is she going in such an all-fired-hurry?"

"To the airport in Charleston, I expect. A flight from O'Hare arrives in an hour. As Marsh said, welcome to Seamew Island, Isaiah Young. I'd stay and talk but duty calls."

He looks out the window as Collins and Barker take a table near the door to the lobby. "The feds have arrived and I've lost my appetite."

I look at him, the social openness is gone, his battleship eyes are cold and dark like pictures I've seen of the North Sea. "Why are they hanging around?"

"Jim, I wish I knew. Taxpayers are footing their bill, and it will take months for Marsh to collect by requisition. Barker did tell me Kevin Stevens was his boss."

Isaiah looks at me, "Who is Stevens?"

Instead of answering, I glance around the dining room as the sheriff leaves. Collins and Barker pick up their cups and follow him into the lobby.

"Let's go to the parlor so Marsh can clean this table."

Matt wiggles his eyebrow. "Fine with me, you're into Maud for three bucks, maybe she'll let you win?"

"Jim, I asked you a question."

Chapter 14

The hotel is quiet. Everyone has vanished. The wing-back chairs before the fire are empty. Their bright flowers of summer are a stark contrast to the day. We help Maud arrange them around a card table set at an angle so no one's back blocks the warmth. Their high backs provide shelter from the sharp currents floating around the long room.

Today, instead of wood, Marsh is using coal for heat. The black lumps shoot small blue flames that remind me of the old farmhouse where we were born. Mom always used coal, which we picked from a seam above the river. I had two one-gallon lard buckets for the little pieces she used each morning to start the fires.

We play Gin Rummy to pass the time and attempt to fill Isaiah in on the events that have swirled around us like the wind and rain outside the long windows. Small ice pellets ping on the tin porch roof with the constant pecking of a flock of hens on a gravel patch. The heavy drapes are closed, protecting us from the storm.

"Halt." Isaiah spreads his cards with a flourish and a bashful smirk. "Gin."

"You dog." He has caught us with our hands full. We tally up and I start a new deal.

"I almost missed it trying to make heads or tails of the tale you've been telling me. I'm confused.

"Jim, you and Mrs. Tosh found the body of the woman on the beach. She was Mrs. Lavin. I've got that much. Who is the guy?"

"The guy Phedra slapped? We don't know."

"No, who is the dead guy?"

Matt answers for me. "Kevin Stevens. He was with the FBI. The sheriff told us this morning, you were there. Barker's boss. I found his body the night before the oyster roast."

Isaiah and I are facing the door. Nialis Lapier almost staggers under the heavy load as she climbs the broad steps leading to the second floor. A bright yellow kerchief covers her hair, but her pretty face is drawn with worry. Two parallel lines crease her forehead above her eyes like she has a headache. Her tray is piled with dishes and two large coffee pots.

Collins, coming down, stands aside to let her pass on the stairs.

"Matt, you're saying there are two corpses."

"Yes."

Isaiah shakes his head, glances up at Nialis, then abruptly changes the subject, "Who rates the special service?"

"The Longers—obnoxious hotel guests. So far we've avoided meeting them. She eavesdrops on every word we say when they're in the dining room. Fanny Longer imposes on the staff. A tray in their room, during this storm!" With an indignant huff, Maud settles back into her chair and picks up her hand.

As Nialis works her way toward the top of the stairs, without looking behind him Wally Longer starts backing down dragging a large trunk. He doesn't see Nialis.

I see the disaster looming and yell, "Longer, stop." He drops the trunk and its weight propels it down the steps on a slide, knocking him down.

Collins turns to the avalanche as I yell. He reaches for Nialis. She screams. He jumps over the bannister to avoid both Wally and the trunk. They crash into Nialis and the loaded tray. Matt and Isaiah are close behind me as we reach the door.

They land in a heap at the bottom of the stairs as Fanny Longer starts down carrying a small case, "Wally, are you hurt?" Before he can answer she snears, "Now you have to unpack. You've got food-stains on your suit."

She rounds on Nialis who is struggling to her feet. "You clum-sy pickaninny! It's a good thing we won't need that tray. We're leaving."

Maud rushes to Nialis, who has a gash on her face and a cut on her arm from the broken china. Blood is seeping through her blouse in the back. She is trying to stand on one foot, holding her leg. Her skirt is soaked from the steaming coffee. Marsh runs from the kitchen followed by Mamma Lou.

"Take Nialis to my apartment." Marsh and Maud help the limp-ing, whimpering girl down the back hall. Maud is holding a snowy napkin to her back, which is rapidly streaking bright red.

Mamma Lou looks at me. Her anger is palatable, "Mr. Young, would you mind helping Mr. Longer put that trunk in his car?" It isn't a request, but a command.

She ignores Franny Longer, "There will be no charge for the damages if you leave *now*." Her cold dark eyes stare at Wally, "Go bring the car to the door so Mr. Young will not get wet. I must see to Nialis."

Orta is quietly putting the remains of the Longers' room service order on the tray, which Isaiah picks up and carries to the kitchen as Mamma Lou wheels her chair and starts down the hall.

As I pick up the trunk, Fanny exclaims, "Well, I never, how rude."

I refuse to answer the woman. Matt holds the door open for us. As I start down the front-steps, Collins, wearing his coat, rushes down the stairs carrying his briefcase.

"Mrs. Longer, I have an emergency. May I bum a ride to the mainland?"

She hesitates, then beams and hands her case to me as if I were a lackey. "Of course, we'd be delighted to help you leave this awful place."

I can't help smiling and waving *bon voyage* as the winged Cadillac lumbers, in the same way Wally walks, through the gate.

When I return and deposit my slicker in the cloakroom, the hall has been swept clean of the debris from the accident. The floor has been mopped. Matt and Isaiah are busy picking up the cards we'd scattered in our rush to help Nialis. They add more coal to the fire and the room assumes a cheery, relaxing atmosphere. We catch up on family news while waiting for Maud to return.

"Sorry I took so long. She's going to be okay, her heavy skirt prevented her from being burned. Her ankle is twisted, and it will be sore for several days. The broken glass cut two deep gashes. Mamma Lou pulled one sliver out of her arm. I held the one across her back together while Momma Lou stitched. It took five stitches to close it. She's sleeping now."

Maud gives a little shake to her head and looks around before taking a drink of her flat Pepsi. She has changed clothes to deep brown slacks and a rough knit sweater with a heavy gold necklace like a collar around her neck.

Barker is reflected in the tall pier mirror above a low marble table in the hall. He walks over to the small windows beside the front double-doors and peers out into the gloom. Then pulling up a chair, he places it beside the entrance to the parlor and proceeds to read his paper. While I'm watching Barker, Isaiah deals a new hand and resumes our conversation as if nothing had happened.

"Maud, the sheriff said you didn't tell him about going shopping with the victim." His question reminds me of a board game Levi got for Christmas one year, *Clue*.

Maud's vitality is shaken. She answers as if grateful for the change of subject. "It wasn't important. She got her hair done while I explored the shops. Matt, what else do you know about them?"

"Maud, I owe Dr. Lavin. He did an emergency set on my arm and shoulder before they put me on the stretcher, which kept the swelling down until they got me to the hospital. Besides, all I know is locker room talk."

"Matt, who are these people? You haven't said much, but you've known them long enough to dislike Phedra's sister."

"Dr. Lavin and Phedra have had it rough."

"Murder is rough."

"Yes, ma'am, but last year they lost their children."

"I know. She told me."

"I can only tell you what was in the papers. They were in the front yard, Phedra and the little boy were struck by a car. Phedra survived. The baby was born prematurely. The baby, a girl, died in her crib a few months later. Talk around town was the mob was using them as an example to Lavin. Then, a few months ago, her father died."

Barker folds his paper and goes upstairs. He has been listening to every word we've said. Old gossip must not hold his interest. I'm glad he's gone when Maud asks her next question.

"Matt, why mob talk?"

"I don't know, but word on the street is he does patch-up jobs for the syndicate and wants out. They can't afford anyone walking around knowing their secrets who isn't part of the company."

"But isn't he Jewish?"

"Maud, not all members of the mob are Sicilian or Italian. That's a television myth."

"Oh. The sheriff questioned us after we discovered Mrs. Lavin. The doctor wasn't a guest in the hotel. I thought he was here the day I checked in because I saw Phedra kissing a man in the parking lot.

"The sheriff tried to locate him at home for notification. He wasn't there. When he came in with his sister-in-law it was the first time anyone had seen him. He isn't the same man I saw with Phedra."

Isaiah is watching Maud grill Matt, who's not enthusiastic about telling what he knows. While Maud is dealing a new hand, I get up and open the heavy curtains, exposing the dirty-gray parking lot. The brightest spots are Matt's red Porsche, which looks mulberry through the gloom and Isaiah's mustard Blazer. The old station wagon and Sheriff Thay's truck are gone. My Rover sits off to one side, its gunmetal body blending with the rain.

Orta sets a tray of sandwiches and pots on the registration desk. She notices me watching her and gives me the high sign before she goes back into the dining room, closing the doors behind her. Lunch today will be alfresco, which is fine with us.

"We don't know anything about Dr. Lavin. Jim has been asking questions, but the answers don't lead anywhere."

"I know, he told me. This mess is Sheriff Townsend's business, not yours." Matt's eyes drill me like a wood bee boring on a post. He doesn't want me to stick my nose in a murder investigation.

Maud ignores him and goes on talking like she's thinking out loud. I'm no longer sure I agree with Matt. He believes I could get myself in a peck of trouble. I hate to admit it, but he's right.

"This morning Sheriff Thay didn't think Dr. Lavin killed Phedra. Lettic started to say something last night, but Dr. Lavin shut her up." Maud discards the three-of-clubs, which I pick up. She knows I'm holding clubs and isn't paying attention to her game.

"Back to Phedra. The night she died she was having dinner with a man. She slapped him and left the dining room alone. She had bruises on her face that she tried to hide under her makeup. The man she slapped wasn't the same man I saw her kissing the day I arrived. The sheriff saw the contretemps in the dining room. He was sitting at the table behind Jim. It was the last time anyone saw her alive."

Isaiah holds up his hand. "Let me see if I've got this correct. Man—Mrs. Lavin was kissing isn't the corpse you found, Matt?"

Matt nods his head. Isaiah keeps counting, "Man—Mrs. Lavin slapped is two. Husband is three." He pulls down his fingers to count while hiding his cards.

"Jim, you forgot, you told me Marsh said a man took her for a drive one afternoon before I arrived. Marsh told Sheriff Thay he was Mr. Stevens—the man Matt found in the oyster bed. He asked for her at the desk, but he wasn't a guest at the hotel."

"Man—drive—dead. That makes four different men. She was a very busy lady. How is the dead FBI agent connected to her?"

Matt and Maud look at me, "Isaiah, no one knows. Neither the sheriff nor we can figure it out. We don't even know why Mr. Stevens came to the island. Marsh's nephew, who we saw carrying him to the island has disappeared. Mr. Stevens took Phedra for a drive before Maud arrived according to Marsh. It was in the afternoon after Maud found her body that we saw him with Shell coming to the island.

"The sheriff suspects something and has for some time. He spends his nights prowling around the island. Checking on things. He was doing that before Mrs. Lavin was murdered. He mentioned his walks the morning we found her. The night before Mrs. Lavin died he stayed outside my cottage long enough to know I was reading a book."

"The nephew is Shell Wallace, the busboy the sheriff was asking about?" I nod as I study my cards.

"Why is it that you all are so chummy with the local sheriff while he is checking up on what you do? You and Dan Sommers have been at loggerheads for years."

Matt smiles as he sorts his hand and interrupts before I can answer, "Except for Maud, there isn't anyone to talk to on the island. Besides, Marsh loves football. Let Jim tell you about harvesting oysters, which was fun until I discovered the FBI guy."

"Matt, hush. Here comes Lettic Forbenshire across the parking lot. She's alone."

"From what I can see that's a classy looking lady."

"Forget it, Isaiah. She's a barracuda. You don't have enough meat on your bones."

The front door bangs open as a gust of wind pulls it from her hand. Her makeup is streaked, but not from the rain. She's been crying.

Marsh closes the door, takes her coat, and escorts her into the parlor to a seat on the sofa. Her sophistication is gone.

Maud spreads her cards face up on the table, "Gin." Then she rushes over and puts her arm around the shaking woman.

I pull a clean handkerchief from my back pocket and hand it to Maud. Maud's hand is pure hearts, she fed me a minnow. Lettic wipes her face as Orta hands her a mug of hot chocolate from a fresh tray of snacks on the front desk. Lettic barely notices the woman.

"Rhodes Thornton's plane was forced to land in Columbia. Engine trouble. He won't get here until tonight. His message was waiting for me at the airport."

Her teeth chatter with a clacking sound as her wild gaze roams the room. "Lemuel will have to stay in that awful jail until Rhodes gets here. They wouldn't let him go on my say-so. The authorities won't listen to me. Lemuel didn't murder that woman. He was with me at the beach house in Michigan." She takes a sip of the chocolate and the cup rattles against her teeth.

Maud pats Lettic's knee in a friendly gesture, but delivers a blunt observation, "You're having an affair with your sister's husband." Maud had warned us of the true nature of Lettic's relationship to her brother-in-law, which gives them both an excellent reason for murder.

"Lettic, she was your sister."

The distraught woman jumps up. Matt grabs the cup of chocolate from her hand to keep it from spilling on the floor. She goes over to the window and gazes out into the parking lot as the sheriff's truck pulls up near the front door. I can see a man hurrying across the crushed shells carrying a small Samsonite shirt-case and a garment bag. Lettic's face brightens then a shade is lowered over her expression.

Phillip Andrews sets down his case and hangs the bag in the cloakroom before he sheds his coat and hat, then looks around. I can see him reflected in the mirror, the same way I watched Barker. Why is Mr. Andrews on Seamew Island?

He spots us and comes to the door. A low gasp erupts from Maud as she springs from the sofa and propels herself into his arms, unmindful of our interested stares.

"Phillip! Why? How did you get here?" Her voice is like a hic-cupping sob. Matt was on the money. Maud is in love with a living man.

"Why? I get an incoherent letter from you. The TV is predicting a major storm along the coast. The phone system is out of commission because of the emergency. You're finding bodies...."

"But we're not involved."

"Let me finish. I came over on the ferry and was picked up at the dock." He gives her a slight shake, then pulls her close. "Finally, it was lonely with a dark house next door."

"But...."

"Maud, I shut off the water, drained the pipes and took your plants over to Elton before I caught my plane. A lot of places along the coast are flooded according to the weather report on the TV at the airport. I know the Youngs, but who is this pretty lady?"

Maud blushes and performs the introduction. Lettic uses one hand smooth her hair as she tugs at her sweater with the other, while Maud grips Mr. Andrews arm. I've never been sure of his age. His sun-bleached brown hair is peppered with silver, but his deeply tanned skin is smooth. His eyes are the brilliant color of an October sky. They pierce the gloom Lettic brought with her into the room. Maud makes no bones to the woman about Mr. Andrews position in her life as they sit on the sofa. She makes sure she is sitting in the middle.

I choke an urge to laugh when Matt kicks me under the table. Sheriff Thay comes through the front door with a strange man. That's a revolving door and it's getting difficult for me to keep track of who's here and who has departed for other shores.

"Rhodes," Lettic all most stumbles over Mr. Andrews' feet as he rises from the sofa. She grips the lapels of the man's jacket as he struggles to remove his coat. "Make them let Lemuel go. He didn't murder that woman."

Maud quickly vacates the sofa for her chair at the card table. Mr. Andrews perches on the arm with his hand resting on her shoulder. This allows Rhodes Thornton to sit near the fire as he pulls the hysterical Lettic down beside him.

"Lettic, calm down. I'll get Lemuel out in morning. He's safe enough in jail today."

Her scream pierces the air, "No. No, you must go now. Lemuel didn't murder that woman."

"Lettic, I can't go back to the mainland. The causeway is washed out."

"But he didn't kill her. He's innocent."

"I'm sure he's innocent. You're not listening to me. My rental car is nose down between culverts of the causeway. The sheriff fished me out."

I glance down at his feet. Rhodes Thornton's trousers are soaked to the knees, dripping water onto the carpet.

Sheriff Thay and Marsh peer into the parlor. A look of surprise registers on Thay's stone-cut features at the stranger being familiar with Maud. Mr. Andrews is twirling a curl of her hair around his finger as if he has done it many times.

Marsh has dry sweats over his arm and is carrying a pair of rubber thongs. "Sir, we have a room ready for you where you can change, then we can dry your clothes."

"Thank you. And thank you, Sheriff. I believe I owe you my life, that throw was perfect. I could feel the car slipping when you spotted me."

Thay nods and whispers something to Marsh. "Jim, may I borrow your Rover?" I toss him the keys, his truck isn't up to a washed-out bridge. He returns to the storm to check the damage on his beloved island.

"Rhodes, borrow a boat. Mr. Andrews came over on a ferry. When it comes back you go and free Lemuel."

"Miss Forbenshire, I'm sorry, but the ferry was having engine trouble. The captain was heading back to its berth for repairs when he left."

Lettic keeps screaming at Mr. Thornton as if Mr. Andrews hadn't spoken.

"That woman in the morgue isn't Phedra. There's been a mistake. That woman isn't my sister!"

"Lettic, let me change and we'll talk. Go to your room. I'll come as soon as I can." He's aware of our listening ears. I'm surprised not to see Barker parked outside the door. He isn't one to miss a conversation.

"Hell Rhodes, forget your damn clothes. There's no one here to impress." Her hands are clenched again as if she wants to pound him. "You aren't listening to me. That bitch at the morgue is *not* Phedra."

"Lettic, Lemuel identified her for the authorities. You aren't making sense and your locker room language doesn't help."

We're trapped against the fireplace. Thay and Marsh are blocking the doorway watching the furious woman as her hands open and close. Red splotches mottle her face. Maud reaches out with a restraining hand as Lettic leaps from the sofa.

She grabs Thornton's lapels and pulls him to his feet then slugs him with her fist. Her breathing is rapid as if she can't breath, "Now, that I've got your attention, you slimy bastard. Look! You've always wanted to look, but didn't have the guts."

Before anyone can stop her, Lettic yanks off her sweater and pulls down her slacks. "My sister didn't have an appendectomy scar, as you damn well know. She had stretch marks. I have the scar. Get your eyes full, it's the last chance you'll ever get. That imposter at the morgue has this same scar. You idiot. It's a good con, but she isn't my sister. Her hair is the same color, and it's cut the same way. But she isn't Phedra." Lettic grabs up her sweater and runs up the stairs.

Chapter 15

We were glad to get out of that parlor. It was like being in a play where every actor had a role but us. Isaiah went to his room to take a nap. He had driven most of the night and was near exhaustion. Maud and Mr. Andrews ran to her cottage to move her things to the hotel, which brought a knowing grin to Marsh's face.

Strangely, I enjoy the walk back to cottage to get my things. It isn't fair to the hotel staff for me to stay in my sanctuary. But, I'm relieved to leave the hotel with it's ugly currents. The people back there are like those heavy preludes of classical music Isaiah plays for a formal concert. They keep repeating, going in different directions without a climax.

The telephone and electric lines went down when the causeway collapsed so the only communication to the mainland is Thay's ship-to-shore radio. Marsh is using the hotel generator for power. We're castaways, which adds to the eeriness.

The wind has picked up and slaps walls of water like wet sheets hung on a line against my face. Marsh says it will blow inland to the mountains by mid-day tomorrow, dumping snow there while sucking up warm air from the Gulf Stream. I want to spend the afternoon holed up in the cottage away from people before I move in with them.

But Matt follows me and his pacing is like being caged with a trapped wildcat. He picks up the shells I've collected, then puts them back in the same spot. He isn't looking at me, but collapses on the foot of the bed I'm using, staring at the ceiling.

"Hey, this isn't bad for a rehabilitation set-up. I'd need a weight bench."

"Not me. Hobbling around on those crutches put muscles in my shoulders I didn't know I had."

"I noticed when you hefted Longer's trunk. Then you've never had any trouble moving an engine block." He keeps tossing a rock back and forth, avoiding my questions.

"Matt, I know you didn't come to Seamew to check on me. I told you I'd promised Kane I'd lay off the booze."

"Most of these ocean front places are closed during the winter. Jim, you weren't anywhere near an alcoholic, but Mom was worried. Kane protects her so he found this isolated resort to park you to recuperate.

"It has helped, the running on the beach. You're slowly getting back in shape. You aren't afraid to put your feet down like you were when you came home from the hospital."

"You're avoiding my questions." He has something on his mind and it isn't the state of my feet. His eyes dart everywhere, not once looking at me.

"All right, to answer the question you haven't asked, but have been holding like a stuffed warthog. The Vikings dropped my contract as Mrs. Longer announced to the world. I can put my name in the pool when the draft comes up, but I don't stand a chance against the young guys fresh out of school. Playing is over for me."

"Do something else."

His head snaps up. "You tried the bottle. Did it work?"

"No, but what has that to do with you?"

"Jim, we didn't have a choice. You love racing and I love playing ball. Those doors slammed shut leaving us out in the cold."

"You own a radio/television station."

"You own a junkyard and a machine shop. I don't want to come home as a failure."

"How do you think I felt? It's the same thing."

"Yes and no. You built engines for other owners before the accident. I got the color job for one game as a handout." He picks up my book from the table beside the bed. The red cover of *The Young Detective's Handbook* gleams in the lamplight. "What's this?"

"A book I'm reading."

"You told me the sheriff watched you read the first night you were here, was this the book? It looks like a book for kids." He is thumbing through the pages. "Why are you reading this?"

"It was the only book I could find on how to be a detective." I feel myself blushing.

Matt is finally looking at me and now I wish he wasn't. "And?"

"Phillip Andrews has offered me a job as an insurance investigator."

"Andrews owns the biggest agency in Brewster...oops...Ono County. I'll never get used to that dumb name."

The lights flicker and then come back bright.

"Yes. I promised I'd give him an answer and now he's here on the island. I thought I'd have time to think about it on the trip back over the mountains. Now I'll need to decide before we go home."

"What gave him the idea you knew anything about insurance." Matt is shaking the book at me.

"I don't. I helped him out when Laurence Bradley staged an accident to collect the insurance on his car. When I pulled the car out of the ravine I showed Mr. Andrews there were no skid marks. We found where he dumped gas in the backseat and set it on fire. It took some asking around, but Laurence was laying off bets with some Capitol City bookies and couldn't pay up. He was going to use the insurance money to get off the hook."

Matt starts to prowl again. He goes to the front window, pulls open the curtain, but the shutters are closed on the outside. "Don't you hate being closed in out here? It's spooky."

"No, it reminds me of Mark's place. Peaceful before you started converting it to a running track. What's bothering you?"

"We've been cooped up for two days, nothing but rain and wind. Some vacation. Now we're stranded until they can repair the causeway or the ferry with a murderer who has killed two people."

"Are you saying the woman and Stevens were killed by the same person? They weren't killed the same way."

Matt looks stunned at his own thoughts, "Yes, they were. Both died from attacks to the neck. The killer had to be tall enough to attack both victims. The woman was what, about five-four? Stevens was around five-ten, so the killer had to be strong and tall enough to strike the neck—near six-foot."

I'm embarrassed. I'd read the part of the book about observing everything and remembering small details. It told me to make notes, but Matt figured out the height thing.

"Well, that lets out Fanny and Wally."

"Damn, those two deadbeats would have been perfect. They were enough to drive a person stir crazy. I wanted to boot her down the front steps to make sure she didn't sneak back into the hotel."

"Now who is the detective?"

"If what Lettic says is true. The woman in the morgue isn't Mrs. Lavin. Who is she?"

"I don't have any idea, but she was living here as Phedra Lavin. Had been for almost six weeks. Maud met her and went shopping with the woman who was murdered. Why was she pretending to be Mrs. Lavin?"

He keeps flipping the pages of the book. "Good question?"

"You're a lot of help. Where is the real Mrs. Lavin? That makes one woman and one kid who are missing, plus an extra woman and a FBI agent dead. Kevin Stevens, the FBI agent, was dumped in the sound. Barker is hanging around listening to every word anyone says. Thay has his hands full on the island with this storm."

"You're right." Matt starts laughing, "Perfect, it's the best solution for your future. You've always been nosey and not afraid to ask questions. Yes, I can see you as a detective." He holds up the book. "Have you learned anything?"

"A little."

"Can you figure out what is happening on this island?"

"Maud asked me to find out who killed Phedra or whoever she is, but Thay told me not to practice anything I learned from a kid's book."

Matt is dead serious, the eyebrow doesn't move. "Jim, I was wrong about Lettic Forbenshire." He takes a gulp of air, "She needs help. Rhodes Thornton is Mike Gallino's main lawyer. He's a front man for some rough people. If what she implied is true, her sister is his mistress."

"How did you come up with that conclusion?"

"Jim, for a future detective you weren't paying attention. Lettic yelled that Rhodes Thornton knew about the stretch marks on her sister."

"But she is Dr. Lavin's girlfriend, isn't she? Cheating on her sister."

"That's the way it reads to me." He pulls my bag from the closet and tosses it on the bed shoving in my clothes. "Get your stuff out of the bathroom. Use some sense. Marsh and Thay have enough to worry about without you playing at camping out."

The wind is hitting the door. "You'd better answer the door." He points as he dumps more of my stuff in the bag.

" Lettic!" She stands there shaking, "Come in." She doesn't even look at me when I opened the door.

"Matt…while I was in town." Her teeth clatter like false teeth as her jaw trembles. "My room…ransacked. Come look."

Matt tosses me my coat off the rocker where I'd draped it to dry, pulling his on at the same time. He slips his left arm around the trembling Lettic and we rush out into the quickening storm.

Her room is a mess. Bedcovers dumped on the floor, the mattress is up-see-daisy, clothes pulled from the closet, drawers pitched, and her suitcase up-ended on the table with the lining ripped out. Matt pushes her into my arms.

"I'll rouse Marsh. Don't touch anything." He takes off running down the hall.

She'd showed us to a small door on the beach side that opened onto backstairs. It led to the upper verandah. We'd left the hotel over two hours ago. Where had she been that she hadn't discovered this mess in her room until now?

We wait for Matt in the hall. I can hear Isaiah tinkering with the piano downstairs. It's beyond him to leave one unless the tuning is perfect, though it sounds good to me as he run a swift series of cords in a minor key like ragtime slowed to a waltz. The soft air comes to an abrupt halt.

Marsh's feet pound down the long hall like African drums beating in the night. Lettic's choked sobs echo Marsh's frantic footsteps as an off beat. Matt followed by Isaiah, brings up the rear. Marsh takes one look in the room and pulls a ring of keys from his pocket. "I'm sorry, Miss Forbenshire, but your room will have to be locked up until Thay gets back."

Small beads of sweat dot his upper lip. "Ma'am, we've never had anything like this happen. I'll give you a room in the south wing until Thay says we can clean up."

It's clear this is beyond Marsh's hotel management skills. He's thinking on his feet and hoping he's making the right moves. Lettic has stepped away from me and slowly nods her head in agreement like she's in a daze.

"Thank you. Let me get my purse, I dropped it on the floor and ran. My head is killing me. I need to take some aspirin, and I have some in my purse."

The shake is back in her voice, but it's flat as if she's caved in. I don't like her, but I do feel sorry for her. She's been pushed to her limits and is teetering on the brink. A large black bag is hanging from her shoulder when she returns to the hall.

Rhodes Thornton and Roger Barker poke their heads out of adjoining rooms to investigate the sudden activity in the hall. Lettic looks their way and hides behind me as if she is terrified of Thornton.

In a strangled little girl voice, "May I have a key, please." She holds out one hand to Marsh and clutches the big purse to her stomach with the other.

Thornton strides up to us. He's in shirt sleeves, baggy pants, and not wearing a tie. Marsh's flipflops make a sucking sound on the heart-pine floor. Barker is still wearing a suit, but remains by his door.

Thornton's voice booms like a bullhorn. "Lettic, what problems are you causing? I told you. Lemuel will be released as soon as I can get to the mainland."

She looks at him with contempt in her eyes, but the fight has fled to be replaced by fear. "Someone trashed my room. The manager is giving me a new one as far away from you as I can get." She turns to Marsh, "Will you show me where the room is located?"

They walk away, Marsh in the lead. Thornton studies them and turns back to us. "Young? Washed out with the Vikings. Didn't recognize you without a helmet. Tell me what in the hell is going on?"

I take a deep breath to see if he's still standing. Isaiah gives a swift shake of his head and heads for the stairs. Matt looks him up and down as if measuring him for a casket before a mountain falls. I kick him and we leave the scumbag standing in the hall.

"Whee. The next time you guys take a vacation, camp out on a deserted desert island." He sits down on the piano bench, takes his left thumb nail and runs it the length of the keys, each tone is perfect.

"Isaiah, what's the word they use when a bunch of dancers are on stage and you don't want them running into each other?"

"Jim, I guess the word you want is choreographed."

"That's it. She trashed that room. Matt, it was staged. You were played for a sucker."

"Me? How did you come up with this wild notion?"

"Her purse, it was bulging and heavy. She had all her woman fixings in it, jewelry and stuff. Her hair wasn't mussed. She wasn't breathing hard when she knocked on the door of my cottage, not like she was when she attacked Thornton. She was wearing that mink coat in a rainstorm, but a wet slicker was on the floor. She was wearing her mink vest under the coat, like she was going for a visit to the North Pole."

Isaiah fingers *do re me* over and over, as Matt plops down on the end of the sofa. He swiftly turns and glares at Isaiah, "Don't you start, don't you dare!" Isaiah just grins, a sassy Isaac grin. They're sharing something older brothers keep from the runt.

"Okay, Little Brother. That's good detective work, now explain."

"It didn't hit me until we were coming down the stairs. We came into her room from the veranda, the door to the bathroom was wide open. She had taken a shower, the wet towels were on the floor. There was water on the floor, which means the shower was recent. She'd been in her room long enough to take a bath and fix her hair. Where was her hair dryer? What's the first thing you put out when you unpack in a hotel room?"

Matt screws his face in a frown, then the eyebrow wobbles. "My shaving kit. I take it out, put it in the bathroom and then I hang up my clothes."

"Because it's the last thing, you stuff in your bag. There wasn't any woman's stuff on the counter in the bath or on the chest in her room."

"Tell Mr. Andrews you'll take the job offer. All I saw was the mess. It looked to me like someone was looking for something. But why?"

"That's what she wanted you to think. To get you to come down off your high horse, I expect. She knew where you were, probably watched you go down to my cottage. When I opened the door, she said your name." They're both looking at me. I throw up my hand, "It was all a bunch of little things, that didn't add up."

"Well, I won't go rushing out into another storm to rescue a damsel in distress. Go ask Marsh for a room. You're still holding your gym-bag."

Chapter 16

I start to put my unfinished letter in the trash, but Phillip reaches for it. I let him read it. The ancient history is irrelevant now that he is here.

January 19, 1976

> *Marsh says the Nor'easter may cut gouges in the land bridge and if it goes we'll be stranded. Orta, one of the maids, tells me it will blow out tomorrow and get warm again. My milk house heater is pumping away, but it's still cool in my cottage because of the big drop in the temperature. Early this morning you could hear sleet hitting the roof, but that didn't last.*
>
> *The phones are unreliable as the authorities are keeping the lines open for emergencies. If the storm knocks out everything this letter may be a few days getting to the mainland.*
>
> *I always wanted to be near the ocean in a storm, but it isn't the fun I thought it would be. Just wind and rain, then more rain and wind.*
>
> *Stay tuned for the next episode, I enjoy talking to you.*

"So you enjoy talking to me?" He lays the letter on the bed and pats it before scooping his shorts off the floor. In all those years when he was fighting the bottle, he never lost the thick muscles in his legs and shoulders acquired from living on a horse. Now he has gained weight from decent eating. If he were to walk down the beach in the summer, it would cause a riot. It's my delicious secret. The fine figure of a man he hides under his Capital City tailored suits is breathtaking.

I'm shameless, but I love those long legs and powerful arms wrapped around me. It's like coming home after a long absence.

"Phillip, I was never so glad in my life as when you walked through the door. But when Rhodes Thornton came in with Thay I wanted to crawl in a hole and disappear."

"Mr. Thornton is Dr. Lavin's lawyer. Why would you be afraid of a man you've never seen."

"That's just it. I have seen him. My red hair is hard to miss, and I was afraid he'd recognize me."

"Why would he recognize you? Miss Forbenshire said the body in the morgue wasn't her sister and proved it rather spectacularly, if I may say so."

"Just like a man. She got the attention of every man in the room.

"The questions no one asked are: Who is she? Why is she dead if she isn't Phedra Lavin? Where is the real Phedra Lavin? Is Lettic correct with her identification or is she trying to pull the wool over everyone's eyes to protect her lover?

"You men were too busy looking at the peep show to consider the implications of these murders."

"Maud, you're attacking your hair with that brush. Let me. I'm guilty as accused. You haven't answer my question. Why are you afraid Rhodes Thornton would recognize you?"

"He is...he is the man the man I saw kissing the woman in the morgue. Whoever she is. He was on the island the day I arrived."

Phillip puts down the brush, goes over to the bed, and sits down. He face is a deep study of concern. "That puts a different complection on the matter. You'd best have a long talk with the sheriff and let him know about Thornton."

"I will the first chance I get to see him alone." Phillip's brilliant blue eyes seep into my soul asking questions he need not contemplate. I smile back at his reflection in the mirror remembering what he said when he arrived.

"I've been lonely too."

"Lonely? With all those men around you?" Little crinkles dance at the edge of his eyes.

"Phillip, stop teasing. You know they're just boys. They regard me as they do their mother."

He looks up from pulling on a sock and I catch the questioning eyes in the mirror before they dart to the closet where our clothes hang side-by-side. Phillip wants to know if I'm comfortable staying here in the hotel with him.

At our ages, why do I cling to ancient appearances? All of his family and most of mine are dead. Loving demands courage. I must tell him the truth. It was easier writing. When I didn't have to look him in the face.

"Phillip, we'll go down and tell the boys at supper. I love you and I'm tired of hiding. It isn't seemingly to take a lover so soon after Rupert's death, but I can't stand the thought of a barren life anymore. I don't want to be married ever again and I don't want to lose you. I saw Lettic Forbenshire look you over like a trophy to add to her collection, as Matt says."

I'm trying to get my hair in some kind of order, but this damp is making it spring out like Medusa's. He comes over to the dresser where I sit and removes my hands, taking a curl and twining it around his finger.

"This curl has the power of a thousand chains. Maud, I'm no prize, one drink and I'm back on the sauce. I made a promise to Marcy before she died. So far I've kept my word, but every day is a new battle I have to wage. And it will be for the rest of my life. Can you live with that uncertainty?"

I'm shaking, there are so many things I want to tell him. "You don't mind not getting married?"

He gives a little chuckle, "No, I'll take you anyway you want. 'Seemingly' be damned. I've loved you for years and you know it. Loving you may have been the only thing that kept me sane when all the ugliness about my sister was the talk of Clydesville and I lost custody of Bill Jr."

He looks back at the closet. "I like our clothes mixed together."

"It didn't take me long to fill my suitcase." My heart made up my mind. I'll need to get another case to take home all the things I've purchased in town. I've been like a drunken sailor on shore leave in an exotic port, seeing the lovely things the stores at home don't carry.

"Finish fixing your hair and we'll go downstairs to face the music from your chaperones. The boys I can handle, when we left they looked like see'nos."

I grab the tie-belt to my dress and wrap it around the fly-a-way as a headband. "See'nos? What are you talking about?"

"You know the three monkeys, 'See No Evil, Hear No Evil, and Speak No Evil.' They had pleased grins on their faces when we left to get your things. The Youngs won't be a problem. It's the sheriff who worries me. He's sweet on you."

There is something in what he says. Flattering yes, but with Phillip present Thay will keep it as friends. He's too much of a gentleman to do otherwise.

I refuse to be baited by Phillip's banter. His teasing is another sign he does love me. Rupert never teased me.

"Do you think they know about their mother and Silas Morgan?"

"What? I didn't. I'll have to show Silas where to find their back gate. Mary Young is like you, a stubborn woman when it comes to marrying. She put a double-barrel to the idea 'boys need a father.' Her boys are grown men.

"Here let me help with that, you're turning into a pretzel."

A back zipper is an excellent reason for having a man around. This wool paisley jersey fits like that black dress Lettic was wearing the other night. Black is one color I'll never wear again. Phillip's Christmas present is heavy around my neck. Have I traded a nose-ring for a collar? If I have, at least its real gold. Imagine me, owning a gold collar.

"What's the name of your perfume? It's all around you, like a cloud."

"It's French and frightfully expensive. I loved the name, so I bought it. Joy."

"It's you and what you give me, joy."

"When we get home?" I see his eyes gleam, as he deliberately misunderstands me.

"Maud, I know the way though the raspberry bushes."

"Are you sure?"

"I've been sure for more years than I care to count."

"Phillip, I love you. But I also love being myself. Not being beholden to anyone."

"Can't you understand? That stubborn streak of independence is part of you. If it were missing it would make you someone else. I love all of you, not just a piece here and there."

I giggle, can't help it. The idea of loving a piece of a person, maybe a finger. He's never mentioned the difference in our ages. I'm five years older than Phillip. Will he leave me when I get old and gray?

"I won't leave the porch light on. The backdoor won't lock."

"It does now, I fixed it before I left. I have one condition. You put a broom across the doorway. We'll jump it together for form."

That still makes a legal marriage in the mountains, but not at home. I don't think.

It's going to be hard to keep my hands off him in public. This afternoon in the parlor I felt like I was posed for an old tintype. He was running his thumb across my shoulder blade. My nipples got hard while Lettic was having hysterics.

"Are you going to wear those?" Phillip is pointing at my feet.

"But, I'll be taller than you."

"Maud, it doesn't matter. From behind you look like a waddling duck when you wear shoes without a heel. In pumps the muscles of your calves move in rhythm with your hips. A feast for this hungry man."

He opens the door to our south side suite and waves me through. My hand fits so comfortably on his arm. It feels like it belongs there. I'm wearing high heels and don't feel gawky with Phillip by my side.

Chapter 17

"Louise Leviticus, you listen to me. Orta is sitting with Nialis, we looked in on her when we came down. There are nine people for supper with only Marsh to do the serving. That's too much in the middle of this storm."

"Miss Maud...."

"One long table, put the food out and pass the bowls. No room service. If they want to eat they can come to the table. Phillip, you and Marsh arrange the square tables in a line and set the places. Mamma Lou can sit at one end and I will sit at the other."

The battle is raging as I come down the stairs. Maud and Mamma Lou are having a difference of option. Sheriff Thay is standing just outside the door, hidden from view and laughing. "She's met her match. Miss Maud has Mr. Andrews and Marsh rearranging the dining room. Mamma Lou is resisting taking orders."

"I'm not surprised. It's hard to for me to explain. My brother, Levi could. He teaches history at the university and knows the right words. Maud and Mr. Andrews eat breakfast at the Kricket every morning before it opens with a group of other folks. Admittance is stiffer than at the country club."

I look at Thay while trying to explain how Maud thinks about what people should do. He knows I'm making hash of our ways. He's enjoying my bumbling around. He waits for me to finish as if he knows what I'm trying to say is important.

"I'm not old enough, though Lon Chambers and Elroy Harris who work in my machine shop and run moonshine are members.

Lon is an Oswego Indian with a dash of colored and a few other things mixed in. That isn't important. It's like they're welded by memories too terrible to share. If I'd show up for breakfast they'd be polite, but I'd be a stranger though they've known me all my life.

"Sure we see stuff about race problems on TV, everybody does, but it doesn't concern us. It's the same way with Wilson who owns the Kricket. He's from New York and different, but he's family, being a cousin to Elton Fightmaster."

Thay looks at me and I nod my head. He understands about Wilson. I can feel my words get faster as they tumble out of my mouth, "How you pull your freight matters. At the Kricket you eat what Wilson puts out and everyone eats at the same table." To get out of the hole I've dug, I say the first thing that comes in my fuzzy mind.

"We'd best go help 'em fix those tables. Mamma Lou has lost the argument."

The lights have been flickering all evening, so Marsh turns off as many as possible to take the strain off the old generator. He puts candles with glass globes to shelter the flames down the center of the tables. The entire hotel is dark, huddled against the storm. I feel those watching eyes I felt the first night I waited for Maud, but I resist the urge to look over my shoulder. I've already made a fool of myself trying to explain hill country manners to Thay.

Matt went back upstairs and rousted everyone to the dining room. Lettic kicked up a fuss, but he wasn't taking any nonsense after what she pulled this afternoon. I was tempted to suggest she clean up the mess she'd made in that room instead of expecting Orta to wait on her. I still can't figure out why she did it. Whose attention was she trying to get? She didn't plan to be stuck in the hall with me!

Thirteen plates are laid for supper, Maud wants everyone, including Nialis and Orta, at the table. Orta brings a platter from the kitchen, takes one look at the table and runs back to the kitchen. Marsh hurries into the room and swiftly removers two plates, leaving five on one side and four on the other. He smiles at Thay, "My sister insists on eating with Nialis to make sure she eats something."

Maud seats eleven people in a master plan where they won't rub against each other the wrong way. Mr. Andrews pushes Mamma Lou's chair up to one end with Barker on her left, followed by Rhodes Thornton, Matt, Marsh, and Thay. Their backs are to the kitchen door. Isaiah is placed at Mamma Lou's right hand with Lettic, myself, and Mr. Andrews spread out down to Maud on the other end.

Lettic is sitting beside me and making a good meal of the simple food. Pork chops simmered in thick gravy, mashed potatoes seasoned with butter and garlic, baked stewed tomatoes, peas mixed with tiny shreds of carrots, and fluffy yeast-rolls. The atmosphere is tense, the flicking candles light up the strained faces of strangers.

Mr. Andrews smiles at Thay. "The blue front-door is very distinctive."

"It's Marsh's formula for thwarting 'haints.'"

Mr. Andrews looks to Marsh. "Haints? Oh, ghosts. Does it work?"

"Seems to, I've never seen one." Thay raises his head, assuming his freezing manner. Mr. Andrews ignores the stiff neck and reaches over to hold Maud's hand.

I start to ask about the plates Marsh snatched from the table, but Matt's fourteen connects with my leg.

Mr. Andrews makes eye-contact with everyone. Like Rhodes Thornton, he's a stranger, but people respond to his open smile.

"A great-uncle of mine always swore he'd seen a ghost, but the family tells the story differently. His mama had ordered some piece goods from Nashville for curtains. Back then everything was brought up the Cumberland River to Creelsboro, the landing on the river. They'd just finished plowing when they heard the steam whistle echoing through the hills.

"Uncle Will was about seven at the time and begged to go fetch his mother's packet. He knew the general store had jars of penny candy. It was near to four miles from the farm to the landing. He took his Pa's fine stallion, Tallboy, and was expected back not long after supper."

The table is quiet, everyone is listening to Mr. Andrews. Maud's face is relaxed in pleased acceptance as if she's heard the story before, but proud to hear it again.

"Young boys were sports for the ne'er-do-wells around the landing who were always willing to help in their development. Uncle Will consumed a bit more than his piece of candy on an empty stomach. He strapped the package wrapped in butcher paper to the pad he was using as a saddle and started for home, his legs barely stretching across Tallboy's broad back.

"It was late and he was busy thinking up reasons to explain his long absence from home. Tallboy didn't need guiding to find his way to the barn. He'd carried Will's Pa home in the same inebriated state after he shipped his hogs-heads of tobacco to Nashville. Uncle Will looped the reins around his fist and fell asleep to the rocking rhythm of the plodding hooves.

"Fog settles in quick in the valleys between the hills along the Cumberland. Will woke up to a fidgeting horse near to pulling his arms out of their sockets. He couldn't slide off because he had no place to climb back on. So he leaned over Tallboy's neck to soothe the frantic beast and succeeded in upchucking the 'lighten he'd consumed. The fog was swirling around near his feet, and to him it seemed as if the horse was pacing through clouds. He couldn't tell how far he'd come because of the thick trees hanging over the path and the fog. Sick and miserable, he heard a sharp crackling sound and looked back to get his bearings.

"Out there! Just beyond Tallboy's rump was a "thing" floating in the dark and dipping down into the fog. Scared out of his wits, Uncle Will took the ends of the reins and slapped the horse, who didn't need urging. But every time he looked back, the "thing" was following him. They raced through the night as if that old stallion was Pegasus. Somewhere in their headlong flight the reins were pulled from Will's sweating hands. Will stretched, but couldn't reach them, as they were caught up in Tallboy's roached mane. The horse had the bit between his teeth and fled in terror from the "thing" that pursued them through the dense fog.

"Tallboy pulled up by the porch. Uncle Will fell off, but hauled himself to his feet. He ran in the house shouting and screaming about the "thing" that followed him home. When his folks got him calmed down and went outside to investigate, Tallboy, head bowed to the ground, was standing in the light from the door sweating and trembling. Uncle Will's mama's package was spilling open. The bolt of cloth was streaming over Tallboy's steaming rump to the ground."

Laughter erupts to Mr. Andrews's funny ghost story. Lettic jerks her head around to stare into darkness as a loud crash shatters the silence outside the windows. The lights flicker and go out. A faint odor of burning rubber mingles with the aroma of the marsh on the currents in the room. This time it's several seconds before the lights come back on dimmer than before. The old generator is having a hard time against the brunt of the storm.

Mamma Lou exclaims, "Why they tell that same story on Edisto Island. But it happened long before steamboats."

"All stories tend to have a common thread, but they make good telling."

Uncle Will's adventures and Mamma Lou's acceptance dispels

the gloom around the table. Everyone starts talking to their neighbors while I concentrate on securing another pork chop before Matt's fork finds the platter.

I hear Isaiah telling Mamma Lou about my winning my first race and am glad the light is dim enough to hide my neck. I wish he wouldn't tell that story. He commands the attention of the entire table without raising his voice. Isaiah is a master teller of family tales. He refuses to look my way knowing I'll try to stop him as he chatters on with everyone listening.

"Jim found an old Chrysler abandoned in a field. It looked like the Bonnie and Clyde car. It took the entire family hacking and sawing to cut down the Slippery-Bark Elm growing up through the motor compartment. That tree had been growing there over thirty years, but the body was still in fine shape, not a spot of rust on it." His voice drones and I slip away from the gloom of murders and storms into the summer heat of a dirt track in August eleven years ago.

Chapter 18

*A*dam strapped the '27 Chrysler to the hay wagon he uses to haul pre-
formed roof trusses to a construction site. He's driving his '59 Chevy
truck with Mom in the seat beside him. Before we start she takes a bottle of
Thunderbird wine and breaks it across the hood for good luck like she'd seen
in a picture of Mamie Eisenhower christening a new battleship. All of my
brothers are in the back of Adam's pickup with me.

Isaiah painted a large nine, for nine bothers, on both doors with
Anderson's Salvage under the number. It looks like I have a real sponsor, but
it's the name of the junkyard where I found most of the parts to build my car.
He is razzing Isaac, his fraternal twin, about some girl he's been seeing on
the sly in Capital City. Isaac isn't taking it kindly, but that's their way. No
one in the family pays any attention to them when they go at it.

I won't get a regular driver's license until next year, but at fifteen I
can legally drive on a track. I've practiced on the back roads away from
the eagle eyes of Will Daniels, our sheriff. He stops by Carl Anderson's shop
often enough to know what I'm doing, but he turns a blind eye. He may be
figuring to borrow the Chrysler since it's the only car in the county that
might run with Elroy Harris's 'Gray Ghost.' He'd love to catch those two
bootleggers.

Cal Osborne's place fronts for a mile on a road near the Cumberland
River, as straight a stretch as you can find in the county. I can climb to 90
in three minutes on that straightaway before I have to make the curve near
Hank Sidmore's orchard. Levi riding shotgun has clocked me, but that's slow
getting up to speed on a good track.

Kane and Abel, our identical twins, will help me in the pits while the *others keep Mom company in the stands. They've staked out the first three rows at the fourth turn of the quarter-mile dirt track. This is the last time we will be together as a family for some time. Kane and Abel are going into the Army and Matt has been drafted by the Minnesota Vikings.*

I'm so scared my teeth are clacking, but I can't afford to admit it. Not in front of my brothers. They've worked hard to help me. Matt has loaned me his university helmet. Kane and Abel got new tires for my car at Sears Roebuck in Capital City. Levi and Mark skipped lunches at the university to help buy the gas. Isaac got my goggles and Mom made my uniform out of heavy twill, with a nine on the back.

After hot laps, we draw for positions in the heat races. I'm in the last one, which makes my hands jangle. The track is drying out, getting hard like concrete and the dust is so thick I can barely see. Can the jalopy handle this rough course?

I want to get it over with, all these guys have been around a while and even though my car looks sharp it's hard to handle on these high clay banks. I lost it four times during warm ups until I got the feel of the track under my feet.

Heat races are for show, I've got my place in the feature...dead last. Seven of us move onto the track for the last heat race. I drew the third starting position on the inside of the second row. My hands are slick with sweat. My uniform is streaked with mud where I've wiped them. The engine is holding together much better than I am.

The flag comes down. It's now or never. The guy behind me gives me a shove. Colors blur and I spin, fighting the wheel all the way, but manage to stay on the track without hitting anyone. Halfway to turn three I'm in last place. Now the best I can do is hold it and eat their dust to avoid getting in a pile-up. I've earned my spot in the feature. Now's not the time to lose it.

The flagman stops the race, I just miss hitting the pile-up between a black Mercury and a blue Chevy when I drive through the dust. I follow the lead car around for a full lap. Another car is down on the brim with a blown engine. We've made two laps and three cars are out of the race. The starter gives us the signal and four cars go full bore for the last five laps.

This dust is awful. I can't see. The crowd is yelling. The race is over. I spot the opening to head to the pits, but through the fog of dust I hear my brothers yelling, "One More Lap."

The dust clears a fraction and I'm into number four turn, skidding sideways toward the flagstand. The flagman drops the checkered flag over me as I fight to stay on the track.

I won!

I'm in a frenzy so high, I'm dancing on the top of the car clutching my plastic trophy and a case of oil.

I hear Matt's voice from the crowd at my feet.

"Earth to Jim, what did you say?"

"Oh! I'm sorry, I didn't hear you?"

"I asked you what you meant when you said 'I won'?"

I'd spoken out loud. Everyone is looking at me. Heat flames around my collar. I'm fighting like I did the night I won my first race to think of something to say when all the lights go out.

The candles light faces, but silence creeps around the room. I can't hear the soft rumble of the generator. We're the center of an island of darkness. Marsh pushes back his chair, but Mr. Andrews stops him.

"Finish your supper—we're fine. Isaiah and I can help you fix the generator. He paid his tuition doing electrical work for his brother. They did my office. We aren't going anywhere."

Momma Lou picks up Isaiah's hand and studies his palm. "You have many talents, which will bring conflict to your life. It won't be an easy life, but your family is strong."

Isaiah wants to pull his hand away, but being the center of attention serves him right for telling that story about me. The intensity of her eyes focused on my brother is as strong as a hypnotist's. I feel sucked into their deep pools and I'm only watching.

She laughs, breaking the spell, "Mr. Young, I have a better idea.

These lovely hands work best on my piano." She lightly strokes his long fingers and closes them over his palm.

"I heard your music this afternoon. Will you play for our guests before we take coffee and desert in the parlor? Marsh and Thay know that generator better than they know this island."

Isaiah pushes her chair across the hall to a spot by the fire. We follow, carrying the candles and line some of them on the black marble mantle and place a couple on the piano.

Maud and Phillip take two of the wing chairs, while Rhodes Thornton and Lettie take the other two. Matt, Thay, and I collapse on the sofa, as Barker pulls the straight chair in from the hall and settles by the door. Marsh scatters a few hurricane lanterns around the hall on small tables and on the check-in desk before he sits down on the stairs.

The soft glow of the burning candles and the fire moves me back in time. I feel like I'm sitting in this room a hundred years ago when all was peaceful and the War Between the States was long past.

Isaiah tinkers with the keys for a moment as we settle back to listen. He opens with the bittersweet Elvis standard, *Cold Kentucky Rain* as if we needed to be reminded of the weather. I wish he'd play something light and cheerful, but he plows right into *Are You Lonesome Tonight*. Then he turns to Marty Robbins's *Old Dogs and Children* and follows with *Burning Bridges*, but I can't remember who did that one.

He switches to a classical piece where I can hear undertones of a song I know. "I know that piece, what is it?"

Matt whispers back, "It's Chopin's *3rd Etude in E Major*. Listen and you'll hear the wind and rainstorm in the finale. The melody was used for the popular song, *'I'm Always Chasing Rainbows.'*"

I relax and listen to the familiar notes, but I'm watching the faces in the room. Their expressions show intense concentration as

Isaiah works his magic across the age-stained ivory keys of the gold-encrusted piano that gleams in the firelight.

A trill of chords and he begins to play the most mournful sounds I've ever heard. Sounds that cry with the wind as it sweeps around the hotel.

"What's that?"

"The work he did for his doctorate. He converted the themes of Schubert's *Unfinished Symphony* to a piano score."

"No wonder the old guy didn't finish it. I wouldn't have completed that tormented music either."

"Sounds like Isaiah has woman troubles...."

A scream echoes down the hall blending with the music. Orta runs into the parlor. Her face is drained of color. Marsh follows her into the room.

"Mamma! Mamma, Nialis has bled all over your bed. She's dead!"

Chapter 19

We stare at the weeping woman like discarded puppets with our slack jaws hanging open. Barker and Thornton rise to start down the hall. Mamma Lou grips the arms of her chair. Marsh grabs the handles and begins to push.

Thay's strong voice haults them in their tracks. "Everyone stay here. You too, Mamma Lou." He runs down the hall to the family's apartment.

Orta is shaking and is incoherent as she tells her story, "The table said someone would die. It was set for thirteen. I looked in on her before I stated cleaning the kitchen. Took her tray to the kitchen."

Rhodes Thornton grabs Lettic's arm and pulls her from the chair, "We don't belong here. This is not our affair. Go to your room and stay there. The show is over for tonight." It's a sharp command as he shoves her toward the door. She hesitates, then obeys him and ascends the stairs without looking back. He casts a swift glance at our blank faces and goes up behind her.

"Mamma, I only stopped...by the bathroom after I cleaned the kitchen."

Orta is sitting on the floor beside Mamma Lou's chair, clutching her hand. Marsh is leaning against the frame of the door, but keeps casting worried looks down the hall.

Barker pulls his chair into the hall and resumes his seat outside the parlor door as if he is our guard. Mr. Andrews moves to sit on the arm of Maud's chair, draping his hand over her shoulder. She turns her face into his jacket. Her body shudders as he holds her close to him. Isaiah silently closes the cover of the piano, and turns to look at us glued to the couch.

Matt's eyebrow floats up his forehead, but no one mutters a word. How could Nialis have been murdered when we were all in this room?

Minutes pass, and they feel like hours, though the hands of the clock on the mantle have barely moved before Sheriff Thay reappears.

"Mamma Lou, there is nothing you can do. She is dead. Her throat has been cut. Where are the keys to that room?"

"Marsh, show Thay where you keep the keys and bring me the spares." Her voice is old and very tired.

"Mamma Lou, take Orta and put her to bed. There isn't anything I can do tonight. Marsh, stay with your mother. I'll find an empty bed down the hall for the night."

Thay turns from his family, "Everyone should go on to bed. The storm will pass. Tomorrow afternoon or evening the weather will begin to clear. I hate to ask, Isaiah. Would you help me repair the generator in the morning?"

"Sure."

"Thanks. Marsh and Mamma Lou will need time to rustle breakfast for the guests without power."

Barker comes into the room from the hall. "Is there anything I can do to help? A crime has been committed on the premises, and that bedroom needs to be secured."

Thay shakes his head, "I'm the officer in charge and I know what to do, so stay out of my way." He stops and looks, as if he has just noticed, "Where's Collins?"

"He went back to the mainland with the Longers before the causeway washed out. Office duties."

"You don't have office duties?"

"Look Townsend, Stevens was my boss and a friend. Someone killed him, like they murdered the hotel maid. I want to know who."

"Reasonable."

I'm listening to every word that passes between them. Where did I hear to be leery of plausible explanations? Why is Barker still here? Is he hunting Shell?

Sheriff Thay shakes his head again as if to remember his manners, but answers in a strange manner that has nothing to do with Nialis' death. "No thank you, the generator house is a tight space. Two bodies are all that will fit, and even then, it's cramped."

From down the hall, I hear Orta's shaky voice repeating the superstition she had voiced earlier, "I know'd someone would die. I saw it on the table."

Chapter 20

"Maud, stop pacing. You're like a cat with a thorn in her paw."

Phillip's voice out of the dark startles me. I'd tried not to disturb him. The strangeness of someone in my bedroom adds to the eeriness of the night sounds in the hotel. Somewhere on the north end of the hotel a shutter is banging with a staccato pulse.

"I tried to be quiet. Footsteps outside our door woke me."

"Maud, earlier someone tried the door. I was awake when you got up."

" I watched you lock it before we retired. Why would someone try our door?"

"No idea. Maybe the sheriff was executing a bed check. He didn't seem pleased when I enticed you into the iniquities of my bedroom."

"Truth be told, I raced you up the stairs."

"A flame-haired older women has me in her thralls."

"Stop teasing—this is serious."

"It is serious, but your laughter evaporates dark shadows and oils creaking doorknobs."

"Phillip, Nialis was murdered while we sat in the parlor enjoying Isaiah's music. I feel so guilty. I knew something would happen to her. That's why I wanted everyone in the dining room where I could keep an eye on them."

"But you couldn't have prevented her death. Sheriff Townsend did the right thing when he sealed the room."

"Phillip, three people have been murdered since I've been on this island and no one knows why, or even if the killings are related."

"Oh there is a connection. That is evident, but what is the "why" the authorities will need to discover. Not you my love, the authorities."

"I must help."

"I...I know, but how?"

"With all of the confusion I never had a chance to tell Thay about Rhodes Thornton."

"Like the rest of us, he is not going anywhere. Your speaking to the sheriff can wait until morning. There may be a perfectly good reason for his being here earlier in the month."

"I don't know. It is obvious he knew the woman in the morgue was not Phedra Lavin. Who is she? Rhodes Thornton knows. You don't kiss a stranger like that and not know them. I believed he was her husband, until Dr. Lavin arrived."

"It is a tangled web we weave when we want to deceive."

"That sounds like something Lon Chambers would say."

"I didn't quote it correctly. It's an old idea from a poem by Sir Walter Scott, but the idea covers many sins."

"I never went to college."

"I only went one semester. We had it in Mrs. Miller's class. Maud, come back to bed. Seventh grade English is a rotten subject for an after-midnight discussion."

"I keep thinking there is something else I must remember. Besides the murders there are also two people missing. They're both afraid for different reasons."

"Don't go fey on me."

"Fey. Where did you get that idea?"

"Maud, I've lived next door to you for twenty years. This isn't the first time you've said something out of the blue that later proved to be true."

"I don't have visions." My mind just tells me when things are true. "Rupert believed I was crazy."

"So he tried to beat out of you what is as natural in the mountains as breathing. Everyone has or had a relative who has the "sight" to some degree or another. He was a stupid man. Your secrets are safe with me. You're trying to live in Methodist Purgatory and it won't work."

"Phillip, what are you talking about? Purgatory is Catholic."

"It's Methodist too, someone telling you how to live, what to believe, or what to see. Trying to make you feel guilty about who you are so you'll drop a larger donation in the collection plate. You have the sight. So what! It doesn't change the woman I love."

"I love you, too. If I know something is going to happen I should be able to stop it. All I've ever been able to do is fret."

"It's time to stop fretting and come back to bed. Maud, it's the middle of the night. Besides, it's cold."

"I'm wearing my heavy coat."

"You're shedding sand on the floor. Every time you take a step I hear a scrunch under your feet."

"But you'll distract me."

"That is my firm intention. When you stop plaguing yourself the memory will come to you."

"Someone else will die. No. There is another person who is already dead."

Chapter 21

The smell of coffee pulls me from a deep sleep. I turn over and inhale the wake-up call. The events of yesterday were so swift and startling I was a long time getting to bed. I stood on the porch watching the storm settle in for a good blow, and listened to the waves pound the shore with the same question, matching their rhythm in my head. Who would kill a hotel maid?

It's still dark. I reach for the bedside lamp before I remember there isn't any electric power. Matt turns over and buries his head under the pillow. My stomach growls when my nose sniffs bacon. Our room must be over the kitchen for breakfast smells to reach me.

I meet Isaiah on the landing carrying a flash light in one hand and rubbing the sleep from his eyes with the other. Together we go downstairs to slip into the kitchen where Mamma Lou is working over an ancient coal-oil range as Marsh pulls a large pan of biscuits from the oven.

"Thank you for coming, Mr. Isaiah. Mr. Andrews said you know electricity. Fix yourselves a bite of substance before you wrestle with the generator. Then we can make you a proper meal."

Isaiah pulls a paper plate from the stack on a shelf and helps himself from the range's warming oven. I follow suit. We know those old ranges from when Mom used one at the farm. Eating in the kitchen feels like home. I don't have that uncomfortable feeling of someone watching me that I have in the dining room.

No one mentions Nialis and I don't ask questions. Talk is sparse when Thay comes in the back door and pours himself a cup of coffee.

Isaiah waves his fork in my face, "Jim can make himself useful. He'll hold the flashlights for us while we work."

I'd never noticed the stone hut that butts up against the backside of the hotel. A large fuel-oil tank standing on stilts above my head is attached to the building. Deep woods of mixed pines, live oaks, palmetto palms, low-growing bushes, and ferns hid it from the beach front. Out here I can smell the ocean and the mud flats that have been exposed as the tide changes. Its like the breezes are caught in a giant Mix Master and don't know which way to stir.

Worn steps lead down into a dark cubbyhole that holds the rank odor of damp, ancient mold, and burned motor oil.

"Where's the main power switch?"

"Marsh turned everything off at the circuit box in the kitchen."

"Need to do it down here too. If we don't, when we try to start it back up the surge can blow the entire system. I don't want to take a chance of anything being hot while I've got my hands back there in the dark trying to find the problem."

"Let me think. This is Marsh's domain, but the switches should be over here on the wall inside the door."

"Jim, hand me a flashlight so I can see what's here."

Isaiah is bent almost double as he studies the panel, flips open the switches and hands the flashlight back to me.

Isaiah, followed by Thay, crawls through the tight space around the generator. I'm bending over to see through the low door. I don't think I could stand being in that cramped, cold box. Though it's warmer this morning than it's been for several days, my running clothes feel good. I've got my rain slicker over them to ward off the heavy mist in the air.

I crouch down on the bottom step with two flashlights and direct their beams to where they tell me.

"Jim, hand Thay one of those lights so I can see behind this thing. I think I've located the problem."

I bend way over and put the flashlight in Thay's back-stretched hand. As the light passes to him something glitters on the mud floor. I pick it up and stick it in my pocket as I back out of the dark, damp cave.

"Hell fire! Someone stripped the wires down to one strand and it burned through, shorting out the works. Idiot could have burned the place down."

"Are you sure?"

"Thay, I'm looking at the scorch marks on the housing. This was deliberate. It won't take me a minute to fix it. Hand me a Phillips screwdriver and those wire cutters. They've got a stripper in the handles. With a heavy coating of electrician's tape the generator will be back in business."

All I can hear are grunts and a few cuss words from the dark pit. Thay backs up and Isaiah follows him because there isn't room between the generator and the wall for them to turn around.

"Here, give me that light and lets see if what I did works." Isaiah's hand is black, like he's been digging coal above the river. A rank odor of decay hits me in the face before I back up the steps.

Thay reaches up with a crowbar and bangs on the tin roof as the top edge of the sun streams over the beach, casting a golden glow on the hotel.

Marsh pokes his head over the porch railing, "We have light. I can hear the grumbling under my feet. By the time you get cleaned up, breakfast will be on the table."

Thay and Isaiah come up the steps talking. "That'll work for a while, but to be safe have someone come out and replace all that wiring."

"Will it work for the next couple of weeks till we can get service from the mainland?"

"It should, but put a padlock on the door. I'd use it for the essentials. How did this storm affect the power on the rest of the island?"

Thay gives a little chuckle. "Storms are a way of life for us. Most homes have emergency generators."

"That problem was intentional sabotage, no doubt about it. Here are the scrapings I picked up out of the mud."

Their faces are streaked with grime, strands of cobwebs are twined in their hair, and the knees of their pants are coated with a thick, black ooze. It'll take a week's washing to get those pants clean if they're not already ruined.

My brain recognizes the rumble of the generator before they close the thick door. In the hotel it's a low background noise, which I thought came from the waves breaking on shore. What's the matter with me? Have I become a stranger to the strokes of a motor?

"Marsh, tell Matt I've gone for a run to work out the stiffs."

"Mr. Jim, he's took an extra cup of coffee down there to wait for you."

Chapter 22

M att is gasping for breath as we sprint for the steps to the hotel. "Whew! It's only been two days since we ran. I'm already out of shape."

"I beat you."

It feels good to win against Matt at anything. He doesn't know I've been running in place to rebuild the strength in my legs.

"The storm packed the sand down so hard it's like running on asphalt. Looks like it too, an oyster gray."

"The bottoms of my feet are burning."

He drops beside me to shake the sand out of his shoes. "Look. Isaiah is down by that high dune where the sea oats are waving."

"Yeah. He must have cleaned up fast so he could catch the light from the sunrise. He was filthy."

This morning we'd run north along the beach, taking a new direction. Isaiah is seated at his easel south of where we're sitting.

"No use waiting for coffee with Mr. Andrews here. Lets go see what he's doing."

We put on our sneakers and trudge down the beach. He's rapidly applying blobs of paint on his canvas with his nose almost in the fresh paint. Isaac says he does that to see how colors blend on the canvas. I can still hear Mrs. Miller's voice in my ear telling me not to use my nose as an eraser when I did it at school. The only parts he's washed are his hands and face. He's still wearing the gunk-covered clothes.

He works fast, using broad strokes which capture strips of light on the stark scene, like the reflections in Abel's photographs. The painted waves roll toward us as if we're standing on the shore facing the rising sun. A pod of dolphins plays outside the beginning of the ocean's first roll toward land. On the horizon is a sailboat with a broken mast pointing to the sun from a bow tilted skyward, as if it's sinking into the sea.

"The colors are perfect. That sailboat stands out like you actually saw it."

Isaiah lifts a pair of binoculars and hands them to Matt. "I did. See, it's right out there." He points to the horizon, but doesn't take his eyes off what he is doing. "It was sinking when I spotted it."

"I don't see it. Wait, yes I do. It's down by the point. Look, Jim." Matt points down to the south where a blunt cliff juts out into the ocean. The sailboat is bobbing in the waves like a broken kid's toy.

"Matt. The broken mast we found the night we harvest the oysters...."

"Right! Get the sheriff. I'll keep it in sight."

As I run for the hotel I hear Isaiah start to question Matt. Maud and Mr. Andrews are coming down the path with coffee. He starts to hand me a cup.

"I can't take it right now. Is Thay in the hotel?"

"Yes, he was talking to Marsh when we left."

"Thanks." I sprint to the hotel as fast as my tired legs will carry me.

Wreckage from the sea is outside the island's jurisdiction. With Marsh riding shotgun, Thay tore out of the parking lot to notify the authorities by radio.

Marsh took one of the skiffs moored at Thay's dock and motored around the island to secure the sailboat. He looked like a small dog herding a bull with little nudges against its legs to send it to a pen. His maneuvers prevented it from being caught in the offshore currents and drifting out to sea until the authorities arrived.

All of this takes over an hour as we waited on the beach sipping cold coffee before returning to the hotel to escape a soft, cold rain. Under the shelter of the long porch we watched the rescue. Isaiah's powerful binoculars brought the sleek lines of the craft sharp and stark against the gray sky.

Late in the morning everyone from the hotel watches from the upper porch as the men of the Port Authority's cutter lace a cable through the gunwales and around the broken mast to begin its slow haul around the far end of the island.

There isn't a name or registry number on the bow that I can see. The wind is picking up as the broken sailboat lists far to the right when the sailors haul lumpy lines over the gunwales.

I spot Thay. He stands out against the seaman in uniform as he helps pull the dragging rigging from the ocean. Then the powerful wake from the cutter lifts the broken vessel upright before it staggers around the headland on its trip to the mainland.

I'm grateful for warm water when I take a late shower before changing into dry clothes to join the others in the dining room for an early lunch. Its been hours since we ate bacon and biscuits smothered with cane syrup in the kitchen.

Mamma Lou and Orta used the leftover mashed potatoes to make pancakes. The buffet is crammed with platters of last night's pork chops, a potato casserole, bacon, sausage, a hot tray of scrambled eggs, hash browns, and bowls of gravy, plus a tray of fresh baked biscuits. A blueberry cobbler and whipped cream sit by the coffee urn. They must have been cooking the entire time we were watching the salvage operation.

There is little talk at our table as everyone digs into the huge breakfast, which Maud says is called a brunch.

The hotel guests are spread out around the room as if they want to be alone with their thoughts, but their eyes are watchful. Barker can't pretend to read a newspaper because there was no delivery this morning, so he stares out into the rain-doused parking lot. A small radio clatters with bursts of static as the announcer reports on the storm and efforts to access the damage.

Inland repairs have all ready begun on washed-out roadways, but for the foreseeable future the ferry will make an afternoon run to the island. Lettic is pleased that Rhodes Thornton can get to the mainland to free Dr. Lavin. Her delighted squeal rings across the room. In spite of to her obvious dislike of the man, she has been sticking close to him all morning.

We interrupt this program to bring you an important announcement.

Early this morning a derelict sailboat was reported off Seamew Island. Sheriff Townsend notified the Port Authority of the drifting vessel and assisted in maintaining contact with the stricken craft until the PA cutter arrived to haul it into port.

Witnesses reported that the body of a man believed to be Hispanic was found tangled in the lines dangling from the broken mast.

The boat was unmarked and the identity of the man is unknown. If anyone has any information about this tragedy please notify the Shore Patrol or this station immediately.

Thank you for your attention as we resume our regular programing.

Instant silence pervades the room at the mention of a body. We didn't see a body from the porch. Was it found in the sailboat? Maud drops her fork and turns a stricken face to Mr. Andrews. He takes her shaking hand and holds it as she struggles for composure.

From the corner of my eye I catch Barker and Thornton exchange sharp looks across the room.

"Damn it. Excuse my language, ma'am. I forgot the station monitors all radio calls."

Sheriff Thay pulls out a chair beside me and sets a loaded plate on the table that can more than match Matt's. He looks toward Maud, "I'm sorry ma'am. I intended to tell you what we found myself...."

Four men in white uniforms enter the dining room. One locks eyes with Matt, who gives him a slight nod, but he continues eating. He knows I caught the greeting and shakes his head.

They walk to the buffet and begin filling their plates. Marsh prepares a space for them on the far side of the room at a round table.

"Please accept my apologies again while the gentlemen are getting their meals. They have arrived sooner than I expected, it looks as if I still have work to do. They are officers of the United States Coast Guard. They disapprove of vessels of unknown origins within our territorial limits.

"Isaiah, they may want to talk to you. It seems you spotted an extremely ugly kettle of rotten fish to include in your painting. They know about it, but I will make sure they do not confiscate it for evidence. I want to talk to you about it to give Mamma Lou for Christmas. It is one of the best renderings the juxtaposition of the joy and sorrow of the sea I've ever seen.

"The dolphins pass the island twice a day and we protect them. During the summer, guests can watch them from the porch, but Mamma Lou will not allow them on the beach while the dolphins feed.

"Please excuse me. I see that Marsh has made a place for me at their table." He squares his shoulders like someone facing a firing squad, picks up his plate and joins the four men at the isolated round table. Every eye in the dining room follows him, but they are seated too far away to hear their discussion. Marsh pulls stands with a heavy gold cord across their corner to insure their privacy.

"All of that white and gleaming brass makes me feel as if I've been grubbing on the beach and forgotten to wash my hands before I came to the table."

Automatically Matt, Isaiah, and I look down at our hands to check for dirty fingernails. Maud's tinkling-bell laugh explodes as she exclaims, "Phillip, we have been standing in the wind on the beach. I can feel sand in my hair."

Mr. Andrews' quip breaks the tension that has gripped our table since the radio announcement. Isaiah is speechless in face of the compliment Thay had extended to his work. He has always been shy about his painting because he puts a private part of himself into each piece. He isn't the same about accepting praise when he is playing music that was written by someone else. Odd, Isaac is the twin who makes up songs—plinking, he calls it.

I wonder how Isaiah would render those weather carved faces above the starched collars. Their presence gives me a feeling of safety against the evil that has stalked this island since we arrived.

Matt shakes his head. "I do wish they'd waited a while. Thay would have had time to tell us about the sailboat and its passenger."

Chapter 23

Everyone retreated to their rooms for a nap after the early morning exertions and the heavy meal, except Lettic and Thornton who drove Lettic's car down to the main dock to wait for the ferry. I thought about checking it out myself, but elected to pack my gym bag and go back to my cottage.

A stack of freshly laundered and ironed clothes are on the foot of each bed when we returned from breakfast. This is a hotel service I'd not considered, but I intend to leave a large tip in appreciation, as my clean clothes were getting sparse. Marsh said several of his cousins had come from Broomtown to help at the hotel, which makes it easier for Orta who was now covering Shell's busboy duties in the dining room.

I love Matt, but sharing a room is something I haven't done since Levi left for college. Matt was restless last night. He was mumbling, so I'd gotten little sleep during the storm.

He doesn't even know when I leave the room for which I am glad. I don't want to go into any explanations as to why I'm leaving.

As I come down the stairs a second wave of dress uniforms without as much brass or gold braid are coming in the front door heading to the dining room. Seems everyone from the Coast Guard cruiser is getting shore leave for lunch at the hotel. They'll miss the potato pancakes, because we didn't leave one on the buffet.

Except for the lack of power, there is no damage to the cottage so I light the fire I'd laid before the storm, then strip, and crawl into a fresh-made bed. I watch the play of shadows on the ceiling and to try to fit random pieces of the events of the past days into a pattern.

My mind keeps coming back to how shocked Maud was at the radio announcement and Mr. Andrews reaction. He knows what startled her into dropping her fork and left her hands shaking. I fall asleep trying to remember what the announcer had said about the body in the damaged sailboat that could have struck her so hard.

It's nearly 6:30 when I finally get myself back to the hotel for dinner, but I'm the first to sit down at our table. Baker is across the room facing the door with his nose buried in a newspaper. I feel like waving to break his concentration, but think better of the idea.

"The ferry brought the papers over this afternoon. He grabbed the *Washington Post, The New York Times,* and my copy of Charleston's *News & Courier.*" Marsh grumbles as he pours water in a glass.

"He's bored. Must be, to read so many papers."

"Humph! He devours them, right down through the classifieds. He's looking for something."

Marsh puts the water glass and a fresh-typed menu in front of me then retreats to the kitchen in a dudgeon. He resents his personal paper being confiscated by a guest.

I still feel sluggish from the heavy brunch and study the menu looking for something light, like a Porterhouse with home fries and coleslaw.

"Tonight I'm hungry for steak." Thay pulls out a chair and sits down beside me. He's in casual clothes, gray slacks with a fisherman's sweater over a plaid shirt. I'm going to have to get one of those sweaters. Matt has one and they're dressier than a sweatshirt. The suit I purchased is too much for the dining room since everything has gone haywire. I've pulled on a flannel shirt over a dress shirt with a tie.

Maybe that was why I felt like people were looking at me. They knew I've never been in a resort hotel and don't know how to dress.

We stand as Maud, escorted by Phillip Andrews enters the dining room with Matt and Isaiah right behind them. Maud is a beacon of color in the dark red Pendleton pantsuit she wore the first night we ate here. Tonight she has a bronze colored blouse under the jacket.

Everyone is of the same mind and orders steak with fixings for supper. Mr. Andrews suggests a bottle of Bordeaux to go with the meal, but doesn't take any for himself. I join him with iced tea as wine does funny things to me.

Marsh sets small plates with pecans, crackers, and a wedge of a white cheese with blue streaks in front of each of us to nibble on while we wait for our steaks. I hesitate to take any of the moldy cheese, but Matt grins. "Go ahead Little Brother, it's Shelton and won't hurt you."

The cheese is smooth and pungent, but the pecans have been dredged in cinnamon, brown sugar, and butter. I could make a meal on the pecans. I've never tasted nuts like these with a faint tinge of orange below the cinnamon.

As we turn to look at Thay for answers to our questions, I catch a glimpse of the sparkling, dark-green earings Maud is wearing. They match a ring on her left hand. It is a large square emerald with a triangle of three good-sized diamonds on each side. She has moved her wedding ring to her right hand and seems pleased by the new addition. Her green eyes in the candle light are the same deep color. I smile at her and she gives me a big wink before turning to Thay.

"We've been waiting all day. Please tell us what you can about the boat and its passenger."

"Miss Maud, a body that has been in the water for at least five days is not a fit subject for a dinner table. Lets wait until after our meal and I will tell everyone what little I know in the parlor over coffee and the Lady Baltimore cake I saw in the kitchen."

Mr. Andrews looks at Maud and then addresses Thay. "How are communications with the mainland coming along?"

Thay laughs. "That I can tell you. The ferry made one trip today so Miss Forbenshire and Mr. Thornton will not be back to the island until around noon tomorrow. The sound is rough and rising due to both the tides and the water pouring into it from the mainland, so it will take several days, maybe a week, to repair the utility lines and begin work on the causeway. If you have an emergency I can use the ship-to-shore in my home, but remember the local radio station monitors all the calls."

Maud frowns, "I'd have thought once Mr. Thornton secured Dr. Lavin's release they would head back to Minneapolis."

"No, ma'am, we have three murders that have occurred on the island. The police will send them back to the hotel until things are cleared up to their satisfaction. Everyone is under house arrest, including myself. We sent Nialis's body to the funeral home by the ferry. They will perform an autopsy, which may tell us more than my brief examination."

"House arrest. Why are we under suspicion? We've never even met the victims."

"Matt, close your damper and let me finish this fine steak in peace. Thornton, Andrews, and I arrived after the first murders. Are we included in the house arrest?"

"Isaiah, that is true about you and Phillip. Thay, I've been meaning to tell you that Mr. Thornton is the man I saw kissing Phadra Lavin when I arrived at the hotel."

"Thank you, Mrs. Tosh. I appreciate having that little speck of information."

Thay's sarcasm steams the wine glasses. Mr. Andrews quickly defends Maud in the same tone.

"Sir, you haven't been available since Mr. Thornton arrived for Maud to have a chance to tell you."

A rueful grin creases Thay's mouth, "Please accept my apologies, Ma'am. Mr. Andrews is correct."

Isaiah pops the last bite of his steak in his mouth and chews in the silence. "I keep thinking about the mystery woman. She had been living in the hotel for six weeks as Phedra Lavin. She was murdered. Dr. Lavin identified her body as that of his wife, but Lettic Forbenshire swears she isn't her sister.

"Maud saw her kissing Mr. Thornton in the parking lot. Jim, Maud, and you saw her slap an unknown man here in the dining room. Maud also said someone had given her a shiner before the slap.

"Marsh says she went for a ride around the island with Kevin Stevens, the FBI agent, who was also murdered."

"That is the scenario in a nutshell of the woman in the morgue. Isaiah, would you like a job writing my reports?"

"I outline. Writer's cramp is a pianist's horror. Seriously, who is she and how do the first two murders connect to the murder of Nialis Lapier?"

I turn to get a good look at Thay. My arm hits Isaiah's glass, spilling the wine he's barely touched across the table, down his shirt, and into his lap. My face flames as I shudder at my clumsiness. I've been so careful to watch my movements after all the bumps and messes I'd made since leaving the hospital.

"I'm...sorry. I can't see...on my left."

Isaiah is using his napkin to mop up my disaster as Marsh hands him a wet towel. "I know, don't worry about it. Accidents happen."

"Marsh, we'll take coffee and cake in the parlor. You and Mamma Lou come too, that way I'll only have to tell about the sailboat one time. Oh, tell the other guest he is welcome to join us."

Isaiah backs his chair away from the table. "I'll go change, but don't say one word until I return." He gives my shoulder a hard squeeze and lopes from the room bent over to hide the mess I've made of his pants.

Chapter 24

Removing the ear-bobs and ring I carefully placed them in their velvet box. "Phillip, I can't wear anything this fine at home."

"Of course you can. The ring says we're engaged. An engagement that will last a lifetime. Who will know the difference if you tell them you caught them with the pincher claws at a Penny Arcade?"

I giggle and turn on the dresser stool to face him. I hadn't thought about it, but I don't mind being engaged to him. It's more comfortable than plain shacking up. A perfect answer for the nosies.

He's lying against the headboard with a bunch of papers in his lap, but he isn't reading them. Reading by coal-oil lantern light isn't comfortable. I've been watching him in the mirror.

"What did you make of what Thay told us after dinner?"

"Maud, that is a tougher question than how to account for some jewelry I couldn't resist buying for you. You knew there was another death, but you didn't ask any questions when you had the chance."

"I had one. It didn't seem appropriate to ask about a dead man."

"What was it?"

I sit on the edge of the bed so he can unpin the collar and not see me blush for my silly question.

"Don't laugh. It didn't have anything to do with the poor man's death. I kept wondering if he had calluses on his hands." My hands still look like they belong to a scrub woman though I've lathered them with Vaseline and worn gloves to bed for weeks.

"Thay said he was wearing what was left of a suit with a money belt around his waist. What caused you to think of calluses?"

"He was in a boat. If he'd done much sailing wouldn't he have had calluses from handling the ropes? Mother had them from hauling up water from the well."

"I see. Yes, you're right. The man may have been a stranger to boats, which caused his death if he got caught in a squall. I hadn't considered that possibility."

I stand and quickly shed my clothes. Then pull my old flannel gown over my undies before I take them off. Our room is chilly even though Marsh laid a fire in the grate. It reminds me of when we dressed for school behind the coal stove. It will be some time before they can repair the power lines to the island, so they turned off the generator when we left the parlor to save fuel. Its funny how you don't miss a sound until it is gone. The hotel is ominously quiet.

"Jim did. He asked if smuggling was involved. Thay shrugged his shoulders, but didn't answer him. Jim told me right after the first murder that the sheriff patrolled the island at night. Could all of these murder have something to do with drugs?"

"Maud, the man had money—Swiss gold money—on him. That indicates he was planning to stay when he came ashore. Gold money hasn't been in circulation since right after you were born. It is still illegal for Americans to own gold bullion."

Watching me shiver as I pull on my heavy robe before hanging up my suit Phillip sets his papers aside and gets up to stir the fire with the poker before putting another log across the coals.

A small table laden with a late-night snack is beside the fireplace. I stick the bottle of Jergens in the pocket of my robe and join him near the fire.

This is a large room with high ceilings and the heat from the fire doesn't warm the room. We move the table in front of the fireplace and pull the wing chairs close to the flames. He props his feet on the fender like the lord of the manor.

"Phillip." My mouth is full of Lady Baltimore cake making myvoice sound garbled. I chew as fast as I can, almost chocking as I wash it down with hot chocolate. "Phillip, Jim mentioned smuggling. What if it isn't drugs, but people?"

"People? That would explain the money. The radio announcer said he was believed to be Hispanic. Seamew is a good distance from the Keys where the boat people attempt to make landfall. The island would be perfect for hiding someone who is entering our country by the backdoor, especially during the winter when it is practically deserted.

"There are stories in the paper and onTV about refugees who've gotten in bad trouble—sunburn and dehydration before the Coast Guard has rescued them. It isn't an easy trip in an open boat to the Keys. It would be almost impossible to come this far north."

"Could he have gotten caught in the Gulf Stream and been pulled north?"

"Maud, I don't think so. I'm not sure how far from land the Gulf Stream lies, but it's much too far to have put that sailboat here. Remember it was drifting south, not north."

It's so comfortable here with him and sharing a midnight meal while we talk. There is a sharp draft coming under the french doors to the verandah. I put my feet beside his on the fender, which gives me a cozy feeling I don't want to end. I think about what he is telling me while I cream my hands. What comes to mind are more questions than answers.

"Then someone would have to meet them out on the ocean to guide them to the island if they weren't accustomed to sailing?"

"Yes, but what happens to the sailboat? From what I could see it was fairly large, built for ocean travel. How did it get all the way up the coast without being seen by some fishermen?"

More and more questions. The ocean is too far from Cumberland Lake to give either of us an experience on which to base our speculation. Few people have sailboats on our lake because the crosswinds between the hills make sailing dangerous. Maybe Marsh will tell us something about oceans. We're going around in circles, but I do have a personal question about Jim.

"Phillip, do you think that little accident with the wine glass will have Jim hiding in his cabin again?"

"No, Maud. His brothers won't allow him the dubious luxury of self-indulgence by which I nearly destroyed my life. There is a hard core of mountain self-reliance that runs deep in him. No one in that family has ever gotten anything except by hard work...they don't know any other way."

"But the boys inherited Catherine Throckton's estate. I saw the settlement papers."

"Oh, were you doing a little peeking?"

"No. Well a little. A body can't help but wonder when the papers are right on their desk."

"That money doesn't mean a thing to him. Racing was his life. I know how I felt when I grew too tall to be a jockey. It hurts like hell to have your dreams smashed because your body can't do what you demand of it.

"Besides, I've seen no evidence of the money being spent except for hospital bills and that ready-to-wear suit. He wears a tie like he's standing on an executioner's block."

"Don't you make fun of that suit. He bought it to take me to dinner. It still had the price tag on the back of the left cuff the first night he wore it. I got Nialis to let me into his cottage to cut it off while he was out running the next morning. He never knew the difference."

"I need to introduce him to my tailor in Capital City. A good suit will last a long time. You're very fond of Jim."

161

"Heavens, Phillip I changed his diapers many a Sunday. Rupert was a big one for church going. I'd save space in our pew for Mary Young and her boys."

"I sat behind you so I could be near you. That is the only reason I've ever discovered for going to church."

"I have funny feelings about church going, and haven't decided what I'll do when I get home. In my experience the worst scoundrels make a point to be seen in church. I remember a poem by Emily Dickinson that said she kept the Sabbath by staying at home."

Sunday is the only day a working woman has to lie in bed and read the paper. Sunday morning in bed with Phillip while everyone else is in church would be delicious.

"Anyway, what about Jim? Physically he's recovered from the accident. Running on the beach has put strength back in his feet and legs. That business of his being a drunk was a stupid rumor that his sister-in-law started."

"Drunk. I never heard that one. Jim or any of Mary's boys for that matter would qualify as teetotalers. It was obvious at dinner that they took no more than two or three polite sips of the wine."

"It's how he looks at himself that wavers. It will take both determination and time for his pride to heal. I learned it helps when you've something to live for besides getting through each day. Are you going to hire him to do your investigative work?"

"Yes, you dear goose. I made the job offer before he left home. It stands. He sees more with one eye than most people see with two, which is what I need when investigating insurance claims."

I push back my chair, scoot the table aside, and turn off the kerosene lamp. Phillip grins, puts the fire screen back in place, and lifts the quilted goose-down cover. It's warmer than the quilts I have at home.

Chapter 25

We have plenty of questions, but Thay doesn't come in to breakfast. Maud and Mr. Andrews tell us about their late night conversation. Without Thay, we're reduced to speculating among ourselves.

The idea of human cargo keeps me busy through the meal. I can't come up with any other solution. The murder of two women and a man is weird. Stevens was FBI. He may have learned about the smuggling. He was having an argument with Shell Wallace when the kid almost ran me off the road. Shell is still missing. Neither the sheriff nor Marsh has mentioned him for days. Barker has ceased demanding he be found. Is he still on the island?

Family is family. They know where he is. Yes, that is the one thing that makes sense. They're hiding him. I'd do the same thing if any of my brothers were in trouble.

Nialis Lapier may have been Shell's steady, but I don't think either the sheriff or Marsh let her in on their secret before she was murdered. Marsh said she was with Shell on the balcony above Maud when she saw Rhodes Thornton kissing the Phedra Lavin imposter. Would that be important to anyone? No, she couldn't have seen the kiss from above if they were in a car when Maud passed. Were they in a car? There had to have been a car because Thornton left the island. Must ask Maud....

"Jim, are you finished?"

"Huh?"

"You've been in a brown study since we started eating. You

haven't heard a word we said. I asked if you're finished eating."

"Almost, why?"

"Orta told us Thay and Marsh are down by the causeway. They're going to fish out Thornton's rental car. We thought we'd walk down and watch. There might be some news about when I can leave for New York."

They're watching me like I'm a visitor from outer space.

"Okay by me."

The sky is clear. We bundle into our coats before leaving, as a stiff wind is whipping around the corner of the hotel. The storm has left a winter cold behind that makes my feet tingle even when wearing double socks with my sneakers.

Matt is grumbling about taking a walk after running four miles before breakfast. There isn't much else to do on the island for entertainment. I light a Pall Mall and he glares at me. Smoking after a meal has always been a pleasure for me.

The marsh is alive with birds. The wind tosses the plumes of the Snowy Egrets. They gleam against the sun as they search through the brown grass for stranded minnows. A rank odor of rotten eggs seeps from the black ooze as they stalk across the mud flats.

Gulls squawk overhead before making a dive into the shallow water that covers the opaque sea of the tidal marsh. A strange black bird with a bright yellow bill is perched on the twisted root of a downed tree by the far edge of the causeway.

A dirty white tug boat has pushed a narrow, flat barge up against what is left of the roadway. The screak of a high-powered wench pierces our eardrums. The birds take flight, screeching and shrieking their displeasure at the humans who've invaded their morning hunt. The calliope of sound bounces around in my head like a monstrous headache trying to explode.

Maud has her hands over her ears to block the shrill whine. Thay is perched on the edge of the washed-out road waving his hands at the cabin of the tug. Two large wreckers are sitting side by side on the far side, with cables hooked to the back bumper of the Lincoln Thornton tried to drive to the island.

The car is nose deep between two huge concrete culvert pipes. The racket stops and Thay jumps down on the barge. Marsh climbs out of the tug's cabin and pulls a steel cable across the platform toward Thay. Together they disappear from view on the far side of the car. Moments later, Marsh races back to the cabin to take up the cable's slack.

The wrecker on the tug-side starts winding up his cable before the second wrecker begins to pull his side.

All hell breaks loose.

Thay starts to stand as the cable on the far wrecker snaps sending the car plunging back down sideways between the culverts. The cable from the near wrecker whips across the platform catching Thay across the middle. The flying cable sends him soaring like a bent sack of corn as we jump for the platform.

I barely hear Isaiah's shout above the screaming of three wenches, but I feel his hard slap on my back.

"You're the best swimmer. Take off your coat. Find him." Matt is shouting in my ear. I shuck my coat and dive. The water is deeper on this side of the tug. My hands plunge in mud. I can't stand on the bottom. I push to the surface to see where I am and trying to spot where Thay landed.

Matt and Isaiah are holding Marsh. "No. Let Jim find him. He's like an eel. You in the water will stir up more muck."

I suck in a deep gulp of air and dive. Muck, smut, it's like swimming through mud. My eye is stinging trying to see through the thick syrup. A sawyer log is floating just under the waterline. Its branches swiping the bottom stirring up swags of silt.

I've found Thay. He's caught in those swinging branches. Inching my way along the log I have to be careful not to get hit by his kicking boots as he struggles to free himself.

I risk a shot to the surface for more air and make a shallow dive above him. A branch whips across my face blinding me. I grab for the collar of his coat and yank with everything I've got. He's still fighting the tree, but I manage to get his head above the water.

I've no choice. He's trying to hit me. I slug him hard enough to make my hand sting. I hook my elbow around his neck and side crawl back to the side of the tug. Marsh and Matt pull him from the water leaving me to climb on the platform on my own.

I've lost my patch in that murky soup. My breakfast follows. I start to shiver like I'm never going to stop. The world goes black.

Chapter 26

"Thank you for saving my boy."

Mamma Lou's whisper near my head pulls me back from the swirling depths of the sound. I start the rise, but her strong hand pushes me back.

"You lie still and keep warm. Everything is fine. Don't want you to take a chill."

"Thay?" My voice croaks like a gigged frog.

"He's fine. Got some broken ribs. Dr. Lavin taped them. Said Thay is going to be very sore from the banging he took from that cable. Gonna have a big bruise where it caught his belt buckle. Isn't the first time he's come home busted up. He's asleep in the other bed."

I turn my head as she points. We're in a room like the one Matt and I shared during the storm.

"I can get up." I pull myself up and start to swing my feet over the side of the bed when I discover I'm naked. Her firm hand pushes me back against the pillow as her face breaks into to a no-nonsense smile.

"I know you can, but you're not going to till morning. I want you and Thay where I can keep an eye on you. I don't want no relapses on my hands."

"My clothes?"

"Those nasty, sea-soaked things are in the washer." Her eyes are laughing at me. "My soup will warm you inside. Later Orta will bring you your dinner. Mr. Isaiah is going to play for us after supper."

I sit up against the pillows and spoon the thick chicken soup in my mouth before she has a chance to start feeding me. She watches every spoonful. I turn my head to the side to hide the hole where my eye should be. It isn't necessary, a large bandage is across my nose and over the missing eye.

"Don't worry, Orta is fixing you a new patch. This damp cloth will help the stinging in your good eye. Now get some rest." She turns her chair for a brief look at Thay, then closes the door softly behind her.

"Best do as she says or she'll slip a dose of laudanum in your water."

"Laudanum. That's a narcotic."

"Opium in alcohol. In her mother's time it was given to teething babies. Nasty stuff, but still used on the islands to handle recalcitrant patients. She wasn't happy when I refused to let Marsh cart us off to the hospital. Matt knew what happen when you blacked out."

"Matt?"

"Hypothermia—a sudden drop in body temperature. He lives in Minnesota. He showed Marsh how to keep us warm until Andrews got the station wagon down there. His treatment was rough, but effective."

"What did he do?"

A shallow chuckle escapes his lips. "It hurts to laugh. They stripped us, bundled us in every dry coat they could get their hands on and laid down on top of us. How much does Matt weigh?"

The question catches me by surprise. "240 or so."

"I was wondering which weighed the most, Matt, or Miss Maud's sealskin coat."

I laugh. "When will we get our clothes back? I'm fine. I'd like to get out of here."

"When Mamma Lou decides. You'll get yours when the laundry

is finished, but I'm going to be stuck here for a few days with this vise Dr. Lavin put around my ribs. I owe you, but I need your help. Will you be my deputy until I'm released from bondage?"

For a moment I think he is teasing, but those cold-sea eyes are dead serious. "I don't live on the island. Is it legal?"

"Jim, I'm the sheriff and can appoint anyone to serve in my place. I know Mr. Andrews has enough faith in you to give you a job as an investigator for his insurance company. Don't deny it. You and Miss Maud have been trying to discover who killed the woman you found on the beach."

"Maud believes I'm able to...find out things. Matt told me to tend to my own business."

"Matt is smart. Triple murders are only part of the problem. The man who died on the sailboat was being smuggled onto the mainland from the island and he wasn't the first. Marsh's nephew got himself involved in a very nasty business. He let a need for drugs pull him into a morass where few get out alive. Then Marsh brought him to me for help. I had a plan to trap them, but everything went haywire."

"Matt recognized Shell's addiction. I've been in-and-out of hospitals since May. Thay, I don't know a damn thing about drugs. Racing demands a clear head of everyone involved. A cold beer comes after the race."

"Someone is running scared. Murdering to eliminate witnesses. Clean up an operation about to go sour. The storm threw a monkey wrench in their plans. I'm sure someone on this island is responsible. The guy in the sailboat was a Cuban hit man who the federal authorities believe was to be delivered to a cartel in Miami."

"How?"

"The sailboat. She isn't as large as cup racers, but snug enough. The *Queen of the Isles* disappeared off Lauderdale with a family of four aboard. The Coast Guard traced the serial numbers on the diesel engines and identified the schooner. Pirates...."

"Pirates?"

"Yes, real pirates operate today to procure vessels for drug transportation. Usually they take ocean-going cabin cruisers, but someone found an easy prey. They captured the schooner, disposed of the family, and she turns up miles from her home port five years later.

"Shell is the loose screw. If they can find him he'll be the next victim. I would gladly save them the trouble and wring his neck if Mamma Lou would let me."

"If I become your deputy who do I answer to?"

"Me. Me alone. So many feds are working this case they may end up arresting each other. Now that the Coast Guard is involved with what is piracy in our territorial waters they're top dog. My guess is the guy's death was an accident over which no one is shedding any tears except those who paid for his transportation.

"This island is my home even if Sherman did give it to the freed slaves during the war. I'm rambling. Will you help me until I can satisfy Mamma Lou I don't need her coddling?"

"Okay."

Our wardens returned our clothes and allowed us to get up long enough to clean up and shave before dinner. I have a huge bandage that covers the left side of my face. A quick peek revealed stitches above my eyebrow and across my nose where the branch sliced my face. There is no serious damage to the previous scar tissue. The bandage does a good job of not scaring people to death.

Dinner was more of the thick chicken soup with biscuits. Orta said we might be allowed real food for breakfast. That is barring fevers or infections. While we were eating our sparse rations, two of Marsh's cousins carried in folding chairs and set them up around the room like we're exhibits at a public viewing.

"What's going on?"

"I don't know. Those chairs are used for visitations before a funeral."

The two men smile at Thay and leave without saying a word. Thay lifts one shoulder in what could be termed a shrug. Imaginary eyes stare at us from those empty chairs. We start laughing like two idiots.

"Hell! My sides…can't take laughing. Question. Marsh said you went after me like a hound after a ham bone. How did you know?"

How did I know! I closed my eye and try to picture the platform at the edge of the causeway to gain time like Levi does when he packs a pipe he seldom smokes. "The cable folded you in the middle. Legs and arms dangling in the air. Matt yelled for me to shuck my coat."

I undid my coat, Matt pulled it from my shoulders. My arms came around and I dived in one movement. My feet hit bottom. No, my hands went in mud first. Pushed to the surface. Grabbed a breath.

"Bird…."

"A bird?"

"Big black bird like a vulture…."

"Cormorant?"

"I'd never seen one…it was perched on a tree root. I spotted it as we walked down to the causeway." I want to tell him to forget this. It isn't important. That's it!

"The bird flew when the winch started screeching. The root moved after you hit the water."

"You're telling me you found me because of a bird and a root."

"Sort of. Thay, there wasn't time to think. Too fast. A sawyer is what we call a moving submerged tree. I saw it, branches scraping the bottom stirring up silt. You were caught in those branches and kicking like mad. Plain luck."

"You pack a hard right. My jaw is sore. I'm grateful for your *luck*."

171

The door bangs open.

Isaiah, packing his yellow Gibson, fills the doorway. Matt is blocking any view we might have of the outside world of the hallway. They've saved me from any more embarrassment.

"You've been lazing while we've been hauling cars out of the drink. Shirking is over. It is time to earn your keep."

People are crowding into the chairs with a few holding children on their laps. All the hotels guests, Orta with her helpers, and I don't know how many of the islanders. They're looking at us like we're the prize steers at the fair.

"Little Brother, Orta was plumb puzzled that a grown man would have these in his pocket."

Isaiah drops my rock and some thimbles on the bed. "I assured her that you have talents other than fishing for sheriffs. Tonight you're my rhythm section. We're going to have a hoedown."

Matt bows and lays a washboard across my lap then drops two large spoons on my head.

"Wait a minute. You pulled cars out of the sound. What *cars?*"

Isaiah's hazel eyes in the lantern light gleam gold like a cat's. They shoot Thay with a hard look that doesn't brook an argument while he smiles with innocent charm. "Don't you remember my Blazer took a swim. Nothing was damaged. It's safely stored in a garage in town."

Quickly, he takes a tall kitchen stool from Mr. Andrews and plunks it down between the beds. "Thay, jog your legs so I can fetch my piece."

Thay moves his legs without saying a word, but the folds beside his mouth are quivering. The crowd parts for Mamma Lou's chair as if she is the guest of honor at her own party.

Isaiah wraps his long legs around the rungs of the stool and begins to adjust the tuning of the Gibson. That guitar is a 1930s store-demonstration model. He found it in a junk store and restored it to perfection. A cherished treasure from when he went without meals to put together money to buy the old wreck. It's always with him like a talisman, but only comes out for special occasions.

He turns to his audience and is on. The same way as the first night he opened for an act at Ryman auditorium in Nashville. This time I'm backing him up, not Isaac, and I can't sing.

"Evenin' Ladies and Gentlemen. Brother Thay and Brother Jim took an unexpected swim in the sound this morning. As you can see, reports of their demise have been greatly exaggerated. But to relieve your minds, we prevailed on Mamma Lou to give them a reprieve while the Youngs make music the down-home-way. Jim needs a bit of cash to pay his hotel and doctoring bill so don't be shy if he passes the collection plate."

All the time he's rattling his spiel warming up the crowd, his swift fingers are picking the melody line of various country standards, constantly changing tempo, and expecting me to keep up. My hands fumble. Then they remember how to work the spoons. I haven't done this since I was in high school, but after a few miscues they recall the right moves.

Matt has heard these songs many times and gives his place by the door to the old man Maud talked to in the parlor. Marsh follows Matt out the door as Isaiah grins at Thay and slams into *Yonder Comes the Sheriff*.

"Two special ladies requested *The Church in the Wildwood*. Miss Maud and Mamma Lou, this one's for you. Slow it down a bit Jim, you're pushing me."

His chatter is keeping everyone looking at us, even Barker and Collins, who've been penned in a corner away from the door. People keep slipping in and sitting on the floor blocking the door. Lettic with a deep scowl on her face and Mr. Thornton are on the far side of the room at the foot of Thay's bed facing away from the door. Maud is sitting on the edge of my bed with Mr. Andrews standing behind her. His hands are resting on her shoulders. He pulled the washboard off my lap to give me room to work the spoons.

Isaiah's clear tenor wraps around the soft tones of the melancholy tune, then builds power as he moves into the beloved spiritual, *Amazing Grace*. He's covering the absence of Matt and Marsh by keeping everyone's attention focused on him. I turn my head to glance at Mr. Andrews and he gives a slight nod. Maud puts the washboard with the thimbles back in my lap.

He holds the sea of dark faces spellbound, like a magician, faces colored by heritage or lifetime spent with the elements. In some cases it's hard to tell which, but the indoor people stand out like spots of milk gravy on a funeral suit.

"Jim is getting left out of this show. Anyone can bang two spoons together. I'm not going to let him sing, don't want you good folks messing up the walls with rotten eggs. We couldn't find a jug for him to huff and puff, but Orta found us a scrub board. I'm proud to bring you a virtuoso performer of wide renown. Ready, Little Brother, to give them a foot-stomping rendition of *Tiger Rag?*"

He slaps the Gibson and gives it a spin on his knee as I drag my thimbles down the corrugated surface. We take off going as fast as my fingers will move through several pieces of wild dixieland jazz. The packed room responds with clapping and foot stomping until I'm afraid the old plaster is going start flaking off the walls. When my fingers go numb on *Orange Blossom Special*, he switches back to gospel with *He's Got the Whole World in His Hands* and *Joshua Fit the Battle of Jericho*. He encourages the audience to sing and clap along with him.

He bounces back and forth from instrumental to vocal with the ease of a master. I hand him the damp towel I'd held against my eye. Isaiah smiles and wipes his sweating brow. He's giving his voice a rest when I notice that Matt and Marsh are back in the room as if they'd never left.

Mr. Andrews lifts the washboard off my legs and I catch a glimpse of his watch. Isaiah has been going strong for over two hours.

He launches into *Dixie* then smoothly glides without missing a chord to the *Battle Hymn of the Republic*. They know he's paying tribute to both sides of that terrible war. The applause shakes the rafters.

"Before laryngitis ends this session I'm going to close by attempting a medley of my favorite Elvis and Sinatra recordings."

He begins with *Tell Me Why*, follows it with the hard hitting *Follow that Dream* and ends with *My Way* as recorded by Frank Sinatra. His fingers caress the Gibson, barely touching the strings for an accompaniment. I put down the spoons and listen along with the silent audience. His mission has been accomplished. I get the message. My brother lectures through his music.

I can hear vehicles starting up in the parking lot and sounds of laughter from the hall. Isaiah is slumped on the stool drinking quarts of water. Exhaustion is leaking from every pore. The room has cleared as people fold their chairs and follow Marsh who is pushing Mamma Lou out the door. No one hangs around to chat like they do at other concerts. Matt has vanished.

I get to my feet and walk to the bathroom for a break I've needed for some time. My legs wobble from lying in the same position. When I return, Thay is waiting for his turn.

Isaiah closes the snaps on the Gibson's case. Then collapses across the foot of my bed with his long legs dangling over the edge. His voice squeaks, "Check the hall. Can't afford eavesdroppers. I nearly choked when I saw that old roommate of Matt's sitting at my feet. Thought he'd blow the whole plan."

"Two rangers from the Port Authority were in the corner in front of Collins and Barker. What in the hell is going on behind my back?"

"Wait for Marsh to make sure everyone has gone to bed. I'm going to my room. I'm plum give out."With that cryptic statement, he almost staggers from the room carrying his beloved guitar. He will be gone in the morning. Isaiah doesn't say good-bye.

"Does your brother often switch from country rube to an educated man in the same sentence?"

"Isaiah is a country man, lived on a share-cropped farm until he left for college. He's earned two extra degrees in music from Vanderbilt same as Jimmy Rogers did in the 20s. Finished before Christmas. Swore to deck me if I called him doctor."

"The look he gave me could have frozen the balls off a brass monkey. What was that first song?"

"*Yonder Comes the Sheriff*. A signal during Prohibition to shut down the bar. Isaiah's way of warning you to be careful, the brass was out of uniform."

"Don't knock Vernon. He commandeered the helicopter."

Matt and Marsh carry rocking chairs into the room. They plop down, pull off their shoes, and prop their feet on the end of my bed.

"*Commandeered* a helicopter?"

"Well...borrowed without permission. It wasn't free. Cost me four fifty-yard-line tickets for next year's Super Bowl plus Blanda's autograph on a ball from his last game."

"That is expensive. Marsh, what have you two been doing?"

"Hold your horses, Thay. It's been a long day...need to consider how to tell you what you won't want to hear."

Exasperated Thay runs his fingers through his hair. "Take your time. I'm in no shape to beat you senseless."Thay's cutting sarcasm can slice brick cheese.

"Why do I have a feeling you've lost your marbles and done something stupid with a military helicopter?"

"Wasn't stupid. Can't let Mamma's grandson be murdered.

Can't let him go to jail either. Mr. Matt knows people."

"He has *aided and abetted* a fugitive from justice unless I miss my guess."

"Mr. Matt's brother was in the same plight. Had to get 'em to the mainland."

"Long and short of it is Shell and Isaiah are off the island. Shell is in good hands. When he comes home in a year or so he'll be free of the roaches he's carrying in his veins."

"Where is he?"

"Under Dr. Lavin's care on his way to a priest and a rabbi."

I'd been following the rapid exchange between Matt and Thay with amazement. Matt is mumbling his way out of an act of kindness.

"You sent him to Elroy and Lon?"

"It was an emergency. Best I could think of."

Thay looks puzzled, "Elroy and Lon are a priest and a rabbi?"

It's a pleasure to watch Matt squirm for a change. "No. They're moonshiners...."

Thay explodes, "Moonshiners?"

"And my mechanics."

"Had to do something. Shell was back in that place. He was wild. Screaming that lice were crawling under his skin. He broke Moses Southly's arm trying to get away. Mr. Matt got banged up too. While he was putting a cast on Moses's arm Dr. Lavin volunteered to go with Shell."

"I'll bet he did. Jim, please, give me a straight answer."

I look at Matt. "J.T. Whitlock flew them west from the mainland?" He nods. Time to let him off the hook.

"Elroy Harris, Lon Chambers, Monsignor Stanley and Rabbi Lehman were members of the same bomber escort crew out of North Africa. The way Elton Fightmaster explained it. They're welded by war. They handle tough problems."

A thought strikes. "What did Mamma Lou say?"

Marsh smiles for the first time, "She arranged the show."

The steam runs out of Thay like a punctured tire. He slumps back against his pillows. Marsh sticks his feet back in his moccasins and pushes himself out of the rocker.

"Breakfast at five."

Matt, favoring his arm, drags himself up. "Almost forgot. Thay, Isaiah left a canvas at your place and so you won't be late for breakfast Vernon left you a souvenir."

He pulls two boxes out of his pocket and tosses them at us. "Yours don't work worth a damn underwater."

Chapter 27

I t's before the dark of the moon when Marsh wiggles my toe. "Get dressed and come down to Mamma's parlor. Coffee and toast. She doesn't want any uninvited ears horning in on a family conference. Thay, Moses Southly is with her."

Thay groans.

"Come on. Take a nap later. Then eat in the dining room with the others."

Marsh lights the lamp and leaves.

"You take first dibs in the bathroom. Then help me up. I don't want them to know how bad I hurt."

I don't need to shave. A thick bandage covers my left eye and extends down across my nose to hide the jagged gash where the tree limb whipped my face. It only takes a few minutes to wash and pull on my jeans. I feel a few twinges scattered around as I ease my arms into my shirt and tuck in the tail. Thay must be aching all over.

He's pulled up on the side of the bed, but accepts my hand and arm for leverage off the edge. Once he's standing his face isn't as white, but it's still pale and drawn. He was in better shape last night or he'd taken something to kill the pain, because I have to help him walk to the john.

Below the elastic wrappings his stomach is one deep angry bruise with other blackish-red marks on his arms and shoulders. It's a struggle to get his pants on. I have to fasten the new watch on his wrist as his fingers are swollen twice their normal size.

We stagger down the long hall like two drunken sailors. When we get to some double oak doors, he takes a deep breath, slides a door into the wall, and walks into the room under his own power.

A huge man whose bald head gleams like polished coal is sitting between Marsh and Mamma Lou. This man is wearing a T-shirt with a regular flannel shirt slung across his back. The left arm of the shirt dangles flat. His right arm is encased in fresh plaster. The cast extends from above his elbow down across the palm of his hand. His fingers, like Thay's are swollen like Polish sausages.

Maud has on one of her turbans, but a few stray wisps glitter in the candle light. Matt's right arm rests in the sling. They remind me of the patients on my hospital ward. Only Mr. Andrews looks relaxed and alert.

"Grab a seat, Sheriff. You don't look any better than the rest of us. Louise had us working most of the night. Jim, I'm Moses Southly, can't shake hands this morning."

Thay collapses into a chair by Marsh, but he made it on his own two feet. I squeeze between Matt and Mamma Lou.

She hands me a plate of toast. Her idea of toast is French toast made with thick slices of homemade bread, covered with pecans drenched in buttered maple syrup. She fills a large mug with coffee and hot milk poured from two separate pots at the same time. Then adds a big dollop of thick whipped cream and grates nutmeg over the cream.

"Let it cool, Jim before you take a sip. It's rich."

"Louise, this is a fine repast, but you want everyone back in their rooms before sun-up. So I'll move this meeting right along and take breakfast home for later. I need to catch some shuteye. I was on the radio most of the night."

"Ohmigod." The expletive sounds strange coming from Thay. "I forgot." Thay's slate eyes dart around the table. "Moses is a licensed ham radio operator. He has call friends all over the world. Broadcasts weather alerts. His backyard is filled with equipment that's tied into the National Weather Service. What were you doing last night?"

"What he means is I provide the TV people with on-the-spot accurate reports of current weather conditions. I'm a meteorologist.

"What was I doing last night? Guiding Mr. Whitlock across the mountains under the radar. Good night for flying, clear as a bell. Picked up news here and there. The body of a sailor washed ashore down the coast. The authorities figure he'd been in the water from six to eight days."

Thay takes a drink of coffee. His hands are shaking. "The Queen required a crew. One at least…maybe two, depending on their sailing experience."

"That's the way I figure it." Mr. Southly looks at me. "Who is the man of color where you're sending Shell?"

"Lon Chambers."

"Figured. Had to be. Graduated from Minnesota State University with honors in 1938. Mixed Indian. He was in the second flight class. Pulled his mechanic out of an exploding fuel depot when it was bombed near the end of the war. Lost his hearing and got burned in the process. I'll pass the word he's in Kentucky.

"So his navigator and tail-gunner ended up a priest and a rabbi. That's a sure way of thanking God—hit him from two sides. The fly-boys will get a kick out of that."

"I don't understand. Lon Chambers was a pilot? He works for me."

"Last night you told Marsh the men flew bomber escort out of North Africa. Mr. Jim, every person on this island knows the story of the Tuskegee Airmen. It's an exclusive club. I was too big to fit in an airplane so I ended up in the signal corps…used Gullah for communications in Italy. Got too close to the shelling."

"What is Gullah?"

"Gullah or Geechee is the old language of the islands, like Gallic is the old language in Scotland. Shell will get help, which is Louise's concern. Your brother is on his way to New York. Mission accomplished. I've heard nothing, but praise for his show. Sorry I missed it."

"Marsh, how did you get Isaiah's Blazer to town?" Thay is peering at Marsh like he's trying to see through fogged up glasses.

"Simple." Matt answers for Marsh. "Vernon, in his full dress uniform, drove it onto the ferry. The Port Authority fellas don't question a Guard Chief Petty Officer. Then he and a couple of his radio men returned in a small launch for the show. Isaiah left with them."

"Why in the hell–excuse me ladies–didn't he leave with his van instead of hanging around?"

"But, Thay." Mamma Lou reaches out and grasps his hand. "I needed him to make loud music to cover the noise of the helicopter. Mr. Isaiah was watching his watch. He did the dixieland with stomping as it came in and then got everyone to singing *He's Got the Whole World in His Hands* as it went out."

Isaiah had on a watch like Matt, Thay, Mr. Andrews, and I are wearing. The washboard…Matt put it on my lap and Mr. Andrews removed it. It was a signal to Isaiah as to when to do the loud stuff and when to stop. He synchronized the show to the sounds helicopter. My brothers are a sneaky bunch when the chips are down.

Mamma Lou takes my hand and squeezes it. "I will write your mother and tell her how blessed she is with her sons."

I can feel the heat on my neck rising, but Matt intercepts the pass Isaiah-style. "Ma'am, that'll be a change. She tells me we're giving her gray hair."

Mr. Andrews puts the real problem back on the table. "You've removed the innocents, which leaves you an interesting assortment of murder suspects." Thay is nodding off, but jerks his head and takes a long drink of coffee. "A woman, two agents from different federal law enforcement departments and a lawyer. Who is the best candidate?"

"I can't see Lettic Forbenshire as a suspect. She came with Dr. Levin. We need to find out everything we can about the men."

"Miss Maud, right now I have so many helpers I'm stumbling over them." His voice is slurred and slow. "Last night I made Jim my official deputy. According to you he *finds out things* so maybe he can find out about Thornton, Collins, and Barker."

"No, Thay. The best man for that job is Mr. Southly."

"Moses?"

"You said it yourself. He has call friends all over the world."

Southly is laughing. He winks at Mamma Lou. "Would you please stop talking about me as if I'm not sitting here? What is it you want to know, Pretty Lady?"

"That's easy, Sir. The same thing Thay went snooping to Dan Sommers about after the first murder."

Maud is right. Money is a good place to start.

"Two are federal agents. Who has money problems or has more money than he should have?"

"If the information is available and I can locate it, who should I give it to? Our sheriff who doesn't have enough sense to go back to bed before he falls on his face or you, Pretty Lady?"

"Jim, of course."

Chapter 28

"When did Collins return?"

"Only way he could have come was on the noon ferry. We were too busy to notice until he showed up in the dining room for supper. Marsh said he kept his room while he was off the island." Matt is talking with his mouth full.

We took a short run on the beach to work up an appetite for this second breakfast. He didn't talk about yesterday, but I learned the hard way that gratitude is like medicine—hard to swallow.

Chicken soup may ward off a chill, but it leaves a man hungry. Maybe Mamma Lou will allow Thay a full meal when he wakes up. She's not about to let him out of that bed. I think she dosed him with laudanum. He was groggy when we got him back to the room. Kept mumbling about a witch.

Maud is glowing when they join us. "Phillip says I'm ghoulish, but I love living on the edge. Hoping, but not knowing, if our plans would work."

"I had to hold her down. It wouldn't have been *seemingly* for her to jump up and down on your bed." The look he gives her is half tender and half humorous.

Mr. Andrews is teasing her. It's a private joke between two people who love each other. Matt looks at me as if he shares my envy at not having someone special.

"May I join you?" Moses Southly is standing behind Matt. He's taller than Isaiah—a giant.

"Thanks. Your nephew made things awkward." Marsh pulls out

a chair for him. "Could you bring me a cup of that fancy coffee I had this morning? Find a cup with a wide handle I can get my fingers through and a straw."

"Coming right up."

"Pretty Lady, the money question will take some time, but I was able to discover a few interesting tidbits."

I glance around the room, but we're alone in the dining room. Mr. Southly's voice is soft, which was a surprise considering his size. I'd expected a loud booming voice.

"Roger Barker, Stanley Collins, and Rhodes Thornton are from the same hayseed burg in Nebraska. Thornton is older by ten years or so. Collins and Barker are first cousins, their mothers are sisters.

"All three served in the military, but Barker is the only one who saw combat. He was Shell Wallace's commanding officer in Vietnam with a rank of captain."

Matt whistles through his teeth. "Talk about connections. They're as twisted as a Celtic knot."

He continues, "None of the three have been arrested, but Thornton has been called before the Minnesota and Illinois Law Review Boards on occasions. Those proceedings are closed sessions. No action was taken against him. Could have been for picking his toenails in public for all we'll ever know. The Minnesota questioning could be serious. The Illinois group is nothing but a whitewash cover for organized crime."

"The rumor in Milwaukee is that he's the front lawyer for the mob."

"Didn't see any names the Chicago Archdiocese could nominate for sainthood among his clients. Now that isn't saying they don't make hefty donations to the church.

"Marsh, damnit. Stop hoovering and sit. According to the doctor, I'm going to have to endure this cast for six weeks. Got to learn to learn to live with it. Besides I want to discuss an idea

I have before I go home. Have you got any suspenders around the place?"

"No. Can't remember anyone wearing them."

"Figured. Will have to call Este Hawkins and have him bring a pair over on the ferry. Make it easier to get in and out of my trousers."

"Moses, Orta needs help starting lunch. What did you want to ask me?"

"Me and my daddy worked on the WPA project that built that causeway. Didn't think it was a good idea then, but it paid eating money for the family during hard times. It has caused problems since the day it was finished. Interferes with the natural flow of the water between the mainland and the island. Fills in the sound and estuaries with silt and mainland trash."

"Moses, we need that road for the telephone and power lines. Hotel guests would have to come over on the ferry. It only runs once a day in the summer. In the winter, not at all, except in an emergency."

"That's exactly what is going to happen for months. Maybe a year until they get around to fixing the causeway since there are so few voters out here to put pressure on the county. Este would change his schedule if there was enough traffic to support it.

"If men can run a cable across the North Atlantic in the last century I'm sure delivery systems have improved enough to run one across the sound. A nor'easter or a hurricane wouldn't put it out of commission for months either. All power lines could be run underground, which would leave the island unspoiled. We'd have decent television service…no spindly towers dotting the landscape that twist and come down every little whipstitch.

"I watched you fish that car out and figured it wouldn't take much to do the same thing with those culverts. Then you could bring in a dredge and clear the channel."

"I don't know. You'd have to talk to Thay and Momma."

"Debris hung up in that channel almost cost Thay his life. When you consider the riffraff that come and go as they please hauling in drugs and murdering people, it's a good idea to be inaccessible. Thay could sleep nights instead of trying to be all to all. He suffers from his daddy's delusion of noblesse oblige. Every person on this island owns a stake in its well-being.

"Good people who appreciate and enjoy what we have to offer will find us. Gutter trash need to find another location to conduct their nefarious activities."

"Are you proposing we dig a moat around the Seamew and pull up the drawbridge?"

"Worked for the knights, kept out the Vandals. The Coast Guard is not adverse to a good harbor and a home-cooked meal now that they have Louise's kitchen on their radar. I know she is resting, so I won't bother her. You think about what I'm saying, Marsh."

"Matt Young, would you sign my cast? I heard your game broadcast, it was good. Stick with it." Matt takes his pen and signs

With Pleasure! Matt Young

"Pretty Lady and gentlemen." He waves his cast around the table. "It was nice talking to you. I see we have company. I'll get back on that other as soon as I hear any news."

I jump up and help him out of the chair.

"Humph! Man of action and good manners, too."

"Pretty Lady." Mr. Andrews similes at Maud. "There goes a wise man. It is a rare sight. Many people are against something just to be contrary. Mr. Southly has considered the causeway from all angles. He maybe right."

Maud is twirling a curl through her fingers. "The information he gave us puts everything in a muddle. I know it all points to Rhodes

Thornton. I can't see him as a murderer. It's too crude. He might order a killing, but he wouldn't dirty his hands to kill himself."

Maud waves at Marsh, who is on his way to the kitchen with Collins and Barker's order.

"Yes, Ma'am?"

"Marsh, would you please loan Phillip the hotel station wagon to go off the island?"

"Miss Maud, you'd have to stay on the mainland overnight." He says it like they'd be out slumming. "The ferry only makes one trip a day."

"I know, but I need to do some shopping. I desperately need another grip."

"Glad to, if you'll pick up some kitchen supplies. Islanders had dinner before Mr. Isaiah's show. Good for business, but hard on the larder. I'll draw you a map to the wholesale warehouse. Leave my list there, and they'll have it ready for pickup in time for you to catch the return ferry."

He digs in his pocket, hands Mr. Andrews his keys, and hurries away to make his list.

"Maud, you could take my Porsche."

"Thank you, but the hotel's wagon will get us off the island without being detained by the Port Authority."

"I don't mind, but why do you want off the island?"

"Phillip, I need another suitcase, but I want to go to the library."

"The library?"

"Libraries keep back issues of newspapers, don't they?"

"I believe so, but...."

"You can help me check the personal ads before the storm. I don't know what I'm looking for, but I'll know it when I see it."

Matt's eyebrow wiggles. Mr. Andrews looks confused. I see where she is going. "Both Collins and Barker read the papers. You don't think they just have a nose for the news?"

"A spy novel I read. The bad guys were sending messages through the paper's classified ads."

"Worth a look. Barker took all of the newspapers as soon as they were delivered from the ferry. Marsh was ticked off because he took his personal copy of the local paper."

"Phillip, we'd best go pack. My train case will do"

He picks up the check, signs it, and drops a tip on the table.

"What are you going to do, Little Brother?"

"Back to my cottage for an *undisturbed* nap."

"Sounds good to me. I'll stop by for a chat."

"Don't. We're not going anywhere. I'll talk to you later."

Chapter 29

I slept through lunch. I have the same feeling I had the first night, that someone is watching me. It's bizarre. Matt and I are the only people in the dining room until Collins and Barker saunterer in with newspapers under their arms.

They stick close, but ignore each other. I've been watching them and I don't think they've said ten words. Every once in a while, Barker will lift his head and look toward the door as if he's expecting someone.

Matt is having a steak salad. The lettuce looks limp, as if it has been left out of the refrigerator. I chose the Oyster Roll, a dozen sauteed oysters served on a long French roll with shredded spinach, sliced tomatoes, cocktail sauce, mayo, and a side of fried onion rings. The oysters were delivered this morning by one of the islanders.

"You heard Isaiah?"

Matt's laughter rings in the empty room. Collins lowers his newspaper to glare as if we've committed a sin in church.

"Couldn't miss it. He was getting in the last word."

"Easier than to listen to than Kane's preaching."

"Don't pay any attention to Kane. He evokes Mom's name when he decides you're to do what he wants. It's a bad habit with him. She made sure we were clothed, fed, and went to school. She wants only one thing, and that is for us to do whatever it takes to make us happy. She told me so herself when I was debating going into pro football.

"What are you going to do?"

"Drop down to Daytona to watch Kyle Petty race. Look around the garages before I head home. Then, with the help of my famous mechanics, make a stab at the future in building engines. It won't be the same as driving, but it'll still be racing."

"You used the wrong word. It's *infamous* mechanics!"

My turn to laugh. I didn't know until it came out my mouth what I was going to do. I get a hateful stare from Barker. I can taste it in the air between our tables. It makes me shiver.

"Are you still cold?"

"No. Just a thought I had. What are you going to do?"

"While your head was buried under the pillows, I took advantage of the decent day. Got Marsh to make me a Ruben and drove to Broomtown. Went sight-seeing. Walked a few rutted paths. Some ended near ruins of old houses, others went to the shore either on the ocean or sound side. I was thinking about what Moses Southly said.

"Every house is as neat as a pin and the barns are in good shape. The island is as close to paradise as I'd want to get in this world. No old wrecks resting in weeds rusting away. Considered asking Mr. Southly if there was an acre or so available on the sound where I could build me a place to wet a line."

"And?"

"Everyone said it was our year to win, went into the playoffs 10 and 0. If I'd been in the game could I have blocked that pass Roger Staubach threw to Drew Pearson? Could I have made the difference to get us to the Super Bowl? Blanda is retiring. The game is changing. I don't want to be an old wreck sitting around rusting.

"To answer your question. I'm not sure I have the stuff to be a television broadcaster, though Mr. Southly said he liked my style."

I glance at his hands. They're bare. He doesn't wear the two Super Bowl rings he has. He's like Isaiah, who doesn't wear his Phi Beta Kappa key. The symbol isn't important, it's the being in the game that counts.

"You own a radio/television station."

"Catherine left me a responsibility. I don't want to be calling J.T. every time a camera goes on the blink. I could stick my nose in the works during the off-season. I need experience to understand what I'd be seeing. Want to find out how things work in media-land.

"I'd be a liar if I didn't admit that, in spite of not being on the field, I enjoyed broadcasting once I got over being scared. Learned how to eat a sandwich bending over so as not to get spots on my tie."

We both laugh and finish our meal in comfortable silence.

We're drinking coffee following a peach ice cream pie for dessert when I remember a box I saw on a shelf in the parlor.

"Would you be up to a rousing game of *Clue?*"

"You mean that awful game Levi got for Christmas?"

"Yep, there's one in the parlor. We don't have anything else to do."

"Agony. I remember the nights he badgered us to play it with him."

Chapter 30

P hillip is helping Marsh unload the station wagon. He ordered enough food stuffs to feed an army. I was afraid the eggs would break when we bumped onto the ramp to the ferry. We hit bottom with a clang.

I'm not sure we found a message in the *Washington Post*. It looks like a weather report. I'll show it to Mr. Southly. He can tell us if we've found anything significant. We stayed in a motel near a major highway and the sound of big trucks rumbled through our room most of the night.

I kick my shoes off and slip my feet into my slippers. Oops. What in the world? Now how did that get there?

Phillip's key rattles in the lock. "Some vacation night. I'm sorry. I thought it would be easier to find our way back to the warehouse this morning. What's that?"

I'm holding one of the shells I'd collected from the beach. It was in my slipper.

"Phillip, someone has been in our room while we were in town."

"Are you sure? What do we have that would be of interest?"

"I don't know, but this shell was in my slipper. I sure didn't put it there?"

"Maud, it's possible you dropped the shell. You didn't hear it fall because it fell in your houseshoe."

"No. I broke a pretty brown striped one washing the sand out of it. Since then I've been careful to wrap them in my dirty step-ins before I put them in my lingerie bag."

"Have you looked around?"

"No, I just sat down."

"Stay there and let me look. You took your jewelry with you, so there isn't anything here to steal. That's odd. My extra jacket is in my garment bag. It was damp, I left it out to dry. The pocket of your fur coat is turned out."

"Our room has been searched. You had the key. How could anyone get in?"

Phillip holds up the room key. It's an ordinary skeleton key. Anyone could get in. "You are correct. Someone has done a rather thorough search of this room. Where is the lingerie bag?"

"In my old suitcase on the luggage rack."

"Take a look."

"Someone's gone through my things. My sweaters were rolled so they wouldn't wrinkle. Not like this...the sleeves are on the outside. The bag is in the wrong pocket. I use the big one for my clean clothes."

"I didn't want to go pawing through you're unmentionables."

Phillip is old fashioned in ways that surprise me. I can't help teasing him, "You don't mind taking them off of me."

"That's different...not a bad idea," he replies with a devastating grin that shatters my intentions.

Thay is sitting facing the door. His hair is free of the sea muck. He has a couple of small razor nicks on his chin. His movements are stiff, but he raises an arm and points to a chair.

I face him across the table. "The sleep worked. You look better."

"Same for you. New patch okay?"

"Better than that bandage. When I looked sideways, all I could see was a lump. Matt said the pack was better than tying my hands to the bed like they did in the hospital to keep me from rubbing it."

"You have eight brothers. Are the others like Matt and Isaiah?"

The question spins me for a lap around the track. "How…what do you mean?"

"Man the ships. Damn the torpedoes."

I consider my brothers and laugh. "You mean take-charge kind of guys? Yeah, I suppose so. I'm the runt. They take turns telling me what to do…except Adam. He's the oldest. He'll say I know what's right and leave it at that."

"I don't have a brother. Tell me about them."

I turn my head to look behind me. Two tables away, but well within listening distance are Thornton, Lettic, Barker, and Collins.

"My brothers are alike in that they've been behind me, even when I quit school to go racing. Mom wasn't happy. Adam didn't finish school either. He's a builder."

"Construction?"

"Has his own business. His love is fine wood working. He constructed the dulcimer and mandolin Isaiah has packed in the Blazer."

"Do you all play?'

"You heard my contribution to our front porch music. Isaiah wasn't funning when he said I can't sing. His twin…."

"He has a twin?"

"Isaac. Nothing alike, even their voices are different. Isaac is a baritone and a bass man. He can make that big fiddle talk. They paid for their schooling playing in clubs. He's a representative in the state legislature."

"Rather young, isn't he, for that job?"

"Yeah, the youngest in the house. Three years ago I knocked on every door in three counties to help get him elected. Need to tough'n up my knuckles before fall for another round."

He nods, but encourages me to keep talking. "You know Matt. He pulled me out of the C9, before it exploded."

"Accidents changed the future for both of you?"

"I didn't know until yesterday what I was going to do. I hate the thought of standing behind the wall, but I'll eventually go home to build engines. Matt's pondering his options."

"You said 'eventually?'" Damn, he's paying attention to every word I say.

"Going to drop south to Daytona. Watch the stockcars give it a go. Real reason is to peek at what they're putting under their hoods."

I grin at him. "It isn't a secret. Machine shops copy improvements. One year a guy develops an advantage, next year everyone has it. Levels the track. Shopping to put Young Enterprises back on course."

I take a sip of the tea Marsh set by my plate. "What is this?"

Thay smiles. "Green tea. Tonight we're having Momma Lou's version of Chinese."

I like Chinese food, but their tea is brackish colored water.

Thay is counting on his fingers. "That's four. You have four more."

I want to ask where everyone else is, but I don't dare, with the ears focused on our conversation. I've never known anyone to be interested in my bothers, but in a strange way Thay seems envious.

How can I explain Kane and Abel to a stranger? We've lived with their weirdness all of our lives.

"The real twins are Kane and Abel. If you saw one and later see the other you'd think they're the same person. The Army separated them for the first time. Kane was stationed in Germany, while Abel went to 'Nam. It was hard for them.

"The two years Abel spent there destroyed something in him.

He arrives and departs within the space of days, not saying anything about his travels. He wanders about the country in an old MG I restored for him, selling a picture or working brief shifts at archeological sites photographing for scientific journals and museums.

"We'll see a photo in a magazine and know without looking at the caption it's his vision of the world. Spare and stark."

"I didn't connect the photographer Abel Young to you."

I nod and continue. "He won a citation for his rough snapshot of the cam shaft from the C-9 driven into that dirt track by the explosion of my life...."

Thay looks at me. His penetrating eyes pitch an ugly truth in my face I'd refused to see. Mom had that photo framed. She keeps it in a closet so I won't be reminded of that horrible day last May. She's trying to spare my feelings by hiding her pride in Abel's work. I plunge into Kane to prevent him from asking questions I don't want to answer.

"Kane manages our money. It started when we got our first paying job. He'd take a bit of anything we earn, still does, and puts it in what we've always called *The Family Fund*. When I turned 21 he used an S-2 incorporation...gave half the shares to Mom and divided the rest nine ways. He's a lawyer." Talking about Kane is as hard as talking about Abel. It means talking about the strange will Catherine wrote the day she was killed.

"Some years back we each inherited money. Some of it was in the form of trusts. The will gave Kane the chore of looking after the money. Matt refers to him as our burden. You know, the perfect one."

"Moses told me Matt owns a radio/televison station."

"True, it was his part of the will. How did he find out about that?"

"Same way he discover that, for a junkyard proprietor, you're extremely well-heeled."

Like a dummy I blurt. "Catherine's money isn't mine."

I finish off the tea to hide my embarrassment. Where is Matt? What's taking him so long to come to dinner? Why in the hell don't the eavesdroppers leave? They finished eating hours ago.

Thay grins—actually, it's a smirk. He's enjoying playing me along. "You have two other brothers. One is in the Marines?"

"Mark, yes. He's a first lieutenant. I don't know what he does. He moves from place to place, and sometimes we don't know his location."

"Sounds like intelligence."

"I suppose, but Levi's our brain. Half the time we don't know what he's talking about. He has a fellowship and is teaching at the university while he completes his doctoral work in the new field of computer science."

Thay is fiddling with his fork. He's running out of questions. "Family or Biblical names?"

I'm wrong, but his question is trivial. "Biblical according to Mom. She named us. Then our father insisted on a warrior's name for the middle. I never knew him. He left when I was a few weeks old."

Marsh is taking his time bending to set a fresh pot of tea beside Thay.

I hear the soft order. "When they leave, immediately lock the door and close the curtains."

In a normal tone he asks, "What are your middle names?"

Marsh parks another pot of tea by my plate. We'll be leaking the stuff if we're not careful. I have to think a minute to remember, so I start with myself.

"There's ten years between Adam and me. I'm James Richard...."

"the Lion Hearted."

"Levi Jackson...."

"like a stonewall."

"Isaiah Grant and Isaac Lee...."

"fine generals, different sides."

"Mark William…."

"the Conqueror."

He's dragging this out as long as he can. I help him by pretending not to know who comes next and counting on my fingers.

"Matthew Henry…."

"of Navarre."

Wow, Thay does know military history. Even Levi had to look that one up.

"Kane Alexander and Abel Kahn…."

A chair scrapes on the stone slab floor. I let out a deep breath I hadn't realized I was holding. Thay shakes his head.

"the Great and Genghis."

Then more chairs scrape, but he keeps talking as if we aren't following every move they make.

"Adam Arthur…."

"King."

"No. Actually, Arthur was a warrior, but never a king."

"I wouldn't want to meet that unit. Three's enough. A master tactician, an honorable man in a dishonorable situation and one without fear or good sense if I remember my history."

Matt slams his hand on my shoulder scaring the crap out of me.

"Now you've had a history lesson compliments of Brother Levi. I didn't think that bunch was ever going to leave."

"Where have you been?"

"Take it easy, Little Brother. You're grouchy because you're hungry. So are we." Signaling for us to remain seated. Mr. Andrews holds a chair for Maud then sits down. Matt slides in beside me.

They've been hiding in the kitchen. Marsh pushes a cart laden with covered bowls beside the table. He hands Thay a huge bowl of rice, who takes a serving and passes it on.

"Where is Mamma Lou?"

"In the parlor tinkering on the piano. Has her eye on the doors to keep the gremlins at bay."

"We'll eat first and then talk." Looking at Matt. "Jim told me about your brothers while I covered the visit to Moses. It's only fair that I tell him about the situation here. When Orta married, Mamma Lou gave her her father's farm between my place and Broomtown. Orta's man was killed in a car wreck. When Marsh returned from the Army she deeded him this end of the island, except the hotel."

Marsh keeps putting dishes on the table in front of Thay.

"Damnit, stop acting like the butler and sit. My neck is too sore to look up to you."

Chapter 31

"Phillip found these in the *Washington Post*. There were five going back to the first of December with the same two bottom rows of numbers. You'll have to share copies, but this is the fifth one. It was in the paper on the 13th of January.

D1:15 – 4B
32.52828936482526
-80.08758544921875

"Moses ciphered the code. D1:15 is January 15th. 4B is four bells, which means 4 AM or 4 hours after midnight marine time. The two rows of numbers are the latitude and longitude coordinates, except they're decimal numbers instead of the degrees and minutes as we learned in school."

Maud beams a smile that radiates her pleasure in knowing her hunch panned out.

"There was one on the 19th I could read. '*ND – Contact.*'"

"Marsh, when did the murdered woman register at the hotel?"

"The book is on the front desk. Best I recall she came in near the first of December or the last of November. I'd have to check to be sure."

"That's all right. Close enough. Jane Doe had a reason for living here and it got her murdered."

Marsh hangs his head. "The ads were a signal for Shell to pick up a traveler offshore."

Thay follows him in his pain. "You're guessing he got paid in snow."

"Sold his soul to feed a devil. He knew his masters didn't know a squall from a trade wind. That's when he started running scared and came to you for help."

"Marsh, remember the morning he brought in the flounder. We were surprised he'd been out. That's when he missed his appointment."

"Covered his tracks by going fishing. He knew I'd ask questions about his being out in that flimsy skiff by himself with a storm brewing. What am I going to tell Mamma?"

"Nothing, absolutely nothing. As far as she is concerned he's out of it. The same for all the law enforcement authorities. The Coast Guard believes he was a sick vet who needed help. They don't need to know he was involved in the smuggling."

"Will this hurt your standing?"

"Don't think so. Family has been bending the law in my name right and left. What's another crimp or two? What we need to find out is who was retrieving the parcel from the island, committing murder, and supplying Shell. He'd be an expendable liability. Last payment would have been uncut. Another junkie dead of an overdose with no questions asked."

The talk between the two cousins hurts to watch. Both are proud men. We'd kept quiet, but it's time to pull them out of their misery.

"Thanks to Maud and Mr. Andrews...."

"Jim, after all we've been through, you can call me Phillip."

"Yes, Sir. Now you know how their system operates."

"Yes, and our killer knows we know."

"How?"

"While we were off island someone did a professional search of our room."

"They what?"

"Jim, whoever did the search knew what they were doing, but dropped a shell."

"A shell?"

"Little mistake that alerted Maud. What were they looking for? I don't know. Maud has no idea. May have just been looking around, but I wouldn't count on it. Too risky. This killer isn't taking risks... just the opposite."

"Is the house arrest still in effect?"

"Officially. The PA is monitoring everyone who comes to the island. You know who's still here. They'll land in jail if they try to leave, which wouldn't look good on their service records. I'm sure the murders are the act of a single person. As Matt oberved, they've all been neck attacks, which indicates military training."

"We're not going to accomplish any more tonight. I'm going back to my cottage for some down-time."

"Mr. Jim, I'll walk you."

"Marsh, I know the way." His dark eyes dart to Thay and back to me.

"Moses has watchers patrolling the island. They won't know you in the dark."

Thay shouts. "He's what?"

"Moses calls it reconnaissance. His thoughts are that all the islanders have a stake. It's their island too. You shouldn't have to take out the garbage by yourself."

"Marsh, there isn't a truck on this island that doesn't need a new muffler."

"Horses. Dark faces don't show at night."

"You approved?"

"Didn't have a choice. He told me what they're doing, didn't ask permission—didn't need to, nohow. So smile as you walk out the front door and drive home to sleep in your own bed. Mine's going to be occupied by me."

Chapter 32

"Jim, don't be obvious, but look over your shoulder. The man Phedra slapped is with Sheriff Thay."

"Maud, are you sure?"

"His face. You can't forget those scars."

"Take her word, Little Brother. Turning around to look is obvious. Bad case of acne leaves pitted scars."

"I wish I could hear what they're saying."

Thornton shepherds Lettic into the dining room from the porch. She doesn't look too happy. She darts away from Thornton.

"Rick. Rick Riley."

Lettic streaks across the room and I turn to watch. She is hugging the stranger. Thornton is left standing inside the door with a scowl on his face, which he instantly hides.

Matt mutters, "Is there a man alive she doesn't know?"

"It's been ages. I haven't seen...."

Lettic has obviously known this man for a long time. We listen in the same way Collins and Barker have spied on us.

"Lettic, Jane and I attended your father's funeral, but we didn't get a chance to speak."

"Oh. Why are you here, of all places?"

"Jane...."

"Your sister. Hell and damnation. The dead woman is Jane. I should have known. Rick, I'm so sorry. Your parents must be crushed."

"Yes."

"That explains why the body looked like Phedra. But how did you know?"

"Her driver's license was mailed to the police. I was listed as next of kin on her application. The police requested my presence to verify their information. Sheriff Townsend and I...."

"Bad ole sheriff won't let me go home." Her voice changes to a spoiled child's whine.

"Lettic, he has a job to do."

"But I didn't have anything to do with it. She was dead when I arrived. Jane was living in this godforsaken hotel as Phedra."

"I know, we had words about it. You and Lemuel didn't recognize her."

"They put Lemuel in jail for killing Phedra. I proved she wasn't Phedra. It didn't dawn on me who she was until I saw you."

Thornton has eased up behind Lettic and takes her arm. She brushes his hand off like it is a horsefly.

Riley turns to Thay, "Sheriff, I appreciate your help. Do you have a room where I can talk to my cousin?"

"Please follow me. Jim, would you ask Marsh to bring a coffee setup to Mamma Lou's parlor?"

"Why was Jane pretending to be Phedra? Where is Phedra?"

Moses Southly invited Matt, Maud, and Mr. Andrews for a guided tour of the north end of the island. I invited myself. We took the Rover to his place under tall pines whose sticky sap spreads a medicinal odor over the salt crisp breeze. He is going back to the hotel for dinner and later Thay will return him to his lair for the night.

As we walk down the shell-surfaced road, Matt gets him to talking about the island.

"It's been in the Townsend family since around 1640. Dolan Townsend tried to buy it from a tribe of Indians who visited the island for oysters. They thought it was a great joke. Indians didn't own land so they sold him the chief's daughter. The island came with her as a marriage portion."

"There's over two hundred years between settlement and the Civil War. Why are there so few people living here now?"

"Indian raids, storms, tides, diseases, snakes, and the sea give no quarter to an islander. A man of any color was lucky to have one son live to pass his land on to. Daughters married off the island, but some took strangers for their mates—new blood."

"Indian raids, but the Indians gave Townsend the island."

"Different tribe who lost their hunting grounds in the original transaction. White men were no longer strangers, they'd learned their ways."

"Then the War changed everything. How did the islanders cope?"

"When the War between the States ended, long staple cotton as a crop was dead, lost their French markets. Thay's great-great-grandfather married his housekeeper, who was born in slavery. He did so to provide a mother for his sole surviving son from his first marriage, and also to keep from having to pay her wages. Cash money was what he didn't have. Out west they'd've called her a 'breed' as she had all kinds of blood, but was white enough to inherit under the existing laws when her husband died.

"She and her descendants got the south end of the island, along with the manor house. Thay's great-grandfather got the middle and built the place where Thay lives. Sherman gave the islands to the slaves, but no one ever settled that one. The north end around Broomtown the federals parceled out to the slaves who weren't slaves in the first place. They had enough sense to keep their mouth shut. Got its name from those who jumped over the broom to prove they were married. Moses has some old pictures of the soldiers and their servants."

"I've seen those. I thought they were colored soldiers."

"Naw. An orderly is a servant. Gets to wear a uniform, but he's still a servant. After the soldiers pulled out, those parcels didn't last a generation. A few were sold to city people. Most traded among themselves to get back the land Dolan and his sons had given their ancestors when their indenture was served.

"Ten families were left to go on living on the land their ancestors farmed. People did what they could to survive. Grew their own foodstuffs, let pigs range in the woods, bred horses, and harvested the sea. Most of the men took to harvesting oysters, which in those times paid good money. Then something started killing off the oysters and they were hard to come by. Oysters became food for the rich. Before that oysters were poor people food, used them for everything from thickening for soups to sandwich stuffings.

"There was a big hotel on the north end that got blown away in the hurricane of 1893. That old hurricane killed a passel more of islanders."

We'd been walking down a rough track through a pine woods where the smell of the sea got stronger with each step we took. In a small clearing was the rock foundation of a house that had obviously burned, and not long ago.

"This was Wylie Ferrals place. He lost his sight and went to live with his daughter in North Carolina. Died a few years back, just after lightening struck the house. Burned during the night. No one knew it until we smelled the smoke the next morning. Doubt if we could have saved it anyway. His daughter wants to sell."

There is a barn off in a grove of small saplings that looks in fair shape. The shingles are still in place. I start walking toward it.

"Watch your step, Mr. Jim. There a passel of rattlers in that barn."

"Understand. Mr. Southly. Please drop the mister, it sounds phony."

He chuckles.

Maud is pointing to the left of the barn. "Where does that path go?"

"To the sound. Good fishing when the tide comes in. Shell Wallace loves that spot."

"You brought me out here on purpose."

"Marsh heard you mention wanting a place. Thought I'd show you what's available. Kinda particular who I have for neighbors."

"Pretty Lady, you be careful too. Cottenmouths drop out of trees."

Maud laughs, "Are you trying to sell Matt a place or run us off? I grew up on the Cumberland River. I learned about snakes when I learned to walk, but ours are copperheads."

Maud cups her hand around Phillip's arm and they wander down the path toward the sound. Matt is walking around the foundations in a deep study. Moses plants his frame on a stone slab that served as the front stoop for the house.

I sit down beside him drinking in the warm sunlight reflecting off the broad leaves of a huge magnolia. My hand rests on the stone's uneven suface. I look down, and see that there is a faint word under my hand.

"What is this?'

"A fancy grave cover one of the Hunters, some of Thay's kin, had brought in. They weren't islanders—married in, didn't last long."

I jump to my feet. "You mean I was sitting on a dead person."

"No Jim. The sea took the corpse. Wylie had the cover drug here, he couldn't stand seeing good stone going to waste when it didn't cover nothing."

"You said the sea took the corpse."

"It did. Hunter chose a resting place on the edge of a cliff facing the ocean. Waves undercut the coffin and washed it out to sea. It was tricky getting this stone on the sled. It near followed the casket."

"It feels awful sitting on a man's tombstone."

"If you look you'll find more than one tombstone used for stepping stones. This island is constantly changing. Washed out and washed in from invasions, diseases, silt from the rivers, hurricanes from the sea, or storm surges. It's not like those mountains where you live, that have been sitting there for millions of years. If you love it, you hang on as long as you can, bending with it until it breaks or takes you."

"Moses. Jim. Matt." Maud sounds frantic. "Come look."

We follow her back down the path. "Where's Phillip?"

"He stayed with the boat."

"What boat?"

"The one that's drowning in the sound. He's trying to snake some of the cushions back to land before they float off."

"Damn city-slicker. Doesn't know a damn thing about tides. Leave 'em be, Phillip. Damn fool deserves to lose them."

The water is murky, but I can see the shadowy outline of an inboard cabin cruiser bobbing and tugging at its moorings. Its lines are snubbed tight around the bottom of an old post. It can't float on the rising waters of the sound. Maud's description is right, the boat is drowning.

I remember my surprise when we came back to Thay's dock. The skiffs hit above the middle of the dock. When we left we had to climb down a ladder. Standing in the skiff my head was above the edge of the dock. Whoever tied his boat up tight didn't know the flood tide raises the level of the sound.

"Humph. More damn work. We'll have to wait until the tide goes out, pump it out, and tow it over to Thay's dock. Nobody is going to want to do it in the dark. Have to wait until tomorrow. Not worth getting someone hurt.

"Shouldn't have been back in this cove in the first place. This is all Wylie's daughter's property. He kept a painter tied to an old life preserver that rose and fell as the tides flowed. Must have floated free during the storm."

I've learned Moses can go on for hours once he gets started. The cruiser isn't going anywhere. It's going on dark. Time we got back to the hotel.

"Come on Moses. I hear Momma Lou's dinner bell. We'll help haul this thing out tomorrow. Do you know who it belongs to?"

"Of course not. When I find out I'll knock some sense into his head. Leave a fine cruiser like that tied where it can't float."

Chapter 33

I leave everyone at the hotel and walk back to my cottage. I can't get the sunken cruiser out of my mind. It was trying to float to the surface. I could see movement more than I could the boat. The stout rope held it fast to the bottom. An aluminum folding chair was chained with a padlock to a tree up the path. Moses said Shell frequently fished the cove.

I think what we've found is where Shell delivered his cargo. How long had the boat been snubbed against the post? The cushion Mr. Andrews had snagged hadn't been in the water for long. We left it beside the chair.

The door to my cottage is standing wide open. I reach around for the light switch before I remember there is no electricity. Then I fumble in my pocket for my keys where I keep a miniature flashlight for finding the keyhole of my garage at night. I stumble against a log someone has dropped.

I kick at the log, which is blocking the doorway. It is soft. Why would Marsh bring rotten wood to the cottage?

I bend to move it so I can get in the door and touch cloth. The beam from my pen light is faint and doesn't reach far, but I run it past the toe of my sneaker.

A leg is sprawled across the door seal. My feeble light follows the leg to the body. A man is lying in a spreading pool of blood barely inside my cottage. It's easy to recognize Rick Riley from the scars on his face. His eyes are wide open, staring at his own blood.

<> <> <>

For the second time this week I run back to the hotel to find Thay.

The first thing the beam of his flashlight hits are my footprints. In the dark I'd walked in the man's blood that is splattered on the steps and inside the door of the cottage. My stomach clenches at the gruesome sight. I clamp down on my tongue and hold my breath so I won't get sick.

Thay opens the shutters of a window and I give him a boost through it.

He sticks his head back through the opening, "Where is your gym bag?"

"On the far bed. I didn't unpack much. What I did is in the bathroom."

I wait outside and begin to shiver. The sun is gone. "My coat is hanging on a peg behind the door."

"Hang on a minute. I must light the lamp so I can see."

"It's on the table by the bed closest to the door."

"Need to be careful not to disturb any evidence."

A faint glow blends through the dark and I peer into the room. He's getting my stuff from the bathroom. From the window I can't see Riley and I'm glad. What my miniature light touched was enough to remember for a lifetime.

A man staring at his own blood.

"Here." The bag comes through the window. "There is a raincoat, a parka, and a windbreaker. Are they all yours?"

"Yes."

"Got to work my way around the body to get to them."

When my coats come through the window. I pull on the parka and hug my sides to get warm. Thay is walking slowly around the pool of blood. The beam of his flashlight comes through the open door, illuminating Rick Riley.

"He was shot. I'll have to move him to close the door. Wait for me. I may need help getting back out the window."

The lamp goes out. Thay's feet come out first, toes pointing toward the sky. He slides out on his back and leans against the side of the cottage. "God, that's hard on broken ribs."

"Why didn't you come out the door?"

"One set of footprints is enough. Marsh has gone to get Moses to call the mainland police. The Port Authority will bring them over. It will take at least an hour or more to get Este's ferry fired up for the ambulance. I can hardly bend over much less document a crime scene using a flashlight and coal oil lamp. I need help for this one. Riley was a special investigator with the FBI. He showed me his credentials this morning before we talked."

"Dangerous to our killer."

"Too dangerous. Come on, I'll carry your extra coats. Anything else in the cabin belong to you?"

"Regular stuff. Couple of books. My suit and clean jeans are in the closet. Extra shirts and underwear in the drawers."

"Get to read any more in the detecting book?"

"Are you serious? In one day I've sat on a man's tombstone and found a body in my cottage. That's enough detecting for anyone."

Everyone has questions in their eyes, but Thay shakes his head and accepts the cup of coffee Marsh has waiting for him. Mamma Lou's chili is welcome.

It's closer to two hours before the mainland authorities arrive. We play half-hearted poker and try to imagine what happened at my cottage. The cards are so rotten they don't provoke enough interest to take our minds off our worries for a single hand. We end up about even-steven.

Marsh has given me a room on the ocean side of the hotel. There isn't any question of sleep. I bundle up in my parka and take several blankets to wrap around my legs out on the verandah to watch the cottage. Right now if I had any liquor I'd break my word to Kane. A bourbon and branch would go a long way toward washing the sour taste out of my mouth.

It isn't but a few minutes before I'm joined by Matt, Maud, and Phillip. They don't say a word. Like me, they put down their chairs and stare into the spotlighted dark. Silence steals across the beach. The lap of the waves is soft, as if waiting for the invaders to leave.

I look over the railing. Barker and Collins are sitting on the landing steps that leads down to the boardwalk. They're using a pair of binoculars, which they pass back and forth to look through the spokes of the railing. I don't know if we can be seen from the cottage, but they're well hidden. Silent spectators in the night. One of them lights a cigarette, but it's quickly put out. I don't think they know we're above them.

Matt sees where I'm looking and touches my arm before he goes to his room. He returns with a pair of binoculars. I can't see anything but the lights through them.

We watch forms moving like specters. The police have set a big lantern below the steps and it looks like there are several inside the cottage. Off to the side is an unoccupied gurney. Shadows cross between the light and the window.

Two men come out on the steps and lift the gurney into the cottage. In a few minutes, accompanied by two others carrying flashlights, they start up the path with their burden. I get up and walk to the end of the porch. The ambulance is sitting with its engine running in the same spot it was the morning Jane Riley was brought up from the beach.

Before they reach the top of the path the sky is filled with a terrible roar. The emergency light of the ambulance begins to rotate sending red circles around the parking lot. For an instant I see a horse just inside the trees, his rider is holding his nose before the red light moves, hiding him in the dark.

A helicopter lands off to the side, its lights spotting the four men with the gurney. One man instantly covers his eyes, turns, and goes back down the path. That man is Thay, I can tell by the sure way he plants his feet on a path he's walked all of his life. Two men jump from the chopper and run bent over toward the ambulance. The rotating blades of the chopper kick up a stiff wind even up here on the porch.

The red strobe stops and the back door of the ambulance opens for the gurney. I can't hear what they're saying over the noise of the engines, but it's easy to tell an argument is underway. The new guys lose. One climbs in the back of the ambulance with the body of Rick Riley and the other returns to the chopper.

A whoosh of sound like a vacuum cleaner sweeps the air around us. The helicopter rises into the air, circling the beach, dipping low over the cottage, with its ground lights working like the spotlight on a stage before it fades in the distance. The silence of the night is slow to return as my ears continue to ring. The back door of the ambulance closes and waits in the darkness as the three bearers slowly walk back down the path.

A long time passes before bobbing flashlights come up the path, the men are carrying cases and equipment. The back door of the ambulance opens and the men slide their burdens into the space by the gurney. It pulls out with its grisly cargo. Out of sight in the front of the hotel I hear a trunk lid slam shut and an engine start. It needs a tune-up.

I glance over the front balcony. The boardwalk steps are empty. Thay stands below, talking to a man. They're casually discussing a fishing trip before the man walks toward the front parking lot.

Thay's voice is a harsh whisper. "Marsh, don't let them smell the coffee. I'll follow them to the ferry to make sure no one gets lost. While I'm gone see what's in the refrigerator. I'm starving. Jim, you all come down the back stairs."

We pack our chairs and blankets back to our rooms. From the verandah I can see round humped forms racing along the beach. Stopping to dig and moving on. They sit on their haunches and poke small clams in their mouths. The raccoons have returned to scavenge on the ocean's leavings. I've watched them from the cottage window on nights when I had trouble sleeping. Off in the distance a small light flickers four times and disappears.

By the time we get to the kitchen door, Marsh has laid out sandwich-makings on a counter. Maud is filling coffee cups while he lays out plates and cutlery on the work table. "It's help yourself," and we do. I'm ashamed at the amount of food that finds its way onto my plate, but everyone seems to be in an advanced state of starvation.

"Whee. I thought they'd never leave. They'll be back early to look around once it gets light. Este is charging the county enough to replace his ferry for the extra trips." Thay is chattering in a streak as he fills his plate and joins us at the table, not even pausing to remove his coat, though the kitchen is warm.

This time Marsh doesn't hover around being servile. He joins us with a deep sigh. "What took so long?"

I look at my new watch. It's 4:20.

"They picked up every grain of sand in the cracks of the floor and bagged them. Virgil Landers had gotten word that some FBI bigwigs were flying in. He wasn't taking any chances of being accused of sloppy local police work. One of his guys told me he almost crapped in his pants when the helicopter landed. Virgil thought 'flying in' meant to the airport."

"There was a man holding a horse just inside the woods when the chopper came in."

"Moses's men. How did you see him?"

"The red light from the ambulance caught him, but when it came back around they were gone. Barker and Collins were watching from behind the rail of the boardwalk steps. They were using binoculars. We tried it, but couldn't see much."

"Their binoculars are fancier than yours. Night vision, probably. Went to a lot of trouble. Virgil couldn't have kept them out. Wonder why they didn't just walk down."

"They were gone by the time you brought up the equipment."

"Moses may be of some help after all. Maybe his man in the woods saw something we didn't."

"Thay, as soon as it was known who was murdered, Lettic ran up to her room. I heard her pulling the chest-of-drawers across the door. It wasn't play-acting like she did to get Matt's attention. She is frightened."

"Maud, keep an eye on her. She may have every right to be scared. If our murderous guest thinks Riley told her anything she is in danger. I don't think he did, Riley was too much the professional. He was giving his sister hell for impersonating Phedra Lavin the night you saw her slap him. She would not tell him who had been knocking her around."

"Did he tell you how he knew she was here?"

"No ma'am, we didn't have that long a conversation before Lettic came in. He left after he talked to her and I didn't see him again until Jim found his body."

"Was Riley killed in my cottage?"

"No one thinks so. From the blood on the porch and the condition of his hands. We think he was shot down the beach and crawled to your cabin. Then died inside the door."

"That's what I figured."

"Your footprints are a problem. Virgil Landers is the chief of police on the mainland. He wants to talk to you and get a statement. I got you out of it for tonight, but he'll bring his stenographer tomorrow. I told him you were nursing a cold and Mamma Lou had sent you to bed. He bought it, since he already knew you'd pulled me out of the sound. Cough and snuff a bit when you talk to her."

"He can put that bandage back on and scare her to death."

"I'm going down to Moses's place and get his men to make sure no one goes near the beach until Virgil and his men get back. I'm guessing, but I suspect he'll have some unwanted company. Marsh, you better prepare for a substantial late breakfast."

"No problem. With the road out, we won't have many in for Sunday dinner."

Chapter 34

Marsh was dead wrong about Sunday dinner. Virgil Landers and his technicians worked the beach and the buffet. Residents on the island came to find out about the new murder. Then the Coast Guard showed up, but they came in waves, which gave the kitchen enough time to get the dishes washed and back on the tables. I learned more than I ever wanted to know about feeding a large crowd of unexpected guests.

Marsh routed all the power from the generator to the kitchen, then used candles on the tables and in the wall sconces. He set his mother to manning the cash register, as there wasn't room in the kitchen for her wheelchair with all the extra help. I ended up running the potato peeler. Mary Tillis, Virgil Landers' secretary, took my statement while peeling apples for pies. Maud proved a fair hand at making pastry and biscuits.

Local reporters and Thay kept the law people out of our hair, but they too managed to end up in the dining room. I heard Vernon Stillsberry give Matt the raspberries about his new employment as a one-handed busboy.

It gets dark about 4:30 in the afternoon. We're sprawled around the big round table in the dining room too tired to even lift a fork. I slip my shoes off under the table to use the stone floor to cool the stinging and burning of my feet. The long night, little sleep, and the afternoon's KP duty has wiped us all out.

At 4 o'clock Mamma Lou declared the dining room closed and locked the doors. Collins, Barker, and Thornton were the last to leave. She had managed to extract Lettic from Thornton's clutches to roll napkins and cutlery. The ladies, including Lettic and Maud are at a table near the remnants of the buffet.

"I don't want to see another egg." Phillip had scrambled eggs all afternoon. It was surprising how many people chose a country ham, biscuits, and gravy breakfast to the huge roast Marsh carved with deadly skill.

When he ran out of beef, he started on a Smithfield ham that had been turning on a spit over a fire pit behind the hotel. I'm enjoying the barbequed smoked ham with green beans and escalloped potatoes. Only perfect, snowy potatoes were mashed. If the peeler missed an eye or bump they went in pans with cracker crumbs, milk, grated cheese and butter. Mamma Lou and Orta whipped up several batches of her little cornsticks for us before the ovens had a chance to cool.

"Thay, find that killer." Marsh demands as he forks a slice of his own ham onto his plate.

"What do you think I'm trying to do? This one's different. Reily was shot at close range on the path below Jim's cabin with his own gun. One of Virgil's men found it this morning caught in a clump of myrtle."

Each of us peppers Thay with questions. "You mean he trusted his killer?"

"Must have to let him get close enough to take his gun. It was broad daylight."

"Did he know Thornton?"

"I don't think so. I introduced them. He spoke to Barker and Collins out in the hall before we came in, so I assume he knew them."

"Maud said she didn't see Thornton as the killer. Your suspects are down to two." I glance at Mr. Andrew's plate. He had salted away slices of the roast beef and is enjoying a Manhattan.

Matt has been watching Lettic. "She looks like death warmed over."

I laugh, "She should. Maud says she spent the night curled up in the closet in her room."

"Now what happens to her?"

"She is going to disappear."

"Disappear."

"Yes. Orta is going to take her to my place and with stay with her. Moses will see that they are not bothered."

Chapter 35

The night is warmer than it has been for several days. A heavy mist clouds the air like frozen fog. I can't sleep and decide take a walk to stir the mold from my brain. I've imagined a dozen tales for the havoc on the island. They're like the Spanish moss that hangs from the live oaks. They twist and they float, yet have no substance.

My slicker is missing from the closet. I put on an extra sweatshirt and my windbreaker. They'll do, as I don't plan to be gone long.

Ah. My missing coat. Matt is wearing it, standing just below the boardwalk landing staring at the ocean and smoking a cigarette. Deep in thought, he shows no awareness of the night around him. It would serve him right for the fright he gave me in the dining room if I sneaked up and jumped him. With this thought in mind I silently move across the verandah to the side stairs.

I don't know what made me look back. A faint sound. An ugly feeling. Matt hasn't moved. A black shadow is creeping toward his back.

Matt! Matt's in danger. I vault the railing, throwing my body at an angle toward the shadow. My feet connect with his neck and shoulder driving him into the base of an iron urn.

I hear splash like a watermelon bursting if it's dropped against the sharp edge of a step when you don't have a knife. I crack the back of my head on the edge of the steps and my right leg crumples under me. I'm flat on the slippery boards and can't get up. Shaking and breathing hard, Matt is tugging at my arm.

A small man pushes Matt aside and grabs my shoulder.

"Roll over, roll twice. Then stay still, Mr. Jim."

"Is he okay?"

"Don't let him up. I'll get Marsh." He disappears in the dark.

The rain is falling in my face. "Matt, feel my leg. I can't feel it."

I watch him run his hands down my jeans. "You damn fool. That's a drop of over 20 feet. Nothing broken."

Can't stand the cold rain. Can't see with water falling in my eye. "Give me your hand, I've got to sit up." My head spins and starts to pound.

"Is he?"

"I think he's dead. Hasn't moved since you fell on him. Thanks, that was close. I'm shaking as bad as you are."

"He's dead! Who is he?"

"Don't know. Black hood."

When the beam of a flashlight hits us we're sitting on the edge of the steps with our backs to the man. Matt's good arm is draped over my shoulder trying to hold me still. My body keeps jerking like I'm having spasms. We both are trying to smoke a cigarette, but our hands are shaking so bad we can barely find our mouths.

Thay's voice penetrates the haze in my mind. "Jim?"

"He's okay. Shock. Doesn't like to kill rabbits."

We refuse to turn around. I can't look at what I've done. He was going to hurt Matt. Had to stop him. Oh my God, I didn't mean to kill him. Had to stop him from killing Matt.

"Sam, ride to Moses's. Have him radio Virgil. Tell him to come quiet. Don't need to wake anyone else up if we can help it.

"What a minute. Marsh, how's the larder?"

"Momma's making sandwiches by now, but it's low."

"Sam, tell Moses to have Este bring breakfast supplies and anything else he can lay his hands on when they come."

"Marsh, take Jim and Matt back. Get them warm. A shot of brandy in some coffee. Hell, I'll go with you. I can't touch anything here until Virgil gets back with his crew. He's going to love coming out two nights in a row."

Pain shoots up my right leg when I put it down to walk. I can't stifle a grunt. I can feel it now in spades. I grit my teeth, lean on Matt for support, and hobble across the crushed shells.

Somewhere…out there in the dark…I've lost my new shoes.

Chapter 36

I make it to the davenport in the parlor and collapse. I'm so cold. I can't get warm. Mamma Lou is poking the grate to get a fire burning.

"Drink this. No arguments." She hands me a cup of steaming liquid that smells like lemons.

"Marsh, get him out of that wet coat. There's blankets in the hall closet.

"Mr. Matt, are you okay?"

"Yes ma'am. I'm fine. Jim...his feet?"

"I'll see to them as soon as I get him warm. You sit."

I'm flying. Flying in the air. I'm falling...falling. My eye pops open and know I've been dreaming. I'm sweating. I feel around the bed, but my hand hits the floor before I remember where I am. I can see the flames from the fire flickering in the crystals of the chandelier above my head. I turn my head to see.

Matt is leaning against the door frame drinking a cup of coffee. He's still wearing my slicker and has his hand deep in the left pocket. On him it looks like the coat is stuffed. I chuckle.

His head comes up from his deep study. "How are you doing?"

"Okay, I guess. What happened?"

"Sleep, you've been asleep." Matt sounds angry.

"For how long?"

He looks at the clock on the mantle. "Less than an hour."

"Mamma Lou said it was normal. You had a shock so you had to retreat. Sorry didn't mean to snap, but I hate watching you run away. Three times in one year is enough. At least its been shorter each time." His eyebrow wobbles and I laugh.

"What did she give me?"

"Lemon verbena tea with a shot of vodka."

I push the blankets off and sit up. Everything is working fine until I put my right foot on the floor. "Ouch, that hurts."

My foot and ankle is wrapped in an elastic bandage.

"You have a sprain. Won't be doing any running tomorrow morning. Mamma Lou did say something about damn fools that jump off porches when screaming would have saved her the trouble of patching you up again."

Marsh comes in carrying a tray with Thay behind him toting a pot of coffee. Thay closes the heavy double doors that slide into the wall.

"Best eat something before Virgil arrives. It's going to be another long night."

"Who?"

"Don't know, has that hood over his head. No one has stirred from upstairs. Don't want to wake them. So we'll have to wait for the unveiling."

I take his offered cup. Not coffee, but hot chocolate. I don't think I'll ever be able to eat again. I pick up a ham sandwich from the tray.

"Matt says he didn't hear a thing until you landed on the man behind him. Jim, take your time. Tell me what happened."

I take Thay through the events as best I remember, leaving out the part about wanting to play a trick on Matt, up until I jumped the railing. I can't tell him what happened after that…it's blank.

I look at Matt, he's still wearing my slicker. I wish he'd take it off and hide it in a closet. I don't want to look at it. He has a strange look on his face. His eyes meet mine. I suddenly know why Matt was attacked!

"He meant to kill me." My voice sounds dead.

"What?"

Shudders pass through me like the sharp pings of a high torque engine just after it fires. "Matt...is wearing my slicker. Matt doesn't smoke. I do. He wanted to kill me."

"How did this get in your pocket?" Matt holds out his hand.

"It's Isaiah's. I picked it up in the generator hut and forgot to give it back to him."

"Jim, it can't be Isaiah's. He gave it to Mom. He only wore it to church a couple of times to please her."

"Then whose is it?" Who reminded me of Isaiah the first time I saw him?

"The recipient's name is engraved on the back. Turn it over."

A door slides back. Barker, starched and polished stands there with his hand extended. "Please, give that to me. I will return it to my aunt."

Matt slowly reads, "Stanley James Collins. Jim, you've been carrying the name of the murderer in your pocket."

"No. The Kappa key belonged to his father. Stan's full name is Stanley Durham Collins."

Thay is furious. "Barker, you've known all this time. What kind of FBI agent are you?"

"One with family. The same as you. When Kevin Stevens was murdered I was in the dark. I knew Kevin came down here to talk to Shell Wallace. I ran into Stan outside the hospital. By the time I got to the island Shell Wallace was gone. There wasn't a damn thing I could do but hang around and watch. Even then I didn't suspect Stan until the maid was killed. She and Stan were friendly when she cleaned his room. Stan's temper is...was fragile. He was known to hit on women. There are two ex-wives who will testify to that.

"But suspicion isn't evidence. I had no idea he was transporting human cargo for the mob in Miami."

227

Giving Thay a moment to digest what Barker has told us. I asked a question that had been bothering me for some time. "How did Collins get back on the island?"

"He had a cabin cruiser."

"The salvage that is now tied to my dock?"

"Salvage?"

"Yes, he put out a tight anchor and tied it on a short line. It was immersed when the tide came in."

Barker sinks down on the straight chair by the door. "Stan never was keen on small details like tides."

I study Barker with disbelief. This government man considers a force strong enough to send five to seven feet of ocean inland twice in 24 or more hours, a "small detail." He can't be serious. Matt's eyes bore into me like an auger on a power drill. I keep my mouth shut.

He has taken off that damn slicker. I'm glad. I'll never wear it again.

"Look, Townsend, I want to keep this as quiet as possible so my aunt won't see it on the national news."

"Fine with me. The local reporters drove us nuts yesterday, but you'll have to talk to Chief Landers."

"Marsh, what do I do with all this food? Este packed my cruiser so tight I barley had room to drive."

Chapter 37

As Chief Landers is leaving he puts a hand on my shoulder. "Don't take it to heart, son. My report will read that Agent Stanley D. Collins died as the result of an unavoidable accident. Your quick action saved a lot of folks a heap of trouble."

Matt helps me up the stairs to end a very long day. When we are about midway I overhear Barker tell Thay, "I want to thank you for your help. I'm bumming a ride to the mainland with Chief Landers. I don't think your problems are over. Stan didn't have either the brains or the finances to manage a smuggling operation."

The front door slams. Thay and Marsh are blowing out lanterns in the lobby. The hotel is dark by the time we get to our rooms. I don't bother with a light, but sink into the rocker beside the bed and prop my feet on it. I know sleep won't come easy.

A soft knock sounds on the door. Matt is standing in the hall dressed in heavy sweats.

"You couldn't sleep either?"

"Nope. Here's your raincoat and shoes. The chief kept the garrotte that was under one of them. Thay said it had dried blood on it. "

I'm glad to get my shoes back. That coat will get left in the closet.

"Got a minute?"

"Sure, come on in."

"Lets go out on the verandah. I checked and it's not too cold."

"For you maybe after living in polar bear county. I'll put on my sneakers and parka, while you carry out the rockers and some blankets."

Bundled up against the wind, sitting in the moonlight, the world seems peaceful. I offer Matt a Pall Mall, but he shakes his head.

I don't look down to the boardwalk, but keep my eyes on the beach watching the raccoons and opossums search for food. I can hear the 'quawk' of the night heron as it flies along the shoals hunting for small fish. The soft onshore breeze has a salty tang I can taste on my tongue.

"How do you do it?"

"Do what?"

"Pass out…go to sleep after an injury?"

"Don't know. It just happens."

"Are you all right?"

"I think so. It was the sound of his head hitting the urn. It was almost like, but different, too, from the sound I heard when that Corvette hit Catherine. I never want to hear it again."

A screech owl calls in the woods.

"Now that is a sound that always gives me the heebie-jeebies."

"Just a night bird who has found prey. It's his victory call."

"Back home they say when a screech owl calls it's the harbinger of death."

"Matt, that ole owl is having a late dinner. What did you want to talk to me about? I know its not about the bird calls we've heard all of our lives."

"I owe you.…"

"You don't owe me a damn thing."

"Yes, I do. The other day you asked me a question about what I was going to do. I avoided answering you."

"I take it you're not going home."

I'll miss Matt. These few days have been like when I was growing up. Though he calls me Little Brother, it's about physical size, not because I'm the runt of the litter.

"No. I must clean out my locker before its contents are put out on the street for the garbage. I'll see if the station will take me as a color commentator."

"Matt, you own a station."

"You own a salvage yard. Who's running it?"

"Lon and Elroy."

"Same here. J.T. found me a manager who knows what he is doing. He had a few nasty things to say about ignorant ex-football players. This way, I learn a new trade, yet I'll still be near the team. Maybe after a while when I watch them take to the field it won't hurt. I had ten good years, but it's never enough."

No, its never enough when you're tossed on the sidelines and discarded. It's costing Matt to be matter-of-fact. He looks out towards the stark gray of the ocean that never seems to be at peace.

The clear air seems to magnify the encroaching sound of the flood tide as it swallows the beach. We can see it as it climbs inch by inch toward to dunes. It has a sound not unlike the squish of soft against hard.

Chapter 38

Thornton is sitting by a window looking out on the parking lot. The morning sun sparkles on the drops of water left from last night's rain. Like Barker, he keeps looking at the door, expecting someone. No one has told him Collins and Barker are no longer around. He had a bit of help sleeping last night from Momma Lou so he wouldn't follow Miss Lettic.

Moses has joined us. Someone has carved him a wooden spoon and fork with broad long handles. They make it much easier for him to eat. Marsh fixed him some scrambled eggs with sausage crumbled in them. The spoon works well for the gravy over broken biscuits.

Everyone is talking in a low voice. Maud, Phillip, and Moses are avid listeners as Thay explains what happened during the night.

Matt and I concentrate on our brunch, since it is after 11 o'clock. He took a run on the beach and I watched him from the steps. My leg feels better this morning. I can put my foot to the floor. I think it is a twist instead of a sprain. If I take it slow I can do a short run in the morning.

"Collins. Phillip, that's what I was trying to remember. When Wally Longer knocked Nialis down with his trunk. Collins was standing beside her on the stairs. She had a slash down her back, but we never found the glass that made the cut."

"You're saying he tried to stab her on the stairs."

"I didn't see it, but I believe so. Mamma Lou had to sew the cut closed. It was pretty deep."

I reach up and scratch the three stitches across my nose from where a branch smacked me when I was looking for Thay. They itch. Mamma Lou said they'd pull right out after a week and wouldn't leave much of a scar. What there is will fad with time.

Between bites of French toast I contribute my two cents. "He got out of here in a hurry. He must have sneaked up the back stairs to come back down like he did. He left with the Longers. You didn't know he'd gone. You asked Barker about him later. I don't remember just when."

Thay holds his hands in a pyramid, props his elbows on the table, and rests his chin on his fingers. "This is guesswork on my part. He didn't go far. Probably just over the causeway. Came back in his boat, sabotaged the generator, removed a witness, and got back to the mainland before the full force of the storm hit. In an open boat that night it would have been a rough, but not impossible trip."

"I didn't see him again until the evening Thornton's car was fished out of the sound."

"Since we're guessing. I'll contribute an observation. The cabin cruiser was only covered with water the one time when we found it."

"Phillip, how do you know that?"

"The cushions would have been long gone if it has been in and out of the water more than once. They were just beginning to float when we found it."

"How?"

"Dear girl. An insurance agent knows when a boat has been scuttled. You'd be surprised how many times a guy buys more boat than he can afford. Rather than lose it to a re-po, he'll scuttle it. Some we get back and others never show up."

"What will happen to the one tied to Thay's dock?"

"Matt, I don't know the laws for property used in the commission of a crime in this state. The authorities may hold it for evidence for a year or so since it was used in a crime. The finance company may want it back if there's a loan on it or write it off as a loss. Then the police can sell it for salvage."

"Jim, can you overhaul a marine engine?"

"Sure, but where? It's a long haul over the mountains, besides it doesn't have a trailer."

"Here."

"Here?"

"Moses is going to show me the property again this afternoon."

I'm not surprised. I know how much going out to Mark's place and spending an afternoon fishing in his private cove means to me. I check on it from time to time and winterize it for him to repay him for using his place.

"Mr. Andrews, would the same apply to the schooner?"

"Sheriff, I don't know. My guess is it now belongs to the Coast Guard. Why?"

"I keep thinking about her. She's a beauty. I could run charter excursions down to St. Simons Island. A couple of good years would pay for her." Thay is smiling like he's dreaming of finding a pot of gold.

Moses and Matt aren't paying the least bit of attention. Using a paper napkin, Matt starts jotting notes about his place.

"The foundations of the house are in place. Isaiah won't be in New York forever. He can help me put in the wiring and the plumbing. I can drive a nail as well as the next person."

"Mr. Matt, you don't want to use nails. They make the wood rot. Building to last on this island, you must use pegs."

"Matt, I looked at the barn. It's in good shape. You aren't going to be needing a barn. Why don't you take a look at converting it to a house?"

All eyes look at me. "Little Brother, that's a great idea."

This is the first time he's put down roots. He shares an apartment with another player in Minneapolis. His eyes shine with enthusiasm. The sadness that has haunted him since he arrived is gone. He has something to live for away from football. Something of his own choosing.

I look at Thay and laugh. "You said you'd not want to meet a unit of Youngs. Better get prepared, they'll be here in a drove."

"Matt, Maud and I would like to join your family for your house raising. She has already made reservations to come back next year. Maybe you'll allow us to use it for a few weeks, when you're not in residence. There are some tax advantages to that kind of arrangement."

Hard, sharp clicks ring on the stone floor from high heel shoes draw our eyes across the room. A determined woman is making her way to Thornton's table.

"Where is my sister?"

"Lettic?"

"She is the only one I have. Where is she?"

"Phedra, I don't know." He rises and smiles at her. "You didn't let me know you'd returned."

"I had no intention of informing you. Six weeks in Vegas gave me time to think about the mess I've made of my life. The divorce gets both Lemuel and you out of my life forever. Where is Lettic?"

"I've been telling you. I don't know. She's disappeared."

"If you've hurt her...."

The pink knitted dress is a bit ratty like she's slept in it for several nights. Lettic is running from the kitchen across the room to her sister.

"Jane was pretending to be you."

"Jane was pretending to be me. Why?"

"Don't know. I'm scared. Jane's dead. She was murdered."

"Jane was murdered." The woman's voice rises.

"Rick came. Then he was murdered. Lemuel went off. I don't know where he's gone."

"That's not surprising. Lemuel always takes the easy way out. I say he's in the Bahamas hiding from his problems."

"He left me with Rhodes. I don't like him. He's mean."

"When I came home to pack my things the maid told me Lettic and Lemuel were here. Why here? I've never heard of this place."

"Phedra, I want to go home. I had to sleep in a closet so no one would kill me. I don't like this hotel."

Lettic is gripping Phedra's arm and shaking it like a bewildered child. Her eyes are vacant. There's nothing behind them, but emptiness.

"You were using me for one of you schemes, you bastard. You knew I would be in Vegas for six weeks. You used me the same way Lemuel let them murder our children without doing one thing to stop them."

Thornton's hold on civilization slips as he stares at the woman-child struggling to wrap herself in her sister's arms.

"Keep your mouth shut, you stupid moron. You've caused enough trouble. All you can do is spread your legs." He reaches out to slap Lettic, but Marsh's hand closes over his arm. "Get your hands off me, Darkie, before I cold cock you."

How Moses got across the room so fast I don't know. His cast slips across Thornton's neck. He lifts him off the floor and grips him in a death vise.

Mamma Lou's voice is hard and commanding. She's holding a dragoon Colt steady as a rock. "Don't think I won't shoot you. I'd be glad to for what you did to my grandson.

"Mr. Thornton, does the name Michael Gallino mean any thing to you?"

I've never seen a man go that white. It's like he died before our eyes.

"Mr. Gallino has a message for you. He said to cut you loose. He doesn't care for the private operation you've been running on his time. Thay, take him to the ferry and chain him to the gunwale. Mr. Barker will be waiting for him on the other side."

Thay yanks Thornton's hands behind him and snaps handcuffs on his wrists. When he tries to struggle Moses tighten his arm to the point the man's eyes are bulging. Thay and Marsh each take an arm and propel him from the dining room. Moses is close behind them.

"Miss Lettic, you go upstairs and put your things together. Orta is waiting to help you. I want to talk to your sister before you leave."

She hands me the old horse pistol, but not before opening the cylinder and dumping the bullets in her lap. She had one under the pin ready to fire.

"Mrs. Lavin, please join me in the parlor." As they go through the door I hear Mamma Lou say, "You sister has problems. She needs your help. Keep her away from men who take advantage of her simpleness."

Phedra Lavin slowly nods her head.

Chapter 39

"**M**arsh, how does your mother know Mike Gallino? He's a recluse. If he's still alive."

"Mr. Mike's word is law. Prohibition. Not Mr. Mike, but his father. Contraband has always come in through the islands, been true for hundreds of years. My grandfather let them use the sound for their trade. Had a good harbor then. He had an honor agreement with Figel Gallino to protected the family from harm.

"Mr. Mike and Moses chat on the radio. He didn't know about Thornton's side business."

"I see."

I'm not sure if Matt does understand. Listening to Elroy tell tales of that time I know the system that existed on the rivers. Men moved shine at night and left payment for those whose land they crossed, usually in the form of a ham or a dressed-out buck.

"Thornton won't live to stand trial. He knows it. He broke the code.

"Keep that to yourselves. Thay is law abiding. Some things he don't know. Never was a reason to tell him.

"Moses, take Matt and Jim to see his new property before Thay gets back. I've got to explains things to him and he's not going to like it."

"But I haven't bought it."

"Yes, you have. Seamew is a siren. She claimed you. Jim belongs to the mountains."

Matt is laughing. "Okay. You win. Loan me some of that white paper you use on the buffet…a tape rule…and a lunch box."

"Matt, I've got a tape in my tool box."

"Would you join us, Pretty Lady?"

Matt's little place is over a hundred acres on the sound side of the island, with access down a rough track to the beach on the ocean. Moses walked us around the perimeter following a worn path. The islanders use the English custom of walking their boundaries once a year. Maud roughed out a map locating fallow fields, the road in, several fresh-water springs, and a good-size pond that is losing a battle with cattails.

After a substantial lunch. We tackle the barn. First, Matt and I take the tape and carefully measure the sides and the ends, checking for loose foundation stones as we go. The walls are board and batten construction, very tight to seal drafts. On the back side there's a door up near the peak for loading hay to the loft. It'll make a fine window with a view of the sound over the trees.

It takes the three of us to lift the double doors so they won't drag. Several stalls of beautifully polished wood run down the west side toward the sound. Now they're packed with horse drawn farming equipment. I inch my way around a curved pronged hay rake. After a struggle with the latches I open windows to let in light. I've never seen a barn so polished and cared for before the dust of ages covered every surface.

Matt is running his hand down the boards. "Race horses?"

"Wylie bred mares with good bloodlines he got on the mainland when they were too old to race. Took better care of his stock than he did his family after his woman died. Let Lottie grow up wild. It destroyed his pride when he had to turn to her for help. She wouldn't come home, so he had to go up there. I took him to the bus station and pinned his ticket on his coat so it wouldn't get lost on the way to North Carolina.

"Thay's father drew up papers for me to have care of the place. I talked to Lottie, she don't want nothing that's here except the money."

Moses takes a ring with one key from his pocket and opens a padlock on an enclosed stall in the back. The lock works surprisingly well.

"Oh!"

"It was his tack room. When Mae Ellen died, he moved all of her fixings out here to the barn. These things belonged to her family. She got them as her marriage portion."

Maud is reverently lifting some bowls on a gleaming table. "These are the willow pattern, but much finer than I've ever seen."

"Her mother ordered them from the Sears Roebuck catalog before the Depression. Other pieces her grandmother got out of boxes of soap. They have a date on the back. I come out every once in a while to check on her things."

Maud lays a hand on Moses arm. "Do you mind if we take the plank table outside for me to use?"

"No, Pretty Lady. This all belongs to Mr. Matt. I won't be coming back." He hands Matt the key, walks out to what was the front step of the house and sits down with his memories.

" Jim, could you pack my pipe for me? Haven't had a good smoke since Shell broke my arm. January is almost over, and it's time to move on."

I hear him mumbling to himself as he takes a deep draw. "'We look before and after and pine for what is nought. Our sincerest laughter with some pain is fraught.'"

We work through the afternoon. Maud sketching diagrams of Matt's plans. We have lots of arguments about where rooms should go and how things should be arranged. Maud wants everything wide open until we explain about support beams for the loft. We end up with three different rough floor plans before we climb into the loft and looked out the hay door.

Matt knew immediately he was wrong. The living room must go up here against the sky. There's plenty of height for even Isaiah to stand up. A sandstone fireplace would look good on the far wall.

"Moses, I won't be farming. Had enough time with my hands on a plow growing up. That doesn't mean I want good fields to go to scrub. You have legal care of the place until deed passes. Do you know anyone who would be willing to lease the tillable acreage?"

Moses is smiling. "Several fellas are looking for a living."

"Know anyone who can use the equipment? It's in good shape, no rust that I can see. If I convert the barn to a home, it must be moved."

"I expect so."

Matt reaches out his hand, which Moses accepts with an innate dignity. "It's a deal. You're my farm manager. I know a ham operator who will let me notify you when I'll be able to come back."

Moses beams as if his prized steer just took first place at the fair.

Matt carefully rolls the sheets of paper covered with our ideas and hands them to me. "Put these in your tool box and take them to Adam. Tell him what you've seen. What I'll need. He'll know how to do it right."

Chapter 40

"What are you thinking about?"

"Nothing really."

"Maud, you have a way of holding your head tilted to the left when you're thinking hard thoughts. Here, hold the coffee."

I am sitting on the verandah waiting for the sun to come up over the ocean one last time before we go. I can see the darker splotches, which are Jim and Matt as they pace along the shore.

Phillip draws a rocking chair beside me, tucks a blanket around my legs, and does the same for himself. The early morning air is brisk, even bundled up like we are. My mother's coat is in a trash bag in Jim's Rover. He is taking it home for me. A fur coat is not the garment to bring to an ocean, it may be warm, but with the fine sand in the air it's a disaster.

"Did you see Lettic when they left yesterday? She was wearing her minks. The sand will be all over that fine Mercedes by the time they get to Minneapolis."

"That's one trip I'm glad I'm not taking. Lettic needs a special kind of help."

"I know. She looks like a grown woman, but she isn't."

"It's odd how the simple and susceptible protect themselves."

"What do you mean?"

"Lettic—she hated Thornton. She instinctively recognized the—for want of a better words—evil in him. Where her much brighter sister didn't."

"He was evil, wasn't he? Is greed that powerful a motive to order people murdered? It seems too simple."

"I don't think Thornton even knew about the killings until he arrived, but he knew who was committing them. I think Collins acted on his own when the smuggling started to fold."

"I'm sorry he died."

"Who?"

"Collins."

"Maud, he murdered four people."

"Yes, but Jim. It seems as if the sandprints of death follow him. Will killing Collins hurt Jim?"

"He is deeply shaken. Anyone would be. It was an accident. He did not intend to kill him. What happened here won't be remembered. Sandprints don't last. They're washed away with each change of the tides.

"He was enjoying working with Matt to make plans for the barn. He agreed to take the investigator's job when he gets home."

"'Gets home?' Isn't he going straight home?"

"No, he is going down to Daytona Beach to watch the stock cars race before he returns."

"Florida. He won't need mother's fur coat down there."

Phillip is laughing so hard he almost spills his coffee. "Speaking of that coat. When did you mother get it?"

"I don't know, before I was born."

"Are you sure the tanner didn't line it with rocks. It weighs a ton."

"I know. I've never worn it at home. It's too ostentatious."

"Ostentatious—perfect. When we get home we will be ostentatious. Shock the neighbors with our outrageous character faults. I will get courageous and knock on your front door."

He has me laughing so hard I have to put my coffee cup on the floor. My face is aching.

"You're not worried about going home, are you?"

"No...a little. When you came out of the porch I was thinking

243

about my garden. My fingers itch to start making a real garden, maybe new curtains for the living room."

"I got infected watching Matt. I'm going to change the inside of my grandfather's mausoleum. There is no room for pain in the house I will live in for the rest of my life beside you."

"Phillip, don't change the outside. I love the Carpenter Gothic style with all the little spindles and curlicues."

"I could paint them like those in San Francisco?"

"That would be ostentatious on a brick house."

"What is going to be ostentatious is your new rug."

"New rug?"

"I'm going to find a furrier in Cincinnati to make a rug for in front of the fireplace in your bedroom out of that coat. We'll keep it hidden in a closet to be rolled out for special occasions to go with your new queen size bed."

"Oh, Phillip look. The sky. That color. Golden apricot of the rising sun makes the sky glow. That will be the color of my bedroom, so we'll remember being happy."

He pulls me from the rocker and kisses me hard with the shimmering illumination of the sun warming the world around us. It's time to go home and make our own memories.

Our bags are sitting in the lobby as we have our last breakfast at Seamew Inn. Matt and I took an early morning run to catch the sun when it came over the horizon. The starkness of the beach was highlighted with deeper colors than it was the first morning I limped along the shore in the dense fog. We took it slow, drinking in the salt air.

Matt left the key to his new place with Marsh and learned the source of Moses's grief. Mae Ellen was his beloved half-sister. Shell was the son the old man couldn't have. Moses filled the role of grandfather in his life. The "fixings" he cared for in the barn were his mother's.

At the look on Matt's face, Marsh told him in no uncertain terms not to insult Moses by trying to give them back, but to care for them and have the old man over to supper to see them loved. We were almost out the door when Matt reached in a sack and pulled out a box of cassette tapes.

Vernon's radio guys had recorded Isaiah's show and made tapes for everyone. I packed mine deep in my gym bag to make sure nothing happens to it before I get home.

I drove Maud and Phillip out to the airport. Matt followed me to see them off. As we're walking back to the parking lot I ask him a question.

"What is the before and after?"

"Where did you hear that?"

"Moses was talking to himself yesterday. Lines, I think, from a poem."

"It's from Shelly's *To a Skylark*."

"Why is January important?"

"The month was named for the Roman god Janus. He's two-faced. Looks to the past and ahead to the future."

"I see."

Matt reaches for the door handle of his Porsche. Its high-gloss red finish is dulled from days of sitting in the salt air of the parking lot."

"First chance you get, have this washed, polished, and under-coated. Do it so rust won't develop. Salt isn't good for metal."

"Your face shows every thought like it's a billboard. Take that tank and get back across the mountains where you belong, Little Brother. You're dangerous."

His engine roars and he is gone.

I put the Land Rover, one of the few things I'd kept of Catherine's, in gear and follow him out to the highway where our roads diverge.

Acknowledgments & Author's Notes

It is with deep thanks to my husband, Ford Nashett, who is the 'Nash' of Nash Black. His help both in providing me time to write undisturbed and his contributions for all things mechanical is important to our story telling.

Seamew Island is fictional, but vaguely patterned after Kiawah and Cumberland Island of the 1960s when both areas were essentially rural, prior to the commercial development of the barrier islands. Today both islands are still removed from more popular southern resort locations and still retain much of their earlier charm.

Edisto Island is a protected wildlife refuge above Hilton Head off the coast of South Carolina. Shards of willow patten china are still found on Edisto Island's beach, but rarely. The reference to the hurricane of 1893 is true.

The tidal periods were developed from a January prediction for Edisto Beach to fit the elements of the story. Full tides move in and out for a little over six hours twice a day. The clock times change because of the overage, and careful attention was paid to make them as accurate as possible. This time overage between the movement of the moon and the earth is the same difference where we adjust our calendars every four years.

Our thanks to Mary Lina Berndt for her careful editing (with a broken wrist) and attention to details.

It is a pleasure to work with the staff of Outskirts Press who have published all the titles from If Publishing Company.

Our thanks to the International Willow Collectors Society (http://www.willowcollectors.org) with whom it has been our pleasure to learn from and share a passion for the willow pattern for over twenty years.

The story Phillip Andrews tells is told in a longer version as "Tallboy's Last Run" in *Haints;* a collection of Cumberland area ghost stories previously publish by the authors. The collection was a finalist for the Independent Publishers Association's awards in its category.

The character Maud Tosh was patterned after a real person. She has been deceased for thirty years, but her cousins still remember her as a remarkable lady who lived into her 90s in the home her grandparents built in DeKoven, KY.

J.T. Whitlock (Lebanon, KY) was a pioneer in the development of radio and televison. He graciously allowed us to use his name. He flew his own plane on humanitarian missions until a few months before his death.

Frogmore is the name of a small town on island of St. Helena, SC. This stew is a summer special when corn is fresh from the field. How much you throw in the pot will depend on the number staying for supper. It was originally cooked on the beach and like Kentucky Burgoo, what it contained is whatever was contributed to the kettle.

Frogmore Stew

16 cups of water
1/4 cup seafood boiling spices (if not available, make your own, recipe
follows)
1 lemon, halved
1 jalapeno chili, seeded and chopped, or 1 canned hot chili
4 cloves of garlic
3 potatoes, quartered
1 lb. hot sausage rolled in balls, browned
6 ears of corn, husked and cut in thirds
6 live blue crabs
1 lb. of large shrimp in the shell
1/2 cup dry white wine
hot red pepper sauce

Place boiling spices, water, lemon, chili, and garlic in a large stockpot. Cover and bring to a boil. Add the potatoes. Return to boiling and cook for 10 minutes. Add sausage and corn then simmer for 5 minutes. Add the blue crabs and cook for 5 minutes. Add shrimp and cook for 4 more minutes.

Remove the potatoes, sausage, corn, crabs, and shrimp from the pot. Place in a casserole and put in the oven to keep warm.

Cook the liquid, uncovered, over medium-heat for five minutes until it is reduced. Add white wine and continue to cook for a further 5 minutes until reduced to your satisfaction. Season to taste with red pepper sauce.

Divide the seafood and vegetables into 6 deep soups bowls. Strain the sauce and pour over the ingredients. Serve immediately.

Seafood boiling spices.

1 tablespoon mustard seeds
2 teaspoons black peppercorns
2 teaspoons hot red pepper flakes
1 or 2 bay leaves
1 teaspoon of celery seeds
1 tablespoon coriander seeds
1 teaspoon ground ginger

Place ingredients in a blender and grind them together. If you must, add salt (1 tablespoon) stirred in after grinding.

If used frequently, this can be made in large quantities and stored in a canning jar with a tight lid in the refrigerator for up to six months.

Cooking notes.

This recipe is for fresh ingredients in season, but substitutions are acceptable. Fresh corn—an Indiana brochure advised for true fresh corn-on-the-cob, build a fire in the field and cook it on site.

Hot dishes are a matter of taste and endurance. Balance the ingredients to your individual tastes. Put a bottle of Tabasco on the table for those with asbestos mouths.

Salt – we provide a grinder of sea salt on the table for those who desire more than the sea provides in its bounty.